TOWN HAUNTS

AN ANNA NOLAN MYSTERY

CATHY SPENCER

Comely
Press

Published by Comely Press

www.comelypress.com

Copyright © 2013 Cathy Spencer

978-0-9917259-8-4

To Agatha Christie, Dorothy Sayers, and Robert B. Parker,
whose wonderful stories inspired me to write mysteries.

Other titles in the Anna Nolan series:
Framed For Murder (Book 1)
Winner of the 2014 Bony Blythe Mystery Award

Discover other titles by Cathy Spencer:
The Dating Do-Over
The Affairs of Harriet Walters, Spinster
Tall Tales Twin-Pack, Mysteries
Tall Tales Twin-Pack, Science Fiction and Fantasy

Connect online with Cathy Spencer:
Subscribe to her blog at
http://cmspencer.blogspot.ca
Like her Facebook page at
https://www.facebook.com/CathySpencerAuthor

Thank you to a great team of beta readers – Alexandra Gall, Barbara Ledger, Ann Pappert, Diana Patterson, and Debbie Welland – and to my editor, Kate Spencer. Cover photo by RDS Photography.

1

It was the middle of the night, but Sherman couldn't sleep. Too many old demons whirling around his brain and pricking at his conscience. Frustrated, he threw back the covers and sat up on the edge of the bed, the soles of his feet chilled by the bare floor boards. Running his hands through his clipped, grizzled hair, he pushed himself up off the bed, jammed his feet into slippers, and limped downstairs in his shorts and undershirt.

The kitchen was dark, but Sherman didn't bother with the lights. He fumbled for a water glass from the cupboard and took the vodka bottle out of the freezer. The blue light from the stove's digital clock was enough to see by as he poured two fingers of Stoli into the glass and put the bottle back. Leaning against the counter by the kitchen sink, he took his first sip. Ahh. The alcohol was cold and smooth going down the back of his throat.

Meaning to count to twenty before taking a second sip, he rested the glass on the sink and looked out the window past the dingy curtains. The house was set up high on a hill next to the Crane municipal cemetery, allowing him to see over the wall into the grounds. For a moment, he thought he caught a flicker of light through the trees. He rubbed his eyes and stared, straining to see it again, but the wind was up and the trees were thrashing. There! He saw the light again, briefly. Maybe it was one of those damned kids up to no good. They had no respect for the dead, knocking over tombstones, spray painting ugly messages on the walls, and leaving empty beer cans right on top of the graves. He'd better take a look, or else he might have a mess to clean up tomorrow.

Forgetting to savour his drink, Sherman downed the rest and hurried upstairs to put on his pants and a warm jacket. It was mid-October in the Alberta Foothills, and the nights were getting frosty. He grabbed his cemetery keys and hobbled down the stairs as fast as his sore knee would allow. Letting himself out of the house, he slid down the damp grass heading for the gate in the cemetery wall. The door screeched as he opened it, and he cursed himself for not keeping the hinges oiled. Easing the door shut behind him, he paused in the flat orange light beneath a security lamp on the ring road.

Everything was still except for the gusting wind. He could see his breath coming out in excited puffs and smelled the sharp wood smoke from the houses on the far side of the church. He shivered as the wind penetrated his clothes. It was too cold to stand still for long, so Sherman crossed the road and set off across the frosty grass. The sky was enshrouded in thick, grey cloud, and it was inky black among the plots. He got his bearings from the familiar tombstones, running his hands over their chilled, smooth surfaces as he hobbled past them. Pausing by a stone angel, Sherman peered to the left, toward the older part of the cemetery. That was the direction the light had been coming from when he had seen it from the kitchen window.

There it was, blinking through a stand of twisting evergreens. He crept toward the trees, taking his time so as not to snap a twig along the way. Was that whispering he heard? He paused to listen, but the branches were creaking too much to be sure, so he kept on. Reaching the evergreens, he edged around them carefully, trailing his hands over their rough bark.

He knew exactly where he was. There was a bench on the other side of the trees with a plot directly in front of it. The words inscribed on the black tombstone read, "Evelyn Mason, Beloved Wife and Mother, November 2, 1954 – March 10, 2012." Evie's grave. He rounded the trees and burst out of hiding.

"What do you think you're doing here?" he hollered. But there was no one there, just the dim outline of the tombstone. He hesitated, sure that this was where he had seen the light.

"Sherman . . ." a voice sighed plaintively on the wind. He jerked his head sideways, trying to follow the sound, but it was impossible to tell where it came from. His hands clutched the bench for support, the metal cold and hard beneath his fingers.

"Who's there?" he yelled, straining to see in the dark.

"Sherman . . ." the voice moaned, emanating from the heart of the plot deep in front of him. His breath came in short gasps, and his legs were shaking.

"Sherman!" the voice shrieked, piercing his ears and squeezing the breath from his lungs. He turned to run and tripped. Clawing at the ground, he staggered to his feet, terrified of skeletal fingers clutching at his shoulder. He tore across the grass and ran between the plots, barking his shins on more than one tombstone. He found the ring road and pushed himself down it, running and hopping as fast as he could. Reaching the door in the wall, he flung it open and staggered up the slope for home.

Thank God he had left the front door unlocked. Once inside, he shot the bolt home and ran upstairs to cower in bed with the ceiling light on. He lay there, his heart thumping erratically in his chest, and willed it to calm down. Mental imaging the people at the hospital had called it after his heart attack five years ago. He swallowed hard and tried to think.

Was he crazy, or had his wife just called to him from the other side of the grave?

Her photograph was on his bedside table in a polished silver frame, the only valuable thing still left. Staring at the beautiful young woman with shining blue eyes smiling into the camera, a snort of laughter burst from his lips. He laughed and laughed until his eyes ran, and he was gasping for breath. The laughter subsided, and he picked up the picture and clutched it to his chest.

"I'm sorry, Evie," he said, his voice cracking.

2

Anna Nolan strode down Main Street in pursuit of breakfast. It was a glorious autumn morning, the air fresh and crisp, the sky a cloudless robin's-egg blue. The leaves on the trees lining the street had turned sunshine-yellow and were dry and crunchy underfoot. Anna stopped outside The Diner and grinned at the scarecrow sitting on a straw bale beside the door. The Crane Chamber of Commerce was holding its annual Halloween contest, and most of the businesses were festooned with cobwebs, spiders, scarecrows, and jack-o'-lanterns. Frank Crow, the restaurant's owner, was a big Elvis fan – he even had one of the King's Vegas costumes mounted in a display case inside the restaurant – so his scarecrow was wearing a black wig, leather jacket, and holding a plywood guitar. Stooping, she kissed its scratchy cheek and went inside.

Mary, The Diner's full-time waitress, was wiping down a vacant spot at the front counter. Thirtyish, she wore her trademark skin-tight jeans, the strings of her white apron tied twice around her pencil-thin waist. Four of the five stools were occupied by truckers dressed alike in flannel shirts, jeans, and baseball caps, their forks scraping on their plates as they concentrated on shovelling food into their mouths as efficiently as possible.

A long, low wolf whistle pierced the silence. Glancing over her shoulder, Anna spied RCMP Constable Steve Walker grinning at her from a table at the back of the room. The rangy, darkly-handsome, twenty-eight-year-old had just finished his shift and was still in uniform, eating his supper before going home to get some rest. Anna beamed as she headed back to join him, a little sashay in her walk.

"Anna Nolan, you are looking fine this morning. Love must truly agree with you," Steve said, leaning back in his chair to look her up and down as she paused beside his table. She was wearing a midnight-blue silk blouse over jeans that cupped her curvy hips, her long, brunette hair flowing over the shoulders of a soft black leather jacket. Anna was forty with a grown son, Ben, in university, and long walks with her dog helped to keep her fit and youthful.

"Thank you, sir, you are too kind," she said with mock gentility, plunking down into the chair across from him. The men at the counter stopped following Anna with their eyes and turned back to their plates.

"Taking a vacation day?" Steve asked. It was Tuesday, and normally she would be on her way to work at eight o'clock in the morning. Work was at the Chinook University in Calgary, where Anna was employed as the administrative assistant for the Kinesiology Department. She had held the position for four years, driving the twenty minutes north to Calgary each day. Her ex-husband, Jack, a handsome charmer who had cheated on her throughout their marriage, had been an actor, and the family had settled in the small town of Crane when he had landed a role in a movie being filmed nearby. Anna had begun divorce proceedings before the shoot was over, however, and when Jack left town at the film's wrap, she and Ben stayed on.

"Uh huh. I had to take a friend to the airport," she replied.

"That's right. I heard that Sergeant Tremaine was back in town last week," Steve said around a piece of toast. "The guys and I were really disappointed when he didn't drop by the station to see us. Here we thought that we had really bonded with Tremaine over your ex-husband's murder investigation, but he didn't take the time to visit his old buddies. I wonder who or what could have been keeping him so busy?"

Anna rolled her eyes. Charles Tremaine was a sergeant with a national RCMP unit that investigated high-profile homicides throughout Western Canada. She and Tremaine had become personally involved during the investigation the previous spring, an investigation in which Anna had figured as the prime suspect. She thought that looking into her ex-husband's personal life would help to find the murderer, and had made it her mission to meet the women Jack had been romancing. Tremaine had discovered the real killer despite Anna's interference, and now they were conducting a long-distance romance.

Mary bustled over to the table to take Anna's order. "We missed you at breakfast on Saturday. Did you sleep in or something?" Anna often met her friends for breakfast at The Diner on Saturday mornings.

Anna braced herself for some extra teasing and said, "I'm sure everyone has heard that Charlie was taking a seminar in Calgary last week."

"Uh huh," Mary and Steve said in unison.

"So, he stayed over for Thanksgiving weekend when it was done."

"And?" Mary asked with rapt attention.

"And, nothing. It's none of your business," Anna said, smiling to soften the sharpness of her retort.

Mary smirked at Steve, who winked back. "How's he getting along with Ben?" the waitress asked. Ben was nineteen, and had moved out of the house just over a year ago to attend Chinook University's computer science program. He was in his second year, sharing a house in Calgary with four other roommates and holding down a part-time job at a building supply store. He still came home every Friday night to have supper with his mom, however.

"They sure got off to a rocky start," Steve added. "First Ben dragged his feet on providing an alibi for his father's murder . . ."

"Ben just got his back up about that," Anna interrupted.

"And then Tremaine brought him in for questioning," Steve said with a grin.

"Yeah, that didn't help." Anna shrugged and smiled. "Ben had Thanksgiving supper with Charlie and me, and no blood was drawn, so I'd say their relationship is improving."

Frank Crow, who was both The Diner's owner and cook, rang the pass-through bell, signalling that there was food for Mary to pick up. The waitress got down to business. "What'll you have, Anna – the usual?"

"No, I made pancakes and bacon at home this weekend. What are you having, Steve?" she asked, peering at his bowl beside the stack of whole wheat toast. He was eating oatmeal topped with raisins and raw apple slices. Anna wrinkled her nose; it didn't look very appealing to her. Steve must be on one of his health kicks.

"I think I need a little more protein than that," she said. "I'll have the Tex-Mex Scramble. And a glass of apple juice, please."

"Coming right up," Mary said, spinning on her heels and walking away.

"So, how's it really going with Tremaine? Are you happy?" Steve asked, scooping up some oatmeal with his spoon.

Anna leaned her elbows on the table. "It's going really well. Charlie's a great guy. I trust him, even though we're apart so much. Not like my ex-husband, that dog. And the long-distance thing is working for me. It keeps us in the honeymoon phase of our relationship all the time."

"Yeah, but how much time have you actually spent together since he left last spring?"

"Well, he had to come back for the trial, so that was four days in July. Then we had his two weeks' vacation in August, plus this past week for the course. That's three and a half weeks. But we talk all the time on the phone. Well, as much as we can when he's not tied up with a case." Anna sighed. "Problem is, every time he leaves, I have to get used to being alone all over again. It's funny. I was fine with not having a man in my life for four years, but now that there's one back again – well, it's hard when he leaves." Anna toyed with the packages of sugar in the bowl on the table while Steve watched.

The restaurant door opened. Anna looked up as a young woman paused in the doorway. Backlit by the morning sun, she was striking in a purple velvet jacket worn over a snippet of floral skirt and high-heeled, scarlet pumps. Her most exotic feature, however, was the smooth cap of flaming-red hair that framed her oval face. The young woman sauntered over to the counter and claimed the empty stool, laying a sheet of paper on the counter top before sliding onto the cushioned seat. The men on either side of her looked up in surprise. Removing smoky sunglasses, she swivelled on the stool to check out the rest of the restaurant, crossing her shapely legs as she did so. Her skirt rode up high enough to revive a dead man's heart, and the truckers gaped at her over their shoulders. The young woman spotted Steve and gave him a half-wave with her fingertips. Steve waved back and beckoned for her to join him and Anna.

"Who's that?" Anna asked, her eyebrows arching as the woman undulated her way through the tables.

"That's Tiernay Rae, the owner of the new store that's going in where Henry's old restaurant used to be," Steve said, mesmerized by Tiernay's progress.

Anna managed to whisper, "You know her? You sure work fast," before the young woman arrived at their table.

Steve rose to greet her. "Tiernay, you are the perfect ending to an uninspired day," he said, whisking out a chair for her. Tiernay smiled at him, and he seemed to lose himself in her eyes. Feeling like a chewed-up dog toy spat out for a meaty bone, Anna cleared her throat. Steve glanced at her before adding, "Let me introduce you to a good friend of mine, Anna Nolan."

"Pleased to meet you," Tiernay said, leaning forward to offer her hand. As Anna took it, she noticed that the younger woman had unusually light blue eyes. Those cool eyes were assessing her. Obviously, Tiernay was sizing up the competition. She needn't have bothered, though; with twelve years between them, Anna had dismissed Steve as potential boyfriend material years ago even though he had demonstrated some interest. Besides, she had Charlie to keep her happy. Releasing Anna's hand, Tiernay sank into her chair and turned her attention back to Steve.

"'Tiernay.' That's an unusual name," Anna said.

"Tiernay is a Celtic name that means 'noble.'"

"Oh. Do you have a Celtic background?"

"No, I'm French-Canadian."

Anna nodded as if she understood, even though she didn't. "Steve tells me that you're opening a new business in Henry Fellow's old restaurant."

"That's right."

"I must say, you've done wonders with the building renovations. It's been an eyesore for months, but it looks terrific now." Henry Fellows, a long-time resident of Crane and a former member of the town council, had owned "Hank's Hearty Home-Cooking," The Diner's only competition in town. The restaurant's kitchen had been demolished by a hit-and-run driver last spring, however, and to make matters worse, Henry had been given a two-month jail term for his involvement with the accident. He was back in Crane, although no one had seen much of the fussy, middle-aged man since his return.

"Thank you," Tiernay said, nodding at Anna's compliment. "Mr. Fellows gave us a really good price because the place was in such rough shape. My brother, Greg, drew up the renovation plans himself. I'm very proud of Greg – he's got an artistic soul."

"What kind of business are you opening?" Anna asked.

"It's called 'Healing Hands' – part store, part massage therapy clinic. I'm a registered massage therapist, by the way. The store will be open in the afternoons, and the clinic in the evenings. I'm not much of a morning person," she said with a lazy smile, "although I'm up with the birds lately. There's so much to do with the store opening this week."

"Sounds intriguing. When do you open?"

"The stars will be in their proper alignment on Friday."

"Really? Are you an astrologist, too?" Anna asked with a condescending smile. She didn't hold much truck with astrology.

"Among other things." Tiernay leaned back in her chair and crossed her legs again. Anna wanted to tell Steve to put his tongue back in his mouth, but kept the comment to herself.

Mary returned with Anna's breakfast and plunked it down on the table in front of her. Catching the waitress's eye, Tiernay said, "Excuse me, ma'am. I'm Tiernay Rae, owner of the new store that's opening across the street. I wonder if I could talk to the owner about putting up a flyer in your window."

Mary paused to consider her, a hand on her hip. "What kind of flyer?"

Tiernay held up the poster for Mary to see. "It's for a cleansing ceremony after the store closes on Saturday night. Everyone in town is welcome. I always do a cleansing ceremony when I'm in a new location, plus I want to get rid of any negative energy left over from the accident."

Mary shrugged and reached for the flyer. "Sure, I'll put it in the window. Frank Crow, the restaurant owner, sits on the town council. He's always happy to promote local business."

"Marvellous. Thanks so much," Tiernay said with a patronizing smile. "By the way, would you bring me a pot of green tea?"

"Sure. Be right back," Mary said as she left.

"Cleansing ceremonies, negative energy, stars' alignment – what's that all about, if you don't mind my asking?" Anna said, picking up her fork and taking a bite of her steaming, peppery omelette. She closed her eyes and chewed slowly, taking a moment to savour Frank's cooking.

"She's a witch," Steve said. Anna's eyes popped open, and she stared at Steve's grinning face.

"Now, don't tease, Steve," Tiernay said, shaking her head at him. "You can call me a Wiccan, if you like, Anna, although I don't like being pigeon-holed by conformist religious definitions. Healing Hands will promote physical, emotional, and spiritual health, however people choose to arrive at it."

Mary returned with a mug and a tea pot, and plopped them down in front of the young woman. "Only had brown," she said over her shoulder as she bustled away.

Tiernay frowned at the pot, poured some tea into the mug, and sipped it warily. Shuddering, she returned the mug to the table before continuing the conversation.

"Steve here, for instance, has an imbalance between his left and right sides. See how his left shoulder is higher than his right? His 'qi'– his energy flow – is blocked, which can lead to a weakened immune system."

One side of Steve's mouth curled upward. "So, how would you suggest I fix that, Tiernay?"

She studied him for a moment. "We could start with massage. I'm sure that I could work out the blockage with my hands. But I could also give you an herbal tincture that would help dissolve the blockage and purge your system."

"I'm not too keen on the purging, but I sure could use a good massage."

Tiernay looked deep into his eyes and said, "Give me your hand." Their eyes locked as he slowly extended it. She took it between her own and held it for a long moment. "It's a little cool," she murmured. "We need to increase your energy flow." She began massaging the flesh between his thumb and forefinger, watching his face as she did so. After half a minute, Steve sighed and closed his eyes.

"That's it. Let the tension go," Tiernay purred.

Anna stopped eating to watch them. "I think it's working. Look, the crease between Steve's eyes has already smoothed out," she said with a sardonic grin. Tiernay ignored her to begin kneading his palm with her thumbs. Steve's mouth dropped open.

"Holding a free clinic, Tiernay?" a baritone voice asked from behind Anna. She turned and saw a stranger standing at her shoulder. He looked to be in his mid-thirties, a tall, lean man with shaggy black hair and a glittering emerald stud in one ear. A prominent hooked nose gave him an aristocratic appearance, but good-humoured brown eyes saved him from seeming haughty. He smiled at Anna, swung the table's remaining chair around, and straddled it. Steve tried to free his hand, but Tiernay clung to it as she continued her massage.

"Where did you pop up from?" she asked, her eyes on her work.

"Oh, I've been all over town," the stranger replied.

Tiernay released Steve's hand with a final caress across the palm and turned her head to gaze at the stranger. "Anna, Steve, this is my big brother, Gregory," she said. "Greg and I are partners in the store. Greg, this is Anna Nolan and Constable Steve Walker."

"Yes, but I'm more of a 'silent' partner. I won't actually be working in the store," Greg said. He gave Steve a casual nod, but took Anna's hand and raised it to his lips in one smooth gesture. "Anna, I'm delighted to make your acquaintance," he murmured, kissing it. Anna's eyes assessed him coolly. In her experience, only a particular kind of man did that sort of thing, and she didn't want to meet another one.

"Don't let Greg bother you. He likes to practise old-fashioned European courtesies," Tiernay said in a dry voice.

"Are you old-fashioned, Greg?" Anna asked, slipping her hand from his grasp.

"No, but it's a good excuse to kiss the hands of beautiful women whenever I get the chance," he replied with an impish grin.

Anna found it impossible not to return his smile. "And how's that working for you?" she asked, leaning back in her chair.

"You'd be surprised how well a little old-fashioned charm works on the gentler sex."

"No I wouldn't. I married a graduate of the old-fashioned charm school myself."

"Lucky you. Still married to him?"

"We got divorced, and then another woman shot him," Anna replied, straight-faced. "So you might want to rethink some of those old European courtesies of yours."

Greg nodded with a poker face. "You'll have to tell me all about him some day."

"Would it do any good?" Anna asked, winning a chuckle from him.

"Oh, I like her," Greg said.

"So, how's the flyer distribution going?" Tiernay asked.

He broke his gaze from Anna's face to heft a leather pouch onto the table. Opening it, he displayed the contents to his sister. "The flyers are half gone."

"Well, we'd better get busy on the rest," she replied, rising from the table. Tiernay was about to say more when she paused, her mouth frozen open in mid-sentence. Her face flushed, and she broke into a sweat.

"No . . . leave us alone," she murmured, staring into the distance.

"Sis?" Greg said as Steve and Anna stared at her.

Tiernay's eyes rolled toward the ceiling, and her knees buckled. Greg grabbed her around the waist as Steve sprang to his feet to help.

"What's wrong?" Greg asked in alarm.

"I just felt this overwhelming sense of evil," she whispered, staring at him with huge eyes. "Give me a moment."

"Here, you'd better sit down," Greg said, helping her back into her chair. Steve reseated himself, watching the young woman attentively. Tiernay closed her eyes and raised a hand to her temple as Greg explained to Anna and Steve, "She gets these premonitions from time to time."

Tiernay's eyes opened. "It felt like something was trying to smother me," she whispered. "I had to fight it off. It's gone now." She pointed across the table at Anna. "It was you! The evil was following you," she declared in a stronger voice. Anna gazed back in astonishment as Tiernay rose and hurried around the table to stand beside her.

"May I?" she asked, lifting Anna's chin and peering into her eyes before Anna had a chance to respond. "You have a very old spirit – even primitive, I'd say. You're strong. That's good. The evil will not easily overpower you."

Anna jerked her chin out of Tiernay's hand and muttered, "That's a lot of crazy talk."

Tiernay's eyes sparkled with anger, and she drew herself up to her full height. "It's not crazy. You listen to me, Anna Nolan. Something poisonous is coming to get you. I frightened it away, but it will be back. As soon as you feel anything, you come and tell me about it. I'm deadly serious about this, do you hear?"

Anna stiffened as she studied Tiernay. She had no idea why this bizarre young woman was trying to frighten her, but she decided to play along until she found out. "Okay, I'll come running as soon as I feel anything," she said, nodding and relaxing back into her chair.

Tiernay's anger evaporated, and she patted Anna's shoulder. "Good. Don't worry, I'm sure that we can handle it between the two of us." Turning to Steve, she added, "Well, Greg and I have work to do. You will come by for that massage sometime, won't you?"

The constable rose from his chair. "I'll be sure to do that. Good luck with your opening on Friday."

Greg stood as well and bowed to Anna. "Wonderful to meet you, lovely lady," he said. "Take good care of yourself." Nodding at Steve, he added, "Constable."

Tiernay trailed behind her brother on the way to the cash register, where she paused as Greg paid Mary for the tea. "Don't forget to come to the cleansing ceremony on Saturday, everyone," she called before sauntering out the door.

Steve sat down with an amused smile, but Anna didn't find anything funny in what had just happened.

"What was all that nonsense about evil following me? Was she serious?"

Steve shrugged. "I don't know. Maybe it's just an act she puts on to promote her business. It doesn't really matter, does it? She didn't spook you, did she?"

Anna frowned. "Not really, but she looked so sincere when she warned me. She seemed to really believe what she was saying."

Steve shivered and rubbed his hands together. "You'd better be careful. The bogey man's coming to get you, and just in time for Halloween."

Anna punched him in the shoulder. "Don't be ridiculous. Tiernay's as phoney as a three-dollar bill."

"Ow," he complained, rubbing the sore spot. "Well, who cares? You know what? I think that Tiernay and her brother are going to liven things up around here. She definitely brightened my day." He stood and stretched. "Gotta go get some sleep. See you around, Anna."

"Tiernay Rae brightened up your day, did she?" Anna mumbled to his retreating back. "Some people just don't have any sense." She forked up some omelette and ground it between her teeth. But, thinking of Greg and his hand-kissing, she smiled.

3

Having two days off made for a short work week, especially since the department was priming for mid-term exams. Anna was kept especially busy trying to sort through the extra printing the faculty had ordered and tracking the essays that were flooding into her office. Just once, she wished that the professors would give her a break and make the students hand in their assignments during class time, but no such luck.

It was Saturday before Anna knew it. She woke up at seven-thirty and glanced blearily at the clock. Normally she enjoyed sleeping late on the weekends, but Wendy, her three-year-old shepherd/labrador cross, lifted her head from the carpet and stared at Anna with her soft brown eyes, and Anna relented and got up. After taking care of her pet's needs, she enjoyed a long, luxurious shower before leaving her cottage on the outskirts of town to walk the seven blocks to The Diner.

It was a dreary day with a fine, cold rain blowing sideways across her face that chilled her. Anna tucked her head inside the hood of her coat and power-walked all the way. Reaching the restaurant door, she rushed inside, stopping on the rubber mat to shake the rain from her clothes. A buzz of conversation and the scent of frying onions greeted her inside the warm, steamy room.

"Morning, Anna!" boomed a familiar voice. She looked up and nodded at Clive Wampole, a tall hulk of a man in overalls and a plaid shirt who farmed his widowed mother's acreage. Clive's chosen mode of transportation was a shiny blue tractor; Anna had missed it parked out front of the restaurant in her haste to get inside. Clive was partially deaf and hadn't heard her come in, but he had felt the blast of cool air from his seat at the counter and swivelled around to check her out.

"Wet enough for you?" he asked. That, and its variants, were part of Clive's standard repertoire. "Hot enough? Cold enough?" Good old Clive, he was nothing if not consistent.

"You bet, Clive," Anna said, patting his arm. She looked around the crowded tables and spotted Mary pouring coffee for Mr. Andrews, a retired rancher who spent most mornings reading the newspaper at The Diner. Anna's book club friends, Erna Dombrosky and May Weston, were seated with him, laughing over a shared joke. May was wearing one of her hand-knit sweaters, an orange concoction with a row of yellow jack-o'-lanterns that clashed horribly with her ruddy complexion. Her steel-grey hair was blunt cut at chin level, accentuating the squareness of her face. Seventy-five-year-old Erna looked cozy in a green wool cardigan buttoned over a tweed skirt, her black pumps visible through pull-on vinyl rain boots. She turned and waved at Anna, her sharp blue eyes twinkling. Anna waved back and was about to join them when Frank's face appeared at the kitchen pass-through.

"Hi, Anna. You're early this morning. Got something important to do today?" Frank, a refugee from the hippies' era, wore his grey hair long and pulled back into a ponytail to complement his full beard and moustache. In his late fifties, he was of medium height with a slight paunch, but his stomach was offset by a muscular chest and arms. Frank had worked hard at manual labour all of his life until enrolling in a cooking school in his early forties. Bankrolling the restaurant twelve years ago had been a strain, but the gamble had paid off and The Diner had become a success. Now

Frank was a well-respected businessman and a member of the Rotary Club.

Anna strolled over to lean against the counter beside Clive. "Morning, Frank. Nope, just woke up early. Is the special ready yet? I feel like something different today." Frank's breakfast special was only available on Saturdays and was one of the reasons why The Diner was so popular with the motorcycle crowd who rode down from Calgary to eat it. It combined rich layers of egg, Swiss cheese, mushrooms, spinach, ham and cream, and was served with baking powder biscuits.

"I just got a fresh batch out of the oven," Frank said. His girlfriend, Judy, yawned as she strolled out of the kitchen, still tying her apron strings behind her back. Judy's teased blond hair was covered by a white Stetson, which she teamed with a plaid shirt, jeans, and boots. She had a full-time job with a local real estate agency, but helped Mary out with the waitressing on Saturdays. Frank reciprocated by keeping The Diner closed on Sundays so that they could enjoy a day off together.

"Morning, Anna," Judy said. "What do you want to drink?"

"How about a hot chocolate? It's so cold and damp this morning, I sure could use one."

"You bet, honey. Coming right up," Judy replied, turning to a stack of mugs on the service counter.

"How's your mom doing, Clive?" Anna shouted into his ear.

"My mother? She's doing good, thanks. The arthritis in her hands is acting up, though. I told her not to start making the pickles without me yesterday, but she wouldn't listen. All that slicing is hard on her knuckles, especially in this weather. I've got a couple of jars for you in the tractor – Mother knows how much you love them." During her first autumn in Crane,

Anna had accepted a jar of Mrs. Wampole's pickles and had choked on the toxic level of vinegar in them. Every autumn thereafter, Mrs. Wampole had sent over two jars of pickles, and Anna had reciprocated with home-made cookies at Christmas.

"Hey, Clive, with Ben in school, I'm the only one at home these days. Maybe I should just take one jar. I wouldn't want them to go to waste."

"That's okay, Anna. Give Ben a jar to share with his roommates next time he visits." Anna smiled, knowing how much her son hated the pickles, too.

Judy squirted some whipped cream into Anna's hot chocolate and placed the mug before her. A moment later, Mary slapped a plate of the special down in front of Clive, exchanging a nod with Anna before picking up a coffee pot and bustling away. Clive grabbed a bottle of tabasco sauce from beside the salt and pepper and splashed a generous dose on his food. Anna shook her head in disbelief.

"Clive, the way you eat that hot stuff, I don't know why you don't have a hole in your stomach."

"Are you kidding? Why do you think I never get sick?" He forked a large piece into his mouth and quickly chewed it. Closing his eyes in appreciation, Clive moaned, "Oh, this is such good stuff."

Anna picked up her hot chocolate and was about to head to her friends' table when something thumped against the outside of the restaurant window. Everyone looked up as Henry Fellows flung the door open and stormed inside. Henry was gangly and habitually neat, dressed in a tie and a tweed jacket, but he wore neither today. His normally pristine shirt and pants were clinging to him, wet from the rain, and his straw-coloured hair was plastered to his face. He glanced around the room, pausing to wipe his dripping nose and push the hair out of his eyes, before darting behind the cashier's station next to the window.

"Hey!" Judy shouted, rushing to intercept him. Henry ripped the notice advertising the cleansing ritual from the glass and waved it in Judy's face. The room quieted.

"What the hell is this? Where's Frank?" Not waiting for an answer, he shoved her into the cash register and bolted through the swinging door into the kitchen. Judy rebounded and ran after him.

A moment too late, Clive shouted, "Hey, wait just one minute, Henry," before jumping to his feet. Together, he and Anna rushed to the swinging door to see what was happening.

The kitchen was small, really only big enough for Frank. The centre of the room was filled with a large butcher-block island, with cupboards, a preparation counter, and appliances crowding the walls. Henry had Frank pinned against the counter and was shoving the flyer into his face. Henry was slim compared to Frank, but there was something desperate about his eyes that made Anna fear for her friend.

"What's this all about, you backstabber?" Henry was yelling. "A cleansing ceremony! Does that mean that I'm so foul that the new owner has to cleanse the store of my presence before she can take over?"

Frank straightened and pushed the flier out of his face. "Just calm down. I'm sure the new owner didn't mean it that way," he said.

Henry scowled. "Don't think that I don't realize how you've all been laughing at me. I paid my fine and I went to prison for two months. Two months – that was no picnic!" he said, his voice climbing until he was shrieking.

Frank held up his hands in a placatory gesture. "I know, Henry. It's been rough on you."

"Well, I've got nowhere else to go until I can sell my house and get out of Crane. But how can I do that when you're encouraging people to laugh at me? You deliberately put one of these flyers in your window where everyone going down Main Street could see it. Damn it, Frank, you're trying to destroy me!" His eyes rolled around the room as Frank said, "That's just not true."

"You calling me a liar?" Henry grabbed a boning knife from the cutting board and jabbed it at Frank. Judy screamed.

"Hang on now," Clive yelled, pushing into the kitchen.

"Get back, Clive," Henry shouted, swinging the knife at him. Clive jumped out of the way and collided with Anna. Turning back to Frank, Henry was grasping the knife handle so hard that his knuckles turned white.

Frank slid over to put the island between them. "No one's laughing at you, Henry," he said, his eyes wary. "They're feeling real sorry about the predicament you're in."

Henry wiped his damp face. "It was a good idea. That drive-through window would have been a goldmine. I put every nickel I had into that restaurant."

"I know. It was a real shame that things didn't work out," Frank said in a soothing tone.

"It's just been so hard," Henry said, his voice cracking. "Clearances. Zoning laws. The town office prevented me from installing it. What harm would a drive-through window have done? When I think of how hard I've worked for the town council, I could kill myself." He stared at Frank through teary eyes.

"No one's worked harder than you."

Henry nodded. "That's right. But no matter how hard I worked, no one listened to me. Everyone listens to you, though. 'Good old Frank and The Diner. He brings all the tourists into town. That Frank, he sure knows what he's doing. Not Henry, though. Henry's a joke.' You said that about me, didn't you, Frank? You made me into a laughing stock!" He waved his knife at Frank while Judy sobbed in a corner. "But I'm not a joke now, am I? Am I!" He slashed at Frank, and Frank jumped back.

"Henry Ernest Fellows, you put down that knife this instant!" a stern voice commanded from the doorway.

Henry cringed. "Miss Dombrosky?" he muttered. He turned to look at Erna, who stood just past Anna and Clive in the kitchen entrance. She was a tiny bird of a woman, but drawn to her full height of five feet, two inches with a purse clenched beneath her left arm, she was every inch the high school history teacher she had once been.

"How dare you threaten Franklin with that knife. Shame on you, Henry. Your mother didn't raise you to behave like a hoodlum. Give me that knife this very instant." She held out her hand, but Henry was immobilised with dread and just stared at her. "This instant, young man!" she demanded. Henry cringed and slowly gave her the knife, handle first. She snatched it from him and said, "I'm very disappointed in you."

"I know. I'm sorry," he said, his head hanging.

"I really think that you ought to apologize to Franklin, too," she added. Henry raised his eyes to Frank's face, but instead of apologizing, he burst into sobs and fled out the back door.

"Well," Erna said with a sniff, dropping the knife onto the counter with distaste. Anna ran forward to put her arm around her shoulders, while Judy hugged Frank. Mr. Andrews, who had slipped unnoticed into the kitchen, removed a cell phone from his corduroy jacket and calmly dialled 911.

"Police, please. Cecilia, that you? Yup, this is Tom Andrews. I'm at The Diner. Better send Corporal Fox Child right over. Henry Fellows was just in here trying to kill Frank. Yeah, that's what I said. What? Nope, no one's hurt.

Uh huh. Right." Mr. Andrews snapped his cell shut and dropped it into his pocket.

Mary crept up behind him, her face incredulous. "I wouldn't have believed it if I hadn't seen it with my own eyes," she said. "Mr. Andrews, when did you get a cell phone?"

"Bought it for myself last summer from the drugstore. On sale. Bought it as a birthday present."

"Well, I never!" Mary said in astonishment.

4

Corporal John Fox Child sat on a stool at The Diner's counter taking notes. A newcomer to the Crane RCMP detachment, he was a clean-shaven, compact man with a wife and two young sons. Anna had seen him playing basketball in the park with a group of guys from the subdivision, and had noticed that he was quick and wily.

Judy and Frank sat on stools beside him, while Anna and the other witnesses sat at a nearby table. The Diner's sign was turned to "Closed," but that didn't stop curious passersby from pressing their faces against the foggy window to peer inside.

"You quoted Henry as saying something about clearances and zoning laws when he was threatening you, Frank. What was that about?" John asked, referring to his notes.

"Yeah, seemed like someone at the town office gave him a hard time when he wanted a building permit for his drive-through window. He came by last spring to talk to me about changing the bylaw, but then he got arrested, and nothing ever came of it."

Steve entered the restaurant through the kitchen backdoor and nodded to the corporal. "There's no sign of Henry, John. I searched up and down the alley, checked his house, and drove all around town. It's as if he disappeared."

"Is his car parked out front of his house?"

"No, it was gone. I called in for the model and the licence number, and had Cecilia radio out a report to all cars."

"Good work."

Steve nodded and took a seat at the table next to Anna while John turned back to Frank. "You might want to stay closed for the rest of the day. If we haven't found him by nightfall, we'll have a car outside your house tonight."

"Ah, I'm not going to do that. I doubt Henry'll come back to bother us. Looks to me like he just blew a fuse."

Judy interrupted him. "Well, I'm worried. What if he comes back with a gun and starts shooting? He could kill everyone in the restaurant."

Frank put an arm around her shoulders and gave her a squeeze. "Okay, I guess we could stay closed for the rest of the day if it'll make you feel better, honey. How about we do a little shopping in Calgary and go out for supper? John can always reach me on the cell if he needs me."

"Sounds like a good idea," John said. "Drop by the station on the way out of town to sign your statement, Frank."

"Sure. I'll be by once we've closed up here."

John nodded and looked over his shoulder at Steve. "We'd better get a uniform to attend this cleansing ceremony at the Healing Hands tonight. From what Frank says, Henry might hold a grudge against the Raes, too." He picked up the flyer and studied it. "The ceremony starts at six."

"I'll go," Steve said. "I'm sort of a friend of Tiernay's. I was thinking of going, anyway."

"Okay, that works. Stick close to the Raes tonight. Escort them home, too. Why don't you walk over there and tell them what's happening while I finish here. I'll catch up with you later."

"Sure, John." The corporal turned back to Frank and Judy, and Steve said, "You coming tonight, Anna?"

"I wasn't going to, but now that all this has happened with Henry, I wouldn't miss it. Erna and May were thinking of coming, too, weren't you?" She looked at her friends, who nodded. "Do you think it'll be safe, Steve?"

"Oh, I don't think Henry will give us any trouble. I can't see him coming into the store if he sees me inside. Hopefully, we'll have found him by then, anyway," Steve replied, rising from the table.

"Right. I guess we'll see you there," Anna said. Steve nodded at his friends and left.

"John, there's something else I think you should know," Erna said, raising her voice to catch the corporal's attention.

"What's that, Miss Dombrosky?" he asked, swivelling on his stool to face her.

"Today wasn't an isolated instance. Henry Fellows has been acting strangely for a couple of weeks. My bedroom faces the street, and I've seen him roaming up and down peoples' front yards at night, muttering to himself. You've seen him too, haven't you, May?"

"That's right," May said. "I've seen him from my apartment across the street from the Healing Hands store. He's been staring into their window at night when no one's around. I don't think he's right in his mind."

Erna added, "His embarrassment at returning to Crane after serving a prison sentence seems to have unbalanced him."

John nodded. "Thank you, ladies. I appreciate the information. We'll have a cruiser out looking for him tonight. You'll be perfectly safe in your homes, but make sure you keep your doors and windows locked."

Erna smiled. "Of course, John. It's good to see that you're a cautious boy." The corporal smiled at her comment and returned to his conversation with Frank.

Anna arranged to meet her two friends at six o'clock at May's Groceries and More. The small grocery store stayed open until nine on Saturday nights, but it was Gerry's turn to work that evening. Gerry was May's son. He had been helping her to run the store since his father's unexpected death from a heart attack six years earlier. May continued to live in the apartment she and her husband had shared over the store, while Gerry lived a few blocks away with his own family.

When Anna arrived, Erna was waiting just inside the door while May had a last-minute conversation with Gerry. The weather hadn't improved much; it was still chilly and overcast, and night was falling quickly. Erna was dressed in a navy trench coat with a floral kerchief tied over her hair, while May was still wearing jeans and her jack-o'-lantern sweater. Anna had been tempted to wear a black dress and a witch's hat to the ceremony, but good manners had triumphed over her sense of humour, and she had worn jeans and a red sweater instead.

Chatting about Henry's bizarre behaviour that morning, the three women crossed the street for the Healing Hands store. A bunch of yellow happy-face balloons tied to an Adirondack chair snapped in the wind, trying to escape. The sign in the store window said "Closed," but Tiernay opened the door before the women had a chance to knock, greeting them with a cool smile.

"Nice of you to come," she said before standing aside. She wore a floor-length green caftan with a plunging neckline and long, trailing sleeves.

"Thank you for inviting us," Erna responded with a genuine smile.

Entering the store, Anna was overwhelmed by a jumble of bright colours and spicy scents. The walls were painted a fresh mint green, and woven mats in vibrant primary colours were scattered across the floor. Trays heaped with incense, candles, and organic teas sat on display tables next to miniature iron cauldrons and carved figures of Buddha and voluptuous Earth Mothers. Near the back of the store, a white cotton couch with plump, melon-coloured cushions was angled next to a wall of bookcases, creating a reading nook.

May elbowed Anna in the side. "Did you get a look at those, doll?" she asked, pointing past the other guests to the wall behind the cash register. Anna turned and saw three studies of a female nude done in ink: one full-faced with arms out-flung toward the sun, another in profile leaning back against a tree, and a third kneeling in shadow on a forest floor.

"They're all of Tiernay!" Anna exclaimed. It was impossible not to recognize the subject's body and hair. How could Tiernay work with nude pictures of herself on such prominent display? Taking a closer look, Anna muttered, "I think that someone has flattered her a little."

All three women turned to appraise the real Tiernay still greeting people at the door.

"No, dear. I think the drawings are quite accurate," Erna said. "She has a lovely figure, don't you think?"

"Humph," Anna replied.

The room was filling with townspeople, about thirty in all, most probably hoping that Henry would make an appearance after his thrilling performance in The Diner that morning. Greg, barefoot in a white cotton tunic and pants, was serving tea from a kitchenette at the back of the store. Steve, who was still in uniform, leaned on the wall beside the front window. He waved at Anna and her friends before strolling over to join them.

"Any sign of Henry yet?" Anna asked.

"Nope, none. My guess is that he's already left town."

"I don't think so," Erna said. "Henry seemed so obsessed with the sale of his house and tonight's cleansing ceremony that I just can't believe he would leave until everything was settled."

Steve shrugged. "Maybe. We'll see."

"Hello again, lovely lady," Greg said, appearing unexpectedly behind Anna. He reached for her hand, but she scuttled back out of his reach. Grinning, Greg said, "Introduce me to your charming friends."

"Greg, this is Erna Dombrosky and May Weston," she said.

"Delighted, ladies," he replied, bowing with a flourish. "So happy to see you tonight. May I get you a cup of tea? We've got a lovely brand of blueberry spice, something hot on a cold night."

"I'll have a cup," May said, but just then Tiernay clapped her hands to gather everyone's attention. Soft music featuring drums and violins began to play from a hidden speaker.

"All right everyone, I think we'll begin," she said, indicating a medium-sized table carved out of driftwood in the centre of the room. There were several items upon it; a particularly handsome knife with a pentagram carved in its handle caught Anna's eye.

"Let me explain what we'll be doing tonight. The cleansing technique I use has been culled from a variety of ancient rituals. We'll begin by burning sage and pinyon pine needles – sage to chase away evil, and pine needles to cleanse. My brother, Greg, will be assisting me. You've all met Greg, haven't you?"

Greg waved as he threaded through the crowd to join his sister at the table. While she waited, Tiernay lit a bundle of sage and blew it out, allowing the smoke to curl toward the ceiling. Greg lit an incense burner containing the pine needles and followed his sister as they walked along the four walls, brushing the smoke before them with large, white feathers and pushing it toward the open door. Anna was glad of the fresh air because the burning scent was reminiscent of a sweaty man who had eaten too many onions.

"Now that that's done," Tiernay said, shutting the door and returning with Greg to the table, "we come to the noisy part of our ceremony. Loud noise drives out evil spirits. Greg and I are going to beat on the instruments you see here on the table, and we ask that you shout and clap your hands with us. Ready, everyone? Let's begin!"

Tiernay picked up a gong and began hammering on it with a mallet, while Greg beat a staccato rhythm on a drum with his hands. Everyone made some sort of noise: yelling, whistling, hand clapping, or feet stamping. Anna smiled at May, who yodelled beside her, while Erna genteelly patted her hands together.

After two or three minutes of this, Tiernay held up her hand for silence. "That was terrific, everyone! I'm sure we chased away all the evil spirits with that noise. For the next part of the ceremony . . ."

But she never got the opportunity to finish her sentence because the music suddenly stopped and the lights went out. It was black inside the store, the only illumination coming from a street light outside the front window. People began to mutter, and someone shoved past Anna, knocking her into a table.

"Hey!" she exclaimed.

"Everybody stay where you are," Steve called from behind her.

"Greg, what happened to the emergency lights?" Tiernay shouted.

The bell on the store door chimed, and a fresh blast of chilly air rushed into the room. Anna looked up from rubbing her knee as everyone fell silent. The dim light from the street lamp illuminated a shadowy figure hovering on the door step. It paused, turning its head slowly, as if searching for someone. Pulling a slender cylinder from its pocket, the figure stepped into the room. The crowd recoiled and a woman gasped. Someone barrelled past Anna and tackled the intruder, knocking him to the floor. People started shouting and pushing, squirming to see what was happening. Then the lights flashed back on, and the music started to play.

Anna craned to see past the people huddled in front of her. Steve was climbing to his feet, the back of his shirt pulled out of his pants and his hair hanging in his face. He had another man by the collar and was hauling him up from the floor. The man twisted in Steve's grasp, and Anna saw his face. It was Sherman Mason, the cemetery caretaker. He looked dazed, and blood trickled from his nose. Steve released Sherman's collar to take hold of his elbow, steadying the wobbly man.

"Sherman, what the devil are you doing here?" he demanded.

5

Steve asked the visitors to clear the store, and ten minutes later, almost everyone was gone. Sherman sat hunched in a chair behind the front counter pressing tissues to his nose, while Steve crouched beside him, asking questions. Tiernay hovered beside Steve, while Greg leaned against the counter with his arms folded over his chest. Anna and her friends sat on the sofa by the book shelves where they were hidden from view.

"How's your knee doing?" May asked.

"Looks like I'm going to get one heck of a bruise, but it'll be okay," Anna said, rolling her pant leg back down.

"Good, because I can't hear anything from back here. Let's get closer so that we can hear what Sherman's saying," May said, springing to her feet and heading for the front of the store with Anna and Erna scurrying after her. Steve glanced up as they arrived, and Tiernay did a double-take.

"You're still here?" she asked.

"We are, dear," Erna replied. "Anna was injured while the lights went out, so we were just resting on the couch until she felt well enough to walk." She turned to Sherman. "You were saying?"

The caretaker glanced at Steve, who straightened up from the floor. "It's not a criminal investigation. If you want to talk in front of them, go ahead." Looking at the three women, Steve added with a wry smile, "Sherman has kindly declined to press assault charges against me."

"It was a mistake. I guess people were a little spooked when they saw me," the caretaker said.

"To put it mildly," Anna murmured.

Sherman nodded and rose to his feet. Heavy drinking hadn't ruined the caretaker's looks; he was still tall and broad-shouldered with a chiselled jaw and a broad forehead, but his shoulders were stooped, and his eyes were bleary. He checked the tissues to see if the bleeding had stopped. Crumpling them in his fist, he tossed the bundle into the trash can under the counter. "As I was explaining to Steve and the Raes here, I thought I'd come by the store tonight after the cleansing ceremony was over, but before everything was locked up. The lights were out and I thought I was too late, but then I heard people talking inside. I figured there'd been a power outage, and I had a flashlight, so I came in to help."

"I'll have the electrician check the wiring on Monday," Greg said. "Something must have got screwed up during the renovations."

"But why wait until the ceremony was over?" Erna asked Sherman. "Why did you come at all?"

He dropped his gaze. "Now that I'm here, Miss Dombrosky, I kind of hate to say. It sounds kind of crazy."

"Nonsense, Sherman, you've always been sharp as a tack. You gave me excellent advice when you were our bank manager." Anna looked up in surprise and stared at Sherman. When had this broken-down old man been a bank manager?

"I understand that you've been going through some difficult times," Erna added, "but why not tell us what's troubling you? Maybe we can help." She laid a hand on Sherman's shoulder, but he stepped out from under it.

"All right. I guess I don't mind you ladies hearing about my business, too. The thing is, I need someone to run a séance for me, and I figured that whoever owned this store might know how."

They all stared at Sherman. Tiernay exchanged a glance with Greg before saying, "I'm not sure that I can help you,

Mr. Mason. It's true that I'm sensitive to the spirit world, but I've never conducted a séance before."

Everyone was silent until May spoke up. "I've been to a séance," she said, matter-of-factly.

"You have?" Tiernay asked.

"Yup. Down in New Orleans. Earl and I went when we were on vacation. There was a medium, a spooky old lady who claimed that her house was haunted by the ghost of a confederate soldier. I must say, the séance was pretty exciting."

"What happened?" Sherman asked, taking a step closer to May.

"Well, it was night-time, plus the curtains were drawn, so the room was really dark. The only light came from two candles lit right in front of the medium's face. She stared at the flames until she went into some kind of trance, and then she started talking in this deep voice, claiming to be the confederate soldier."

"I don't think that I could do that," Tiernay said.

"You never know until you try," Erna replied. "Besides, there's more than one way to communicate with the dead. Table rapping, Ouija board, automatic writing . . . Just who are you trying to communicate with, by the way?" she asked, turning back to Sherman.

"My wife," he said, meeting her eyes. "I think that she spoke to me in the cemetery last Monday night."

"Really? How fascinating. What did she say?"

"Nothing. She just called my name. Three times. But it felt as though she were trying to tell me something."

"I wonder what it could be? How did she sound?"

"She sounded unhappy, Miss Dombrosky. Angry, even."

"Oh my, that's not good. Can you help him?" Erna asked, addressing Tiernay.

The young woman frowned. "I suppose I could try, but I'm new here, Mr. Mason, and I haven't got a coven together yet. The support of other sensitives helps me to focus my powers. I'm not sure how effective I could be without them."

"Not a problem," Greg said. "What about these three lovely ladies? I'm sure that they'd be happy to help." He gestured at Anna, May, and Erna, his face breaking into a grin. "The maiden, the mother, and the crone."

There was an awkward silence that seemed to hang on much too long. "I beg your pardon, Greg?" Anna finally said in a cold voice, angry that he had insulted Erna by implying that she was a crone.

"The triple threat of the Wiccan religion," Greg hastened to explain. "The three faces of the Earth Mother. I didn't mean any insult," he added, looking at Erna.

"Oh, no," Tiernay hurried to say. "People don't think of the crone as an ugly old hag anymore. Today we revere the mature woman for her wisdom and experience. You're beautiful to us, Miss Dombrosky."

"Why, thank you, dear," Erna said with a smile.

"But, Greg, don't be ridiculous," Tiernay countered. "Anna can't represent the maiden. She's much too old. How old are you, anyway – forty-five?"

"Forty," Anna replied, gimlet-eyed.

"You see, I'll have to be the maiden."

"Figuratively speaking," Anna quipped.

May snorted, and Tiernay glared at Anna before turning to her brother. "I don't know. A séance could be dangerous, don't you think?"

"You know what precautions to take."

"Excuse me," Sherman said, breaking into their conversation, "I don't exactly understand what all this Earth Mother talk means, but I'd be grateful if you could help Evie and me. The whole experience was pretty unsettling. I don't mind telling you, I haven't liked going into that part of the cemetery since."

"Evie?" Tiernay asked.

"My wife, Evelyn. We could hold the séance at my house, if you like."

The young woman paused to consider. "Yes, if she's lingered, her spirit might still be strong in the house. We might even have a manifestation. Okay, Mr. Mason, I'd be willing to try if these ladies will help me." She gestured at the three friends. "May has experience with séances, Anna's spirit is strong, and Miss Dombrosky has a lot of orange in her aura."

"Is that good?" Erna asked.

"Definitely. Orange is a sign of power and the ability to control people. You'd be a very useful person to have in our group, Miss Dombrosky."

May smiled and put an arm around her friend's shoulders. "I've always known that about you."

"Thank you," Erna replied. "What do you think, Anna?"

Anna shrugged. "It sounds to me like someone was pulling a prank on Sherman. It's three weeks to Halloween, after all." She addressed the caretaker directly. "Was there any sign of someone being there – someone other than your wife's ghost, I mean?"

Sherman paused, looking uneasy. "There was a light before I got there. I saw it from the back of the house."

"What kind of a light?" Tiernay asked.

Sherman shook his head. "Just a light. It was bouncing between the trees."

Greg exchanged a look with his sister. "Lights are often part of a spirit manifestation, aren't they?"

"That's right," Tiernay said, her breath coming a little more quickly. "Sometimes a spirit isn't strong enough for an ectoplasmic manifestation, but it can manage light. You should have told us about this before, Mr. Mason. I find the light very promising."

"Sorry," he said, falling silent. Tiernay turned to stare pointedly at the other women.

"Look, don't get me wrong, I'd like to help," Anna said. "Just tell me when, and I'll come to the séance."

"I'll need a couple of days to make preparations," Tiernay said. "Fortunately, I don't have many massages booked yet, so my evenings are mostly free. How about Monday night? That gives me two days." She looked at Anna and her friends, who nodded. "What do you think, Mr. Mason?"

"Fine with me. The sooner the better. I have an old table in the dining room big enough for all of us, I should think."

Tiernay looked at her brother. "Greg, can you help me to set up beforehand?"

"Sure. Whatever you need."

"All right, Mr. Mason, I'll do it. Shall we say 8 p.m., everyone?" They all nodded.

"Good. I'll see you then," Sherman said. "You've all been very helpful. I appreciate it." Without another word, the caretaker exited the store with Erna and May following him a moment later. Tiernay took Greg aside for some private conversation, leaving Anna alone with Steve. She started.

"Hey, I forgot all about Henry Fellows with everything else that's been happening. Did you see him?" she asked.

"No, not a sign of him." He pointed at May and Erna through the store window where they chatted on the sidewalk. "I think they're waiting for you. Hadn't you better get going?"

Anna straightened from where she had been leaning against the counter. "Trying to get rid of me?" When he didn't reply, she shrugged and said, "See you later, Steve."

But before she could leave, Steve took hold of her arm. "Listen, Anna," he said, gazing down into her eyes, "make sure that May gives you and Erna a lift home tonight, okay?"

Anna paused, her expression curious. "Why? May always drives Erna home, but I usually walk."

"Well, don't. Not tonight, anyway. There's some weird stuff going on around town, and I don't want you taking any chances." He released her arm. "Just do what you're told, for once."

Anna frowned, not liking his dictatorial tone. Steve's stern expression softened into a smile. "Come on Anna. As a favour to me. If anything ever happened to you, Tremaine would have my hide."

Anna shook her head in exasperation. "All right, I'll ask May to give me a lift, too, if it's so important to you."

Steve smiled and patted her head, but she knocked his hand away in exasperation. His smile widened into a grin. "That's a good girl. Night, Anna."

"You just be careful yourself, Steve Walker," Anna sputtered after him as he headed toward Tiernay at the back of the store.

6

Instead of driving her friends home straight away, however, May invited them to her apartment for a confab. Once inside, she bustled about her tiny kitchen preparing mugs of cinnamon spice decaffeinated tea. While she was working, May asked Anna to add two logs to the wood-burning stove, the apartment's principal heat source.

"Sorry it's a bit chilly in here," May said. "I didn't expect to be at the cleansing ceremony so long, and the fire's burned down. Thanks Anna. Just leave the door open – I like to watch the wood burn." Anna nodded and joined Erna at the kitchen dinette.

May flicked off the harsh ceiling light and slid a pumpkin-shaped ceramic plate heaped with chocolate finger cookies onto the table with the mugs of tea. The flames from the fire cast dancing shadows over the women's faces as they leaned in to talk.

"Now, tell me about the Masons," Anna said. "In the four years I've lived here in Crane, I've only known Sherman as the cemetery custodian, and I never actually spoke to Evelyn. I had no idea that he had been a bank manager once upon a time."

"You're the historian, doll," May said to Erna. "Tell Anna about Sherman and Evelyn."

"Well, let me see," Erna said, settling more comfortably onto her vinyl-covered chair. "Sherman came to manage the bank thirteen years ago. I remember that he'd had a good position at a bank in Calgary before that, but this meant a promotion for him. My, he was such a good-looking man back then. Tall, broad-shouldered, with a big head of blond hair. The way he wore it combed back from his face always reminded me of a lion's mane. He had an air of authority about him, too. Not loud or showy, but just there below the surface. He was well-respected in the community, wasn't he, May?"

"Oh, yeah. Everybody listened to him," May said with a nod.

"He brought Evelyn and their three young sons with him. He could have commuted from Calgary, but he wanted to be part of the community here. Sherman had a beautiful two-storey home built for his family on Robin Street. I'm sure you've seen the house, Anna – the one with the stonework at the end of the cul-de-sac?"

"Uh huh, I know the one you mean. It's beautiful."

"Yes, and Evelyn loved that house. Her people have a farm somewhere south of here, but they've never been prosperous. Evelyn was the first of her family to attend university, as a matter of fact. She and Sherman met while she was going to school in Calgary. She was a few years younger than he, so Sherman already had his business degree and a good job at a bank by the time they met. Evelyn was very proud of him in the early days."

"She was just plain proud about everything," May said, breaking into Erna's reminiscences. "She used to lord it over the rest of us in the Catholic Women's League. Remember? Chairwoman of the social committee. Never thought anyone else's taste was as good as hers. Used to look down her nose at my store, too. Not a big enough selection for her, and our produce wasn't fresh enough, either. She bought her groceries in Calgary."

"I remember," Erna said, patting her friend's hand. "She was a proud woman. Social status meant everything to her.

Poor Evelyn. It just about killed her when Sherman was fired."

"What happened?" Anna asked, looking from one friend to the other.

The two women exchanged a glance before Erna continued. "Well, about seven years ago, there was a big investigation at the bank. It was very hush-hush. No charges were laid, but Sherman was fired. The gossip was that he had been skimming money. He started having a problem with alcohol after that, and they had to sell their lovely house. The scandal was hard on the boys, too. Their schoolmates teased them, and the eldest son got into fights." Erna sighed. "I felt very sorry for that family."

"Then what happened?" Anna asked.

"Well, Sherman tried to run his own investment business for a time. He gave me some very sound advice, but the business failed after just two years. People had a hard time trusting him, I suppose. He had some health problems after that, and Father Winfield gave Sherman the caretaker's job at the cemetery and rented them the house next door. Evelyn had to take a job with the town office to help out. That's when she started being so reclusive."

"Yeah, she dropped out of the Catholic Women's League and everything. Used to walk around town avoiding people. Snubbed me cold at the Post Office one day. Not that I ever did anything to her," May said.

"She was probably afraid that people were glad she'd fallen on hard times," Erna said.

May shrugged. "If they were, it was her own darn fault. If she hadn't been so patronizing when she'd had money, people might have been more sympathetic when she lost it. I don't think she had a friend in the world at the end."

"I think you're right. It was all very sad. Anyway, Evelyn insisted that her sons go to university no matter how hard things got, and between the boys' educational expenses and Sherman's drinking, they spent everything they'd had. The youngest boy finished his bachelor's degree just before Evelyn died last winter."

"I remember thinking that her death sounded kind of fishy," Anna remarked.

"Yes, and tragic," Erna said. "What she was doing in the town office alone after hours? No one ever knew. And why was she in the basement? The only thing down there was the archives. Anyway, they didn't find her body until the next morning. She had been gone quite a while by then, her neck broken from the fall down the stairs. The mayor had to tell Sherman. If Sherman hadn't been under the weather the night before, he might have noticed that Evelyn was missing, and they could have found her sooner. Not that it would have made any difference, but she wouldn't have been alone all night." Erna paused for a moment to reflect.

"I remember that the town took up a collection to help pay for her funeral expenses," Anna said. "Poor Sherman, he must have been devastated. Didn't he go missing about that time, too?"

"Yes, although he was back in time for the funeral," Erna replied. "It broke my heart to see him standing in the front pew with his sons, wearing an old suit from his banking days. The jacket just hung on him. I think it took everything he had to get through the service that day."

"His boys don't come around to see him anymore, that's for sure," May said. "The only person he ever talks to is Father Winfield. He comes around the store once a week to pick up food, though. Canned stew, soup, eggs, bread – that's all he ever buys. I told him once that I didn't see how a man could live on that, but he just shrugged. I hear he's in the liquor store at least once a week. That's where his money goes, you can bet. And that beautiful head of hair. All grey, and I'm sure he cuts it himself with the kitchen scissors. It's a crying shame."

The women sipped from their mugs in silence.

"Poor man," Anna mused. "And now he thinks his dead wife is calling to him."

"More likely a delusion brought on by alcohol and remorse," Erna said. "I wonder if it's right to hold this séance, considering his state of mind. Perhaps Evelyn's death is becoming a morbid obsession with him."

"I never looked at it that way. We don't want to push him over the edge," May said, her face troubled.

"But if this séance helps him to feel better, maybe he'll finally make his peace with Evelyn's death. Wait a minute," Anna said, brightening, "we could make sure that the séance helps. What if Tiernay fakes a message from Evelyn? Something about forgiveness and telling Sherman she still loves him. That would help, wouldn't it?" She looked at the other women. "Do you think that we could talk Tiernay into doing it?"

"What a wonderful idea," Erna said. "I'm sure that if I explained it to her, she would want to help Sherman. I'll drop by her store tomorrow to broach the subject. Between the four of us, I'm sure that we can come up with a convincing plan."

"Great. If there's anything I can do, just let me know," Anna said.

"I can jostle the table with my knee, or knock on it, or something," May said.

"I'll suggest it to Tiernay, and we'll see what she thinks. Well, this is all very promising. I'm actually looking forward to the séance now that I think it might do Sherman some good," Erna said.

"With or without Tiernay's help, we'll make sure that it does," Anna replied.

7

Anna felt good as she strode through town on her way to the séance on Monday night. Not only was the weather milder, but she felt safe walking alone at night again now that Henry Fellows no longer posed a threat. She had stopped in at May's to pick up some milk on the way home, and had learned that the police had found Henry's abandoned car on a side road just two kilometres south of Calgary. He could easily have walked to the city from there, and the Calgary police were looking for him. Happily, Henry was no longer Crane's problem.

Feeling safe from human attack didn't stop Anna from hurrying by the cemetery once she had passed St. Bernadette's Catholic Church. There was something spooky about a graveyard at night that unsettled even the most rational of people, including herself. As she rushed past the cemetery gates, Anna spotted the caretaker's house through the trees and thought how lonely it looked all by itself. It was quite on the outskirts of town. Her own cottage was the last house on Wistler Road before it headed into the countryside, but she liked her privacy and had Betty and Jeff Hiller living next door, if she wanted them. Sherman had no one.

Tonight there were two cars parked out front of the caretaker's house, one of them May's old Buick, and the other a red sports car belonging to Tiernay. No doubt May had given Erna a lift, even though the older woman lived just three blocks away from Sherman on the other side of the church. As fit as Erna was at her age, she was cautious and didn't like walking alone after dark.

Anna paused on the sidewalk to study the house. Two over-grown ash trees blocked most of the light from the porch lamp, leaving the yard steeped in gloom. The white stucco gleamed like bone through the branches, and the roofline drooped over the second storey. Anna shivered, thinking how creepy the house looked, and hurried up the cracked cement walkway to the front steps. The porch was small, just big enough to hold a folding chair and a low plastic table. At least Sherman kept the porch floor painted and swept. She knocked on the door with her knuckles and stood on a hunk of worn outdoor carpet, waiting for someone to let her in.

Sherman opened the door dressed in a pair of faded jeans with a nubby brown cardigan over a greyish-white shirt. Anna noticed that his feet were bare inside a pair of bedroom slippers.

"Come in," he said, backing into the foyer and indicating that she should enter.

"Nice night," she said, stepping onto a mat and bending to untie her shoe laces.

"Keep them on. It won't make any difference to the carpet."

"If you're sure?" Anna asked, straightening. She closed the door behind her and looked past Sherman into the living room. He was right about the carpet. It was a threadbare grey-blue, its pattern practically obliterated by years of passing feet. The furnishings – a sagging velvet couch, a spindly-legged wooden coffee table, a rocking chair, and an ancient television on a metal stand – looked like cast-offs from a church garage sale. The room was devoid of any knickknacks or personal decoration except for a framed family portrait hanging over the couch. Anna ventured into the room to study it by the light of the single lamp. In the picture, a younger, handsome Sherman stood behind a seated blond woman with three boys grouped around her. Sherman was wearing a tailored navy suit with a white shirt and red-and-blue-striped tie. His thick, golden hair was combed straight back from his forehead, just as Erna had described it.

"Your family?" Anna asked, gesturing at the picture.

"Yes," Sherman said, pausing to look. "That's Robert, Michael, and Douglas, my sons. And Evie," he said, pointing to the woman.

Anna scrutinized Evelyn. She looked to be in her early thirties, a pretty woman with ash blond hair swept back into a chignon, her cheeks rosy and her blue eyes confident. A peach rose corsage was pinned to the chest of her blue-and-white printed dress.

"She was lovely," Anna remarked.

"Yes, she was," Sherman said, tearing his gaze away from the portrait to look at Anna. "The others are waiting in the dining room. It's this way."

He led her down a gloomy panelled hallway into the dining room. Tiernay, May, and Erna were already there, seated at a rectangular table atop a plain wooden floor. The tabletop was bare except for a box of matches beside a brass candelabra holding four unlit white tapers. The women looked up as Anna and Sherman entered.

"Welcome, Anna," Tiernay said in a ponderous voice. She wore a floor-length, skin-tight, black velvet dress with plenty of décolletage and long, fitted sleeves. Her only ornament was a coiled silver snake pendant with amber eyes that nestled on a silver chain in her cleavage. Her light blue eyes were rimmed with kohl, and her lips and fingernails were tinted to match her incandescent red hair. Anna smothered a smile; Tiernay looked as though she were auditioning for the role of "creature of the night" in that get-up.

"Sherman, please take your seat at the other end of the table," the young woman said. "Anna, sit here next to the door."

"Can I get you a cup of coffee first, Anna?" Sherman asked, hesitating. "It's only instant, I'm afraid."

"Thanks, but I'm not a coffee drinker," Anna said. She slid into her assigned seat and waved at Erna and May across the table while Sherman sat down.

"Greg was here earlier to help with my preparations," Tiernay said. Anna looked around the almost vacant room, wondering what preparation she meant. The only other piece of furniture was a small black cabinet situated to the left of the door. It held four multi-coloured candles inserted into crystal candlesticks.

"We've sprinkled St. John's Wort around the room and burnt yarrow to protect against psychic attack. I'm going to cast a circle of protection. I want you all to imagine it encircling the room and shielding us against evil." Tiernay picked up the box of matches from the tabletop and walked to the cabinet. Striking a match, she lit the green candle first.

"This goes in the north corner of the room," she said. Carrying the candle there, Tiernay crouched to set it on the floor. "Guardian of the earth, protect this coven against evil," she intoned, waving her hands over the flames three times. She rose in one fluid motion, bowed, and returned to the cabinet. Choosing the red candle, she lit it and carried the candle to the southern corner.

"Guardian of fire, protect this coven against evil," she prayed. She followed the same procedure with the blue and yellow candles, calling upon the elements of water and air for protection. When she had finished, she rejoined the others at the table.

Removing a dainty black silk pouch from her cleavage, Tiernay said, "I've chosen a stone or a crystal for each of you.

I want you to kiss it and place it in the centre of the table to form a protective ring." Opening the drawstring, she poured the objects into her palm and handed one to each person.

"A fire agate for strength and courage for Anna, a white selenite for peace and safety for Erna, a black obsidian to thwart negativity and enhance resilience for May, and a purple amethyst to open psychic channels for Sherman. For myself, I chose amber to melt opposition." They all kissed their stones and laid them on the table top as bidden, making a colourful ring around the candelabra.

"Now that we're protected, we can begin," Tiernay said. "Sherman, light the candles, if you please." Sherman rose and lit each of the white tapers with the match shaking in his fingers.

"Thank you. May, turn off the ceiling light." May rolled her eyes at Tiernay's imperious tone, but jumped up to flip off the wall switch, dousing the electric chandelier. In the flickering candle light, the room assumed a magical quality, no longer bare and forlorn.

Covering her face with her hands, the young woman muttered a string of words to herself, raising her head to finish more audibly with, "Mother Earth, we find our strength in you." That done, she gazed in turn at the others.

"Let's join hands," she directed, holding her hands out to Anna and May. When Anna took Sherman's hand, she found it cold and rough. She watched him out of the corner of her eye, wondering how he would react to the upcoming events. His face was anxious, and his attention was focused entirely upon Tiernay.

The young woman peered toward the shadowy doorway. "We are here tonight to summon the spirit of Evelyn Mason," she intoned. "Evelyn, Sherman heard you calling to him in the graveyard last Monday night. He believes that something troubles you. We want to help you to find peace. What disturbs your slumber?" She paused, and Anna held her breath, wondering what Tiernay had in store for them.

Nothing happened. Tiernay seemed content to wait, however, staring into the shadows. The other women waited in silence, glancing at each other and around the room.

After a minute had passed, Tiernay added, "Please don't be afraid, Evelyn. Speak to us. Tell us what's wrong. We're your friends. We can help you." She waited again, her chest rising and falling with slow, measured breaths, her eyes staring into the doorway. When another minute had passed without result, she turned her gaze upon Sherman.

"Why don't you try summoning her?" she suggested.

Sherman licked his cracked lips. "I wouldn't know what to say."

"Tell her that you love her. Let her know that you're worried about her."

He nodded. "All right, I'll give it a try." Peering around the room first as if his wife's spirit might be hiding in the corners, he licked his lips again and said, "Evie, it's me, Sherman. Are you okay, honey? I thought I heard you calling to me in the cemetery the other night. Is there anything you need, Evie? Anything at all?"

He paused, and suddenly there was a loud rap on the table top. Everyone jumped; everyone except Tiernay.

"Don't be afraid," she said, squeezing Anna and May's hands. "We've made contact. That's excellent. Just keep holding hands and maintain the circle. Try to focus your inner eye on Evelyn." In an encouraging tone, she added, "You're doing fine, Sherman. Keep talking."

Sherman cleared his throat before saying, "Are you there, Evie? Is there anything you want to say to me?"

As they waited, Anna thought she heard a tinkling sound. She glanced at May and Erna, wondering if they could hear it, too. May winked and Erna nodded. After a few moments, the sound grew louder, and Anna realized that it was music. It sounded odd, however, as if it were being played on an old-fashioned player piano. It was just a fragment of a song, the same two bars of melody being played over and over again.

"Where's it coming from?" May asked, looking over her shoulder.

"I'm not sure," Anna said, craning her head upward. "From above us, maybe?"

"I recognize that melody," Erna said. "It's 'Lara's Theme'."

"What's that?" Anna asked.

"From the movie *Dr. Zhivago*," Erna replied.

"Sherman, is there some significance to this music?" Tiernay asked. Anna turned to look at the caretaker. His eyes looked haunted.

"Evie loved that movie. She used to have a music box in her bedroom that played that song. It sounded just like this. I don't know what happened to it. I haven't seen it in months."

"Good, we're making more progress," Tiernay said. "Stay focused, everyone."

Anna looked at the group seated around the table. Tiernay's eyes were closed in concentration, Sherman's face was haggard, May looked impatient, and Erna was staring fixedly past her toward the hallway.

"Look," Erna said in an urgent voice, nodding toward the door. May gasped as Anna turned to see.

A white fog was seeping into the doorway. It accumulated on the threshold, thickening into a cloud until the sill disappeared, and spilled out over the floorboards. It crept in tendrils across the floor, inching its way toward the table. Holding her breath, Anna watched the fog reach her feet and felt its moist cold wrap around her ankles. Staring as her shoes disappeared, she heard an odd wheezing sound coming from nearby. She turned to look at Sherman. His breath rattled through his open mouth as he stared at the fog.

"It's okay," Anna said, giving his hand a squeeze. For pity's sake, this little show was supposed to help the poor man, not give him a heart attack. She gave Tiernay a sharp look, wishing that she would get on with a comforting message from Evelyn, but the young woman didn't notice her. She was staring into the candle flames, oblivious to everyone around her.

"Tiernay," Anna said, giving the young woman's hand a shake, but Tiernay's eyes were fixed and unblinking, glittering strangely in the candlelight. She didn't seem to hear.

"Tiernay, are you all right, dear?" Erna asked.

As everyone stared, Tiernay's mouth dropped open. "Sherman," she whispered, her lips moving while the rest of her face seemed set in stone. "Sher-mannn."

"Is that you, Evie?" the caretaker asked, his expression strained.

"Murder," Tiernay muttered.

"What's that?" he asked.

"My murder must be avenged," Tiernay said in a monotone. Anna stared at her. Was she insane? This was so not the message that she was supposed to give to Sherman.

"Avenged?" Sherman said, his voice cracking over the two syllables.

"I suffer. I cannot rest. There is no peace while my murderer lives."

Sherman gaped at her, his face a mask of horror.

"Stop it!" May hissed.

Slowly, the young woman turned to Sherman, fixing him with terrible, staring eyes. He recoiled from her gaze, ripping his hands from Erna and Anna's.

"We are bound together in both worlds," Tiernay said. "You cannot escape me, Sherman." He moaned and buried his face in his hands.

Erna rose from her chair, marched around the table, and thrust herself in front of Tiernay. Grasping the young woman's shoulders, she gave her a good shake. Tiernay's head bobbed up and down like a limp doll's, but her eyes remained fixed and staring. Erna took hold of her chin and slapped her hard across the face. The sound reverberated around the room. The ceiling light flashed on, and Tiernay slumped, face-first, onto the table.

Sherman broke into a sob, his shoulders heaving. Dismayed, Anna jumped up from her chair and hurried to slip an arm around his shoulders. May stood beside the light switch, staring at Erna.

"Well!" Erna said with a frown. "This is certainly not what I expected."

8

They got nothing useful from Tiernay that evening. Erna had to use smelling salts to revive her, and when the young woman awoke, she protested that she could not remember anything after the fog had appeared in the doorway.

"Evelyn's spirit possessed me," she groaned, holding her head in her hands.

May bustled over to take command of Sherman, releasing Anna to join Erna and Tiernay.

"I've got to go home," the young woman insisted. "My head's splitting."

"I don't know, dear. You don't look as if you're fit to drive," Erna said.

"I'll take her," Anna offered. "That's your red car out front, isn't it?"

"Yes. Thank you, Anna," the young woman said, glancing up at her with genuine gratitude in her kohl-streaked eyes. "I really don't feel up to driving."

"That's okay," Anna said. "But what are we going to do about Sherman?" May was talking earnestly with the caretaker, who looked shrunken, huddled in his chair. After a moment, she nodded and got up to join the others while Sherman stumbled from the room, turning on the hallway light as he passed.

"Sherman's coming home with me tonight," May said, her face determined. "He's just gone to collect a few things. We'll drop you off on the way, Erna." Erna pursed her lips, and May added, "Well, we can't leave him here alone tonight.

Not after what she just said." She jerked her head toward Tiernay.

"But your apartment is so small. Where will you put him?" Erna asked.

"On my couch. He won't mind," May said, glaring at Erna as if daring her to add any more objections.

"Whatever you think best," Erna said, dropping her eyes.

Anna nodded. It seemed a practical solution to her. Sherman looked far too upset to remain alone in the house tonight, and none of them were going to volunteer to stay in this spooky old place with him.

"Well, if that's settled, let's go, Tiernay," Anna said. "You look like you're just about dead on your feet." She retrieved the leather pouch the young woman had slung over the back of her chair and hung it over her shoulder. "You can pick up the rest of your séance stuff tomorrow."

"Whatever you say," Tiernay replied, rising unsteadily to her feet.

Anna slid a steadying hand under Tiernay's elbow and turned to her friends. "I'll call you tomorrow," she said, wiggling her eyebrows suggestively at May and Erna. They had to hold a war council to figure out how to fix things with Sherman. Erna nodded, and Anna led the tottering young woman to the door.

"So, what was that all about?" Anna asked as soon as she and Tiernay had fastened their seat belts after climbing into the car. She put the VW sports car in gear, checked over her shoulder, and made a U-turn back toward town. "You were supposed to help Sherman tonight, not terrify him. Now he's afraid to stay alone in his own house."

Tiernay laid her head back against the headrest, allowing the air pouring through the windows to blow across her face and tousle her hair. "I don't know what happened. I told you, I don't remember anything after I saw the fog coming through the doorway."

"You're kidding, right? Come on – Sherman's not here – you can tell me the truth. How'd you do the fog, by the way?"

"Greg did it. He rigged a machine inside the black cabinet in the dining room. I activated it with a remote and made the rapping noise on the table, but that's it. That's all I did. Everything else was one hundred percent genuine." She closed her eyes.

Anna gritted her teeth, but didn't say another word until she pulled up in front of the young woman's home. Tiernay and Greg lived in a residential neighbourhood one block north of the Healing Hands store. Their house was a two-storey timber frame with three naked poplars vying for space in the stony front yard. Anna turned off the ignition and glanced at Tiernay, who drooped against the seat. Anna had earned her living as an actress for a couple of years after her marriage to Jack. As far as she could tell, if Tiernay were play-acting, she was seriously committed to her role.

"What can I say? How can I believe such a fantastic story?" Anna asked.

Tiernay opened her eyes to gaze sullenly through the windshield. "Believe what you like. You'll see. I only hope it isn't too late."

"Too late for what?"

"The evil I sensed following you. Maybe it was Evelyn's spirit searching for her murderer. We've got to help her before she gets desperate and takes matters into her own hands."

Anna paused to think. Why was Tiernay so insistent in maintaining her ruse about a ghost? Of course, she had faked the entire séance. What did she have to gain by withholding the truth? It just didn't make any sense.

The porch light was on, and Anna nodded toward it. "Is Greg home to help you?"

"I don't know," the young woman said. "I'll try calling him on my cell." She pulled the phone from her bag and punched in the numbers. The phone rang several times before it was answered.

"Hi, it's me. No, the séance didn't go well. I'm not sure. Listen, I'm out front in the car, and I'm feeling pretty shaky. Anna drove me home. Can you come out and help me? Thanks." Tiernay tossed the phone back into her bag and covered her eyes with one hand. "My head is killing me."

"What about the rest of the illusion? The music? How did you do that?"

Tiernay uncovered her face to glare at Anna. "I'm not going to keep repeating myself. Everything except the fog and the knocking was real. I had nothing to do with the music."

Anna wanted to shake the petulant expression right off Tiernay's face, but the front door opened in the nick of time and Greg came bounding down the porch steps in a green silk shirt and tight-fitting jeans. He looked anxiously toward them as he padded barefoot to the curb. Tiernay swung the car door open to greet him.

"What happened?" he asked, bracing a hand against the hood and leaning in toward her.

"I never got the chance to deliver our message. Evelyn's spirit was still in the house. She got past all of my defences," she said in a plaintive voice.

Greg shook his head. "How is that possible?"

"I've never dealt with a haunting before. She's so angry, Greg. I wasn't expecting it. She asked Sherman to avenge her murder." Greg whistled, and Tiernay nodded. "That's why she's still inside the house. Now that I know how strong she is, I won't make the mistake of confronting her on her own territory again." She held out her hand to her brother. "I'm so drained. I need to sleep. Help me inside, will you?"

"Sure, honey," he said, taking her hand and pulling her out of the car. Once she was standing on the curb beside him, he swept her up into his arms, and she nestled her head against his chest and closed her eyes. Glancing back at Anna, Greg said, "Wait for me until I get her settled. I'll be right back."

"Okay," Anna called through the window.

Cutting across the yard, Greg bounded up the front steps and whisked Tiernay inside. Anna got out of the car and locked the doors, leaning against it and waiting for Greg's return. If she couldn't get any information out of Tiernay, maybe she could worm the truth out of him.

Biding her time, Anna stared up at the night sky. The clouds had parted, and there was a sprinkling of stars across the firmament, but the temperature had dropped and the wind was up. Anna blew on her chilled fingers and tucked them under her arms. She wished that Greg would hurry; it was getting late, and she had to get up early for work the next day.

He came out of the house ten minutes later dressed in a knee-length black wool coat and a black watchman's cap, a natty tweed scarf tied around his neck. Anna was beginning to tremble from the cold by then. He trotted across the yard and was at her side in seconds.

"Sorry to keep you waiting. Tiernay wanted me to help her with a cleanse to get rid of any residual energy from the possession. Can I give you a lift home?" Noticing that Anna was shaking, he put an arm around her waist and rubbed her back.

"Th-thanks," Anna replied, her teeth chattering. "Any longer and I was going to get back inside the car and turn on the heater." She dropped the keys into his hand and waited for him to unlock the doors before climbing inside. Greg turned the heater on full blast before peeling away from the curb.

"Where do you live?" he asked.

"At the end of Wistler Road, just on the way out of town," she said, stretching her toes toward the lukewarm air blowing on her feet. Greg executed a sharp U-turn and headed in the opposite direction.

Anna peeked at his face as he concentrated on the road. The black beard stubble, combined with the wavy hair sticking out from under his cap, gave him a roguish look. A whiff of musky cologne reached her nose, and she sniffed appreciatively. Charlie didn't wear scent, but it smelled good on Greg.

"Feeling any warmer?"

"Starting to. Thanks. So tell me, what's the deal with the séance?"

He turned and smiled at her, his warm brown eyes glinting with humour. "You don't beat around the bush, do you, Anna?" She stared at him, waiting for him to confide in her, but he shrugged instead. "Things didn't go as planned."

"I'll say. Tiernay scared Sherman silly. Why'd she do it?"

"Evelyn had a different message in mind, I guess."

Anna paused, backpedalling mentally. She hadn't realized that Greg believed in Tiernay's magical powers. She was treading on shaky ground here.

"Do you believe that Tiernay was really possessed?" she asked slowly.

"I've seen some freaky things happen around my sister. She is seriously gifted. Believe me." Anna remained silent, frowning out the windshield as their headlights swept up the road. "You don't believe in ghosts?" Greg asked, glancing at her. "I'm surprised to hear it. I thought you were a good, church-going Catholic."

"What's that got to do with it?" Anna asked, her eyebrows arching. "Sure, I believe in an afterlife, but not in ghosts. Not ghosts strong enough to rap on tables or possess people, anyway. Otherwise, the world would be knee-deep in them with all the people who died violently or unhappily, right? That just makes common sense."

Greg shook his head and looked back at the road. "I don't have a clue how it works, Anna. All I know is, if you're open to the possibility of a spiritual world, you have to admit that hauntings and possessions can happen. How else can you explain all the ghost stories we still hear, even in our modern, scientific world? Besides, Evelyn's manifestation may have had something to do with you and your friends being there tonight."

He turned onto Wistler Road and was rapidly approaching her house. Distracted, Anna pointed at it through the windshield.

"It's there, the bungalow with the wood siding and the ivy."

Greg nodded and turned into her driveway, pulling up close to the garage. He shifted the car into park and let it idle. It was cozy with the heater whirring away, and the fatigue of a long day was catching up with Anna. She sighed and turned to Greg, studying his face in the garage light she had left on.

"What did you mean when you said that the three of us being there tonight might have had something to do with Evelyn's manifestation?"

Greg rested his hand on the back of her chair. "Ever been part of a witches' coven?"

"What? Of course not. Don't be silly."

He shook his head. "I'm not being silly, Anna. Tiernay thinks that you ladies have something special. Maybe you don't feel it when you're on your own, but when the three of you get together with Tiernay as your focus – boom!" His long, eloquent fingers drew a mini-explosion in the air.

She laughed. "That's crazy."

Instead of answering, Greg slipped his hand into her hair and let it flow through his fingers. Tensing, Anna stopped laughing to watch him. He removed his hand from her hair, letting it rest upon her shoulder.

"I've wanted to do that since I first saw you," he murmured with a mischievous smile. "You have such rich, dark hair – I just had to touch it. And your cheekbones and jaw line are gorgeous." He traced a finger along her jaw. "I'd love to draw you sometime."

"You mean like the way you drew your sister?" Anna asked, gently pulling away. "You did those nude ink drawings of her, didn't you?"

"Guilty," he said, returning his hand to her shoulder. "Does the naked body make you uncomfortable?"

"Sometimes. It has a lot to do with who's naked."

He snorted and put his hand back on the steering wheel. "That's honest, anyway. You know, Constable Walker had a talk with me earlier. He wanted to make sure that I knew about your corporal."

"Sergeant."

"Sergeant. It's a long-distance romance, I gather?"

"That's right."

His chocolate-brown eyes were bottomless as he gazed into hers. "Long-distance romances can be pretty lonely, Anna. I plan to be in Crane for a long time."

Anna unfastened her seatbelt and reached for the door handle. "I'm kind of a solitary person, Greg. I'm doing just fine." She opened the door and climbed out, turning back to look at him.

"Well, you know where to find me if things change."

She shook her head and closed the door. As Anna circled around the front of the car, Greg touched two fingers to his lips and raised them in a salute. She shook her head again and followed the driveway to the front porch. Waiting until she had her key in the lock, Greg tapped the horn softly and backed down the driveway. She waved with one hand and watched him drive away.

Anna shivered in the frosty night air. Thank heaven she had Charlie to keep her on the straight and narrow. Greg was awfully tempting with his deep, rich voice and seductive eyes, but she'd never been one for one-night stands, even when she'd been an inexperienced young woman released from the confines of small-town life into the big, bad city of Toronto. She had grown up a lot since then, but, oh, it would have been easy to have made a fool of herself with him tonight. Still, she barely knew Greg. Muttering a grateful prayer for keeping him at a safe distance, Anna let herself into the house and bolted the door.

9

"Thanks for letting me stay, May," Sherman said, taking the blanket and pillow from her and setting them down on the couch. He hovered beside it, uncomfortable now that he was alone with her in the small apartment.

"That's okay," May said. "I wouldn't have stayed at your house with Evelyn's ghost traipsing around, either. Can I get you a cup of tea? I've got camomile. It'll help you sleep."

He shook his head.

"How about a glass of wine? I've got a nice red open."

He glanced up at her in surprise. The whole town knew that he sometimes had a drink too many. Most people wouldn't have offered him alcohol under the circumstances.

May smiled. "Come on, hang your coat up in the closet and kick off your shoes. I'll get the wine and meet you back at the couch." Sailing into the kitchen, she pulled glasses from the cupboard and retrieved the bottle of wine from her pantry. The pantry door was just about closed again when she reached back inside and grabbed a box of ginger cookies. Shuffling back to the couch, she set the wine, glasses, and cookies down on the coffee table before sitting down beside Sherman. She poured two generous glasses as he placed his second shoe on the floor and handed him a glass.

"This is nice, isn't it?" she said with a smile. "Earl and I liked to have a drink in the evening before going to bed. Cheers!" She held up her glass, and they clinked their glasses together. Sherman took a deep gulp while Erna picked up the box of cookies.

"Can I let you in on a secret?" she asked.

"Sure," Sherman said, feeling even more uneasy.

"I know it's not very sophisticated, but I like to dunk ginger cookies in my wine. Ever try it? They taste great." She held the box out to Sherman, who stared at her like she was crazy before reaching inside for a cookie. May helped herself to one and picked up her glass. Together, they carefully dipped their cookies into the wine. Sherman studied his for a moment while May popped hers into her mouth. Taking a bite, Sherman chewed the fragment slowly while May watched him.

"Good, eh?"

Sherman grinned and took a second bite while May reached for another cookie.

Anna called Erna from work the following morning to report that both Tiernay and Greg were sticking with their possession story, but suggested that the three of them should meet with Tiernay anyway. Erna said she'd walk over to Healing Hands after lunch to talk with the young woman, and would get back to Anna. When Erna called later that afternoon, she said that Tiernay had a massage at seven, but could with meet them at May's store at six.

Erna, May, and Tiernay were already there when Anna arrived at the appointed time, Erna sitting on the stool behind the cash register while May and Tiernay leaned against the counter. The four women quickly began rehashing the events of the previous evening. As Anna expected, Tiernay insisted that she had been possessed at the séance. Erna nodded thoughtfully, while May rolled her eyes.

Tiernay caught the scepticism in May's face. "You're not a believer, are you, May?"

"Course not," the older woman said.

"But you went to that séance in New Orleans."

"Only for entertainment. I didn't believe that the spirit of a dead confederate soldier was actually speaking to us through that phoney-baloney medium." She looked at Anna. "You're awfully quiet. You don't believe that Tiernay was really possessed, do you?"

Anna shrugged, preferring to appear undecided. If Tiernay thought that she and Erna were open-minded about spiritualism, the young woman might let down her guard and reveal what she was really up to. Tiernay looked at Anna in surprise.

"You're not serious? It's all a load of bull kaflunkers," May said, her face reddening.

"How's Sherman doing?" Anna asked, trying to deflect the explosion she knew was building inside her friend.

May audibly exhaled. "He's okay. We killed a bottle of wine last night, so he was finally able to sleep. I made breakfast for us this morning and told him that he could stick around for a few days, if he wanted to. I haven't seen him since."

"I'm glad to hear you're looking after him. He looked so shocked last night," Erna said. "I think that he's still very vulnerable about his wife's death."

"What about his wife's killer?" Tiernay asked. The conversation came to a dead halt as Anna, May, and Erna turned to look at her, Tiernay staring defiantly back at them.

"You're not seriously suggesting that Evelyn was murdered, are you? For Pete's sake, the police thought it was a straightforward accident at the time," May said, growing excited again. "The town office is old, and the basement steps are steep. Evelyn's fall was an accident. The only mystery about her death was what Evelyn was doing down there."

"May's right," Erna added. "There wasn't a hint of gossip at the time. It would have been all over town if her death had seemed suspicious."

"What about security cameras?" Tiernay asked. "At least we would know who was in the office with her when she died."

May snorted. "Are you kidding? In a town this size? We don't have the money to buy security cameras. Besides, why would the town office need them?"

"What does Sherman think, May?" Anna asked, trying to change the subject again.

"He didn't want to talk about it last night or this morning, but you saw how shook up he was." May glared at Tiernay. "Why'd you have to go and say all that crapola? I thought you were going to tell Sherman that Evelyn was at peace and everything was hunky-dory."

"I didn't say anything. Everything you heard came directly from Evelyn. I was only her mouthpiece," Tiernay snapped.

"Don't be ridiculous!" May looked like she was about to launch into a tirade when Erna laid a firm hand upon her arm.

"Let's not go into that again, dear. It's so unproductive." May clamped her mouth shut and folded her arms over her chest, looking like steam was going to pour out of her ears. Erna looked at Tiernay.

"Let's assume that you're right. Let's say that Evelyn was murdered, and that her spirit can't rest until it's avenged. How would you suggest that we proceed?"

"We have to hold another séance," the young woman said with a determined expression. "But not inside her house – she's too strong for us there. We might want to try the cemetery this time."

"You've got to be joking," May said, her voice rising.

"We should talk to Sherman first," Anna said quickly. "If we hold another séance, he'll want to be there. But before we talk to him about that, let's ask him if he knows anything useful about the circumstances surrounding Evelyn's death."

"Like what?" May asked.

"Like, was she upset before she died? Was something bothering her? I don't know – maybe she was taking some kind of medication that made her feel dizzy and lose her balance on the stairs."

"What does that matter, if she was murdered?" Tiernay asked.

"I just want to look at all the possibilities," Anna said, holding up her hands in a "let's all cool down" gesture as May took a step closer to Tiernay.

"Look, we can't make him go through all that again," May said. "He must have covered that with the police back when it happened." She jerked her head at Tiernay. "Why doesn't she just admit that she made a mistake and tell Sherman that Evelyn wasn't murdered after all?"

"I'll do no such thing," Tiernay said with a sniff. "That was a legitimate possession, and I'm not going to sully my reputation by saying that I made the whole thing up. It's so hard to get people to believe as it is."

"All you care about is your business, but nobody gives a rat's ass about it. You scared Sherman, and now you have to fix him." May's chin jutted out as she glared at Tiernay.

"Ladies, please calm down," Erna said. "It does no good to inflame the situation. I must say that I agree with Anna, though. Sherman has had several months to think about Evelyn's death. Maybe he can shine some light on the events leading up to it. I think it's worth a try, don't you?" Erna looked at May with a pleading expression on her face.

"Is he upstairs?" Anna asked.

"Maybe," May replied, relenting a little. "It's supper time. Let's go find out."

May avoided Tiernay as she marched over to the door to flip the store's sign to "Closed." The four women flocked upstairs to find Sherman watching the news and drinking a can of beer in May's recliner. He sat up with a thump, his eyes darting from one face to another.

"What is it?" he asked.

"Nothing, Sherman," May said in a soothing voice. "We just want to talk to you about Evelyn."

"Oh," he said, slumping back into the chair and looking wary. "Why?"

Erna sat down on the couch next to his chair. "We're looking for a little more information about how Evelyn was feeling before the accident."

"Accident?" he said with a bitter smile. "Are we back to calling her death an accident again?" No one said anything, and Sherman sighed. "She wasn't very happy, if you want to know the truth." He clicked the remote to turn off the television.

"Why wasn't she happy?" Erna asked.

"She was angry with me. She wanted to move away from Crane and start fresh somewhere else, but I was against it."

"How come? Wouldn't that have made life easier for you?" May asked, pulling over one of the dinette chairs to sit down beside him. Anna and Tiernay took their places on the couch beside Erna, listening eagerly.

"No. We both had jobs in Crane, and Father Winfield was renting the house to us cheap. Evie wanted to go back to Calgary, but who would have hired me there?" He averted his eyes, the colour in his face deepening.

"Was she on any kind of medication before her death?" Anna asked.

"Medication?" Sherman looked up in surprise. "Well, she had to take a tranquillizer to help her sleep. They made her feel groggy in the morning at first, until the doctor cut back on the dosage. But that was all worked out weeks before she died."

"Why couldn't she sleep?" Anna asked. "Was she stressed about work?"

"Sometimes, but there were things she liked about it, too. She was proud of how quickly she picked up the computer system, for instance, and she was praised for re-organizing the filing system. But she didn't like having to talk to people about their taxes or the town by-laws. They would get upset with her, and she found that hard. She used to talk to me about it at night. She said that it wasn't her fault – that she didn't make up the rules."

"Was anyone in particular upset with her?" Erna asked.

"The contractor putting up the new houses in the subdivision last winter was a problem. He'd be in two or three times a week about something or other, and he always wanted answers right away. And there was Henry Fellows. He had that idea about a drive-through, but there was some problem with the zoning laws not allowing it. He got angry with Evie one day. Said that since he was a member of the town council, he deserved special consideration, and he wasn't going to stop until he got it. Evie came home really upset that night. She said that Henry had shouted at her and treated her like dirt, like she was a nobody. She was crying."

Sherman stopped, his emotions overcoming him. May leaned over to pat his arm, and Erna said, "Poor Evelyn. We're sorry to drag up such unhappy memories."

He nodded. "I wish I could have saved her from that kind of unpleasantness. Evie wasn't used to dealing with unhappy people. But we couldn't get by without her pay cheque." He stared at the floor again. "It wasn't the life I promised her when we got married. I'm sure that she was disappointed with me." He clambered to his feet. "Excuse me ladies. I need some fresh air." Sidestepping the couch, he rushed from the room.

"Sherman, your jacket," May called after him, snatching up his coat from the back of a kitchen chair and hurrying to the door with it. They heard his feet pounding down the stairs, however, and May returned still holding the jacket.

"He'll miss it. It's cold outside," she said, slipping it back over the chair. She sighed. "I wish we hadn't done that. He's upset enough as it is. It's not fair, kicking a man when he's down."

"I'm sorry, May," Erna said. "We don't seem to have learned anything useful, have we? Evelyn was an unhappy woman, but she didn't seem frightened or worried before she died."

Tiernay said, "All the more reason to hold another séance."

"Not that again," May groaned.

"Look, Evelyn is very unhappy. If we don't do something about it soon, things could get pretty ugly around here."

"How so?" Anna asked.

"I can't say for sure," the young woman said, "but it stands to reason. A spirit strong enough to get past my defences wants revenge on her murderer. If we don't find some way of appeasing her, Evelyn may decide to take matters into her own hands. Believe me, we don't want that kind of trouble. And she'll remember us. We were the ones at the séance. She'll focus all her unhappiness on us."

May said, "You are seriously loony tunes, Tiernay. You've got to stop all this garbage about séances and leave Sherman alone. I, for one, won't have anything more to do with it." She turned to Erna and Anna, her eyes searching their faces. "What about you two?"

Anna looked at Tiernay. "I think we have to do what's best for Sherman. We've dredged up a lot of unhappy memories and upset him with all this talk of Evelyn being murdered. Why don't we just let things settle down for a while?"

"I didn't think you were a true believer," Tiernay huffed, turning her back on Anna to regard Erna. "What do you say, Miss Dombrosky?"

"I'm afraid that I agree with Anna. I'm more concerned about the needs of the living than of the dead." May smiled triumphantly, sure of her friends' support. Tiernay shook her head and got up.

"Well, I must say that I'm disappointed in you ladies. I thought that you wanted to help Sherman and Evelyn, but you're afraid to deal with the truth. I've got an appointment in five minutes, so I'm leaving. You know where to find me when things start to go wrong. And they will go wrong, I promise you that." She strode out of the room with her head held high, and they heard her clatter down the outside stairs.

"Witch," May muttered.

"Now what?" Anna asked.

"I think that we should wait and see what happens next," Erna said. "We don't know if Tiernay truly believes in what she says, or if she and her brother are up to some kind of chicanery. Meanwhile, I will apprise Steve of what's happened so that he can keep an eye on Sherman and the Raes' store. We must be prepared for trouble."

"I agree," May said, "but if Tiernay and her brother are up to something, I'll be the first to know it. Their store is right across the street, after all, and I've got binoculars."

"Just be careful," Erna said. "If you see something that worries you, don't try to handle it alone."

"You bet. I'll be on the phone to you and Anna right away, first trouble I see." But looking at the stubborn expression on her face, Anna wasn't sure she believed May.

10

It was Thursday night, two days after the discussion with Tiernay and just past the supper hour. Anyone happening to look in the window of May's Groceries and More would have seen May and Gerry shouting at each other beside the produce section. Gerry, tall and sturdy with a balding, egg-shaped head and a full beard, was waving an apple at his mother. May was standing next to a trolley heaped with grapes, clutching a scissors in one hand and a bunch of grapes in the other.

"Look, Ma, I'm not making it up," Gerry was saying. "They were gossiping about you at the liquor store when I went in this afternoon. They stopped as soon as they saw me standing behind them, but I'd heard enough by then to realize what they were saying."

"Come on, Gerry. Cindy is an idiot. She should know better than to gossip with the customers. The liquor store should fire her, no matter how short-staffed they are."

Gerry tossed the apple onto the pile in exasperation, and had to catch a couple before they rolled off. "But Mike and Heather aren't. They're on the Parent-Teacher Association with me, for Pete's sake. And they were all laughing about you and Sherman being shacked up together."

"Well, we're not. The poor man is devastated, that's all. I'm just trying to help him," May said, cutting the bunch of grapes in half with an emphatic "snip" and dropping them onto the heap.

"I know. I get that. But, enough already. When's he going home?"

May slapped the scissors onto the trolley and wiped her hands along her apron. "I can't just kick him out. The séance was only three nights ago. Where's he going to go?

"Home. He's a grown man!" Gerry said, waving his hands in the air.

May shook her finger in his face. "I don't care what the fools in this town say. I'm not going to toss Sherman out. Case closed." She swung on her heels and stomped to the front of the store while Gerry stared after her, fuming.

"Of all the stupid nonsense," May muttered as she rounded the display counter and picked up a box of chocolate bars from the shelf beneath. "A man his age, bothered by some stupid gossip." She stepped back around the counter and began stacking the bars onto the display.

A minute later, Gerry stalked down the aisle with his coat flapping open over his apron. "I'm going home on time tonight. Susan's holding supper for me."

"Good. Get going. No one told you to hang around," May shouted, watching him over her shoulder as he stamped past her. The bell pealed as Gerry flung the door open, letting it bounce against the wall before storming through it and out into the night.

"And don't break the door just because you're having a temper tantrum, you fat-head," May yelled after him.

Across the street, the sign on the Healing Hands' door was flipped to "Closed," and the lights were turned off. Steve Walker was in the curtained cubicle at the back of the store stripping down to his briefs. A shaded lamp was turned on low in the corner, and half a dozen glowing candles were spread along the top of a bookcase containing magazines. Steve grinned as he heard classical music playing with the sound of running water and bird song embellishing the sweet violins. Typical relaxation music. At least it wasn't pan pipes; he couldn't abide that. Mounting the padded, sheet-draped table, he flopped onto his stomach.

"You ready, Steve?" Tiernay called through the curtain.

He pulled the white sheet over the lower half of his body and positioned his face into the terrycloth-covered head rest. "Sure, come on in," he called back.

Tiernay whisked the curtain aside and stepped into the cubicle, pulling the curtain closed behind her. Her flip-flops smacked against her feet as she walked up to the table dressed in a pair of pink shorts and a white cotton t-shirt that exposed a lot of smooth, tanned skin. She leaned over to switch on a space heater, her shirt creeping up her back as she did.

"Don't want you getting cold," she said, pushing a squeaking cart to the head of the table and pausing to inspect its contents. Selecting a plastic bottle from among the others, she squirted oil into her cupped hand and rubbed it between her palms. The scent of lavender and orange infused the air. Gently, Tiernay laid her hands onto Steve's wide shoulders.

"Temperature okay?"

"Perfect," he murmured, gazing down at her feet.

"Okay, I want you to relax," she said, tracing easy circles over his shoulders. "Let all the tension drain out of your body onto the table. I'm going to start easy and increase the pressure as I work at that blockage in your chi."

"Sure," he said. He exhaled slowly and let himself enjoy the sensation of her strong hands kneading away at the tension in his neck and shoulder muscles. It had been a little crazy at work this week, what with Henry's attack on Frank and subsequent disappearance, and he had put in a couple of extra-long shifts that had left him feeling worn-out. It was good to have some down time just to relax and let everything go.

Tiernay worked in silence for a few minutes, gradually increasing the pressure and alternating flat-handed strokes with kneading as she worked along the base of his neck and down his right shoulder.

"Have you ever had a massage before?" she asked, finding the trouble spot and concentrating on it, her thumbs jabbing into the tight muscle knot. Steve's breath whistled through his teeth as he inhaled sharply.

"Breathe in through your nose and out through your mouth. Don't fight me, Steve. It'll feel better soon," Tiernay said as she applied steady pressure with her thumbs.

"When you stop," he muttered under his breath, fighting not to rise up off the table. After a couple of excruciating minutes, she left the tender spot and began thrusting her palms deep into the tissue along his spine. Steve exhaled and let himself relax again.

"I've had a couple of massages at the gym, but nothing this deep before."

"Okay." After several minutes, she worked her way to his lower back, brushing her palms along his hips and stroking back up again. "Well, this is different. I combine therapeutic massage with Chinese pressure point. It should open the blockage, but it may take two or three appointments before your energy flow is rebalanced."

He grunted in reply.

She worked in silence, and Steve began to feel disembodied as she pounded and manipulated his body. He allowed his mind to drift with the music, listening to a gentle shower pattering upon a lake. Warm air from the heater blew crossways against his skin, and he felt cocooned by the pillows and soft sheets lying under and over his body.

He was drowsing and almost asleep when Tiernay rested a hand upon his shoulder. "Time to turn over onto your back," she said.

Steve opened his eyes and raised one hand, wiping a spot of spittle from the side of his mouth. Geez, he felt rubbery, as if he had been flattened by a truck. Would he have enough energy to climb down from the table when she was finished? Summoning a reserve of strength, he flipped over, holding onto the sheet with one hand to keep his lower half covered.

Tiernay lifted his arm back onto the table and sat down on a stool by his head. She squirted more oil into her hands, and the room filled with a different scent. Something earthy and nutty, with a rich undertone of spice. Was it cloves? He could almost taste it in his mouth, the smell was so strong.

She rubbed her hands together and slid her palms down his arms, firmly at first but easing up on the pressure as her hands climbed back up his chest to his shoulders. She did this a second and a third time, and Steve felt his body slide forward and roll back as if he were being carried on a wave. Her fingers danced up his arms a fourth time, and she began concentrating on his right shoulder again.

"So, tell me, Steve, is there anyone special in your life?" she murmured.

His eyes flickered open as he tried to focus on her question. A face flashed before him and was gone in an instant. "No. Someone a few months ago, but it didn't work out."

"Bummer," Tiernay said. She hummed along to the music under her breath for a few seconds. "Was she a local girl?" She was working on the problem spot again, but either it had released some or it was numb, because it hardly hurt this time. His head felt woozy, though. Must be the massage had increased his blood flow.

"Not a girl – a woman," he muttered.

"Aaah haa," Tiernay replied, drawing out the vowel in each word as she rolled the cords in his neck before stroking under his jaw and along his throat. It was a curious sensation, and it made him feel oddly vulnerable. She began massaging his face, working her way up his jaw to his temples.

"Do you still see her?"

"Mmm. Every week," he said, almost too exhausted to speak. Tiernay said nothing for the next few minutes as she rubbed his scalp with her fingertips. It felt so good that he moaned. She left that and worked soothing fingers down the back of his neck.

The strokes became firm, slow, and rhythmical. He felt as if he were floating on a lake, bobbing gently up and down as her hands pushed him down and pulled him up again. "Do I know her?" she asked, pausing, her lips so close that her breath warmed his ear, her arms encircling his upper body.

"Yeah," he said, more of an exhalation than a word, his soul stripped open before her. "Anna."

Another minute passed as she worked her magic on him. "Anna," she repeated huskily. "I had a hunch." He was hardly aware of her voice, just her hands as they slid down his chest and across his belly. His eyes were closed, but as she spoke, he felt her leaning into him, close enough that he could feel the warmth of her skin.

"I think that we can do better, Steve," she said, whispering in his ear, his flesh fused with her hands as she carried him further and further with the mastery of her craft.

Outside the cubicle, the basement door inched closed, and a latch clicked noiselessly back into place.

It was nine o' clock; closing time. May was standing in front of the store entrance, locking the door. She stepped out from inside the screen and let it bump closed behind her. Turning around and lifting her eyes to the sky, she sniffed eagerly at the sharp, cold smell of decaying leaves and almost-snow in the air. She loved this time of year when the lethargic heat of summer gave way to the revitalizing chill of winter. The wind gusted against her cheeks as she gazed at the tiny pin-pricks of light in the velvety-blue sky next to the elegant slice of moon. Taking a deep, cleansing breath, she blew it out through her lips, letting go of the tension in her shoulders.

She shouldn't have allowed Gerry to get to her like that. Poor kid, he was so middle-class, letting the small town gossip bother him. There was nothing so freeing as growing old and not giving a damn anymore. She smiled smugly. But she had always felt that way, not caring a flying fig for what other people thought. She and Earl. What a team they had made. Damn, how she missed that man, especially at night when she turned out the lights and there was no one lying beside her in the dark. It had been kind of nice, the last couple of nights, hearing Sherman's rough snores drifting through her closed bedroom door. Maybe things might progress beyond friendship? She chuckled to herself. What would Gerry say to that?

Something creaked close by in the wind. A tree branch? She cocked her head to listen. There was a rustling sound in the bushes along the front of the store and a loud, "meow." May relaxed. Probably the next door neighbour's old tom, on the prowl for his lady-love again. She dropped the keys into the pocket of her quilted coat and shuffled down the stairs, letting her hand slide down the wooden railing for support. These days her sixty-three-year-old ankles always ached after the long hours in the store, and she had to take her time on the stairs afterward.

Reaching the sidewalk, she followed it along the gravel parking lot until it turned left at the side of the building. Turning the corner herself, she hesitated. Damn. The bulb had blown out at the top of the stairs beside her apartment door. The Diner was next door to her, but its security lights shone on Main Street and the back alley, leaving the space between the buildings and her apartment stairs in heavy shadow. Maybe she should try calling home on her cell? If Sherman were there, he could open the door and turn on the foyer light for her.

It was nippy, and she gathered her coat more closely around her. Nuts, she was acting like a scaredy-cat. She'd walked the short distance home from work in ice, rain, and fog, and she could certainly find her way in the dark. Stepping forward with one hand feeling the wall beside her and the other outstretched, May groped her way through the blackness, walking the ten yards or so to the base of the stairs. Touching the first step with the toe of her shoe, her face broke into a smile. Nothing to it. She gripped the railing and hauled herself up, counting as she went.

Bottom step, second step, third step, fourth. Her foot was reaching for the fifth when something blacker than the encompassing shadows surged up before her and towered over her head. A mouldy-smelling cloth skimmed over her face. She gasped, sucking it into her mouth. Spitting it out again, May shouted and beat both hands against it. The spectre leaned forward, and she overbalanced, tumbling backward. Her body thudded as she collided with each bone-rattling step on the way to the sidewalk. Smacking onto it, she collapsed into a heap. The spectre floated down the stairs and hovered overhead for three long seconds before dissolving into the gloom beside the building.

May lay unconscious on the sidewalk with the wind blowing tufts of hair around her face. Only the old tom cat noticed her predicament. He touched her face with a damp, inquisitive nose before he, too, was gone.

11

The shrill ring of the telephone woke Anna up. Grabbing for the receiver and pushing the hair out of her face, she glanced at the clock on her bedside table. It read 11:29 p.m.

"Hello?" she muttered.

"Anna, it's Erna. Get over to May's right away. She's been hurt."

"What! What happened?" Anna asked, flinging off the covers.

"She fell down her apartment stairs. She called me on her cell. I just called 911. Get moving!"

Without bothering to say goodbye, Anna slammed down the phone, jammed her feet into her slippers, and almost fell over Wendy, who was scrambling up off the floor.

"Wendy, down!" she shouted, pushing the startled animal back onto the floor. Grabbing her purse, she raced down the hallway for the front hall closet, where she grabbed a jacket and threw it over her pyjamas. She ran outside, slammed the door shut behind her, and jumped into her car parked out front of the garage. She backed quickly out of the driveway and tore off down the street, headed for town. Erna had no car, so she couldn't get to May unless she walked. She must be worried sick about their friend!

All kinds of desperate scenarios flitted through Anna's mind as she drove. How had May fallen down the stairs? Was she seriously hurt? At least she'd been well enough to call Erna for help. Slamming on the brakes and careening into the parking lot, Anna stopped her car and ran along the front of the store. It was pitch black as she turned the corner toward May's apartment, and she had to feel her way more slowly. Where were the lights? No wonder May had fallen.

"May!" she shouted, but her friend didn't answer. After a few yards, Anna spotted a small white light shining low on the ground. She hurried toward it and was able to make out May, stretched face down on the sidewalk. Reaching her, Anna saw that the light was coming from May's cell phone, still open in her hand. May moaned, and Anna fell to her knees beside her. Fumbling in her bag, Anna found her own cell phone and flipped it open to provide more light. May's eyes were closed.

"May," she said, gently tugging at her friend's shoulder, "wake up."

The older woman's eyes fluttered open, and she looked up at Anna. Her face was grey and creased with pain.

"My leg," she groaned.

Anna turned to look, and saw that May's left leg was turned out at an unnatural angle. She cringed and turned back to her friend. There was dirt embedded in May's cheek, and Anna brushed it away. "Don't move, the ambulance is on the way."

"Ghost," May muttered.

"What?" But before she could ask what she meant, Anna heard an emergency vehicle screaming toward them. She jumped up and dashed around the building to the parking lot, where the flashing lights of the ambulance momentarily blinded her. As she ran up to the passenger's side of the vehicle, the window rolled down, and a young man peered out.

"She's around the side," Anna shouted, just before the siren cut off. "She fell down the stairs and broke her leg. Bring a flashlight – it's dark." She jumped back as the door swung open, and left the paramedics to collect their gear as she hurried back to May.

"They're coming," she said, kneeling down again and holding her friend's hand. May's eyes blinked open, and she squeezed Anna's hand to show that she understood. Two minutes later, a gurney came rattling down the sidewalk as the two men rounded the building and trotted toward them, bouncing a bright flashlight beam off the wall until it focused on the two women on the ground.

Anna got to her feet and backed onto the apartment stairs to make room. But then she thought of Gerry, and hurried back to retrieve May's cell phone as the paramedics started their examination.

"What's her name?" the middle-aged man asked.

"May Weston," Anna replied as she eased May's fingers from her cell.

"How old is she?"

"Sixty-three." The man nodded. "I'm going to call Gerry," Anna said, patting May's hand. "Her son," she said to the paramedics.

Hurrying back to the stairs, she scrolled through the phone's menu, finding Gerry's name second on the contact list, right under Erna's. She called his number, but his wife said that Erna had already called, and that Gerry should be there any second.

"We need more light," the younger paramedic called, holding out a bunch of keys. "We found these in May's coat pocket. See if you can open the apartment door."

"Sure," Anna said, scrambling to her feet. She grabbed the key ring and ran up the stairs, using her cell phone to light the way. Fumbling with the lock, she tried key after key before finding the correct one and opening the door. A dim light shone from a lamp on a side table in the living room; May must have left it on.

"Sherman!" she shouted, feeling for the switch on the foyer wall. The ceiling light flashed on, and light poured out the door and down the stairs. "Sherman!" Anna called again, taking a few seconds to check the bedroom and the bathroom. He wasn't there. Anna checked her watch. It was almost twelve o' clock in the morning. Where was he?

She left the apartment and descended halfway down the stairs. Gerry had arrived, wearing a parka over his pyjamas. He glanced up at her, and Anna waved. Together they watched the paramedics brace his mother's neck and leg, flinching when May groaned in pain. When the men had May settled on the gurney and Gerry was following them back up the sidewalk toward the parking lot, Anna called, "Where are you taking her?"

"Oilfields Hospital," the middle-aged paramedic called over his shoulder just before the group rounded the building and disappeared.

Anna nodded. Oilfields wasn't a very large hospital, but it was close to Crane and could probably provide May with the care she needed. She sank down onto the stairs, deciding to stay out of the way until her friend was loaded into the ambulance, but the chill from the wooden stairs penetrated her pyjama bottoms, and she shivered. No point in getting cold. Anna trotted back into the apartment, where she pulled one of May's home-made afghans from the back of the couch and wrapped herself in it. Leaving the door open to provide light, she climbed down the stairs backward, studying each step as she went. Reaching the bottom, she peered up at them again. They looked perfectly sound. Maybe May had tripped over a shoe lace and bumped her head in the fall? Evelyn's ghost had been preying on all their minds since the séance, so it wasn't too farfetched that she would mention a ghost after a bump on the head.

Anna frowned. What had happened to Sherman? Was it just a coincidence that he wasn't home, or had he somehow been involved? She heard an engine start up; the ambulance was leaving for the hospital. Climbing the apartment stairs once more, she left May's cell phone on the coffee table and rummaged through the kitchen cupboards for light bulbs. There was no point in Sherman tripping on the stairs in the dark, too, whenever he got home. Choosing an outdoor bulb from the collection, Anna went outside to replace the burnt-out light. Only it wasn't burnt out. There was no bulb in the socket at all. She stared at it, wondering how she had missed seeing it before. Someone had deliberately removed the bulb, maybe even hoping that May would be hurt. Whoever had done it, it sure as hell hadn't been a ghost. Anna shook her head in disgust. Who would want to harm May?

"Anna? Anna, are you there?" she heard someone call. It was Erna. Shoot, she should have called Erna as soon as the ambulance had arrived.

"I'm at the apartment," she shouted. She ran down the stairs and met her friend, dressed in a wool coat, scarf and hat, as she came around the side of the building.

"Erna, you walked all the way over from your house at this time of night?"

"I had to. I couldn't sit at home worrying about May. Have they taken her to the hospital?"

"Yes, you just missed her. Her leg was broken in the fall." Erna's lips pressed together into a tight line. Anna took her arm. "You've got to come see this," she said, leading the elderly women up the stairs and indicating the empty light fixture. "Look at what I just found."

Erna stared at the socket. "Do you mean that the bulb was missing when May came home?"

Anna nodded. "Someone wanted to hurt her."

Erna turned to look at Anna, her eyes troubled. "I hadn't expected that. This changes everything." She glanced inside the apartment. "Where's Sherman? What does he have to say about May's accident?"

Anna shook her head. "He's not here. I don't know where he is."

A crease appeared between Erna's eyes. "Maybe we should search for him, Anna. With what just happened to May, he could be in danger."

Anna stiffened. She was angry at Sherman for not being here when May needed him; it had never occurred to her that she should be worried about him instead.

"Let me just screw in this bulb so that no one else falls down the stairs, and we'll go look."

But they didn't have to go far. Just as they were about to climb into Anna's car, Sherman appeared, limping toward them. There was something odd about the way he held himself; he moved as if he were a mechanical man. It wasn't until he joined the two women that Anna could smell the alcohol on his breath.

"Ladies," he said, tipping his ball cap, "Why are you out at this time of night?" Anna wrinkled her nose and backed up a step, folding her arms over her chest.

"We came to help May," she said, a grim expression on her face. "Where have you been?"

"At Kennedy's for a nightcap." Kennedy's was the local tavern, situated right on the edge of the highway before entering town. "But what's that you said about May?"

Anna studied his haggard face in the parking lot security light. His eyes were bleary, but he looked concerned.

"She fell down the apartment stairs and broke her leg."

"No! How is she?" His shock seemed real enough.

"Someone removed the bulb from the outside light so that she couldn't see when she came home from work. After her fall, she must have lain there for hours."

Erna turned to look at her while Sherman stared back dismally. "That's horrible," he said. "Poor May."

"What time did you leave for Kennedy's tonight?" Erna asked.

"I'm not sure," he responded, looking confused. "May was still in the store. I waved at her when I went by, but I don't think she saw me."

"Was the outside light on when you left?" Erna asked.

Sherman strained to remember. "Yes, yes, it was. The sun had set, so I'd have noticed if it wasn't on."

"Was anyone hanging around the side of the building?" Anna asked.

"No."

"Or in the parking lot?" He shook his head.

"You were gone a long time for a nightcap," she added.

"There was a football game on. I stayed until the end."

Anna studied him coolly, like a bug under a magnifying glass. "Too bad you weren't here when she fell. You could have helped May right away, rather than leaving her out in the cold for hours."

Sherman gaped at her, his skin looking pasty. Anna didn't care if she was twisting the knife into the wound; he shouldn't have been out drinking when May needed him.

Erna gave her a sharp look before taking Sherman's arm. "I'm sure that she'll be fine. They've just taken her to the hospital. She'll be well looked after there."

"Are you going to the hospital now?" he asked Erna.

"No. Gerry is with her. We'll call in the morning to see how she's doing. Why don't you go to bed, Sherman? It's late, and we're all tired. We'll let you know how May is once we hear in the morning."

"All right," he said, looking grateful. "Tell her I can work for her in the store, if it helps. I worked with May a couple of nights this week, so I know what to do. Tell her I hope she feels better soon."

"We'll be sure to do that," Erna said, patting his arm. "Off you go. Get some rest."

Sherman nodded and limped his way through the parking lot. Anna and Erna watched him until he disappeared around the side of the store. Erna sighed.

"Come on, I'll take you home," Anna said, turning toward the car. She clicked the remote to unlock the doors, and they climbed inside. Starting up the engine, Anna pulled out of the parking lot and turned right onto Main Street.

"How can we be sure that he wasn't home when May fell?" she asked.

"I've heard that he often frequents Kennedy's. I'll ask around."

The edges of Anna's mouth twitched into a small smile. "Your network of spies again?"

"I know a lot of people, so I hear a lot of things." She stared at Anna. "That remark you made to Sherman about finding May was pretty harsh. Is something bothering you?"

"Bothering me? Someone deliberately hurt May tonight. Of course I'm bothered. Aren't you?"

Erna's eyes flared. "I may not look it, but I'm furious with myself. I've been expecting trouble ever since the séance, but I thought that it would be directed at Sherman, not at May. I thought that he would be safe as long as they were together."

Anna glanced at Erna before turning right off Main Street. "What are you talking about? Who did you think would be after Sherman?" The streets were deserted, but she slowed down for a yield sign anyway.

"The Raes. Certainly Tiernay, and maybe Greg, too."

"You think Tiernay and Greg are behind this? Why?"

"I have no proof, Anna, so this is pure conjecture, but to establish her reputation in town, I should think. Let's look at this logically. Either Evelyn's ghost possessed Tiernay on the night of the séance, or Tiernay faked it. If we discount a true possession, we must ask ourselves why she would do that. To make us believe that she has genuine occult powers seems the obvious answer."

"I agree. Tiernay is some kind of egomaniac. She wants everyone to think that she's important."

"Possibly. It might be self-aggrandizement, or it may be a ruse to bring business to her store. Or it might be part of a larger scheme."

"What larger scheme?" Anna asked, pulling up in front of Erna's house and letting the car idle.

"What if Tiernay intends to hold more séances? She could charge a handsome fee for her services while asking people to do things under the guise of following their departed loved one's wishes. She could easily defraud the gullible of their life savings. Perhaps she and Greg have already done so elsewhere, and their reputation just hasn't caught up with them yet."

Anna considered Erna's words for a moment. "Do you really think that's likely?" she asked.

But Erna seemed lost in her own thoughts. "If Tiernay wants to build a reputation as a medium, there have to be consequences for Sherman not acting upon Evelyn's alleged desire for revenge. Tonight's accident may have been intended for Sherman, not May. If something had happened to him, Tiernay could have said that Evelyn was punishing him for not obeying her wishes. And who better to pick upon than a recluse with a drinking problem and guilt associated with his wife's death? Sherman is the perfect victim, and Tiernay has chosen us to be her stooges!"

"And you think Tiernay's plan backfired, and May became the victim instead?"

Erna turned to her. "It's possible. Tiernay may have been late arriving at May's apartment, or Sherman may have left for Kennedy's earlier than usual. If Tiernay was waiting for him on the steps when May came home, she would have been forced to attack May instead. Either attack could be blamed upon a spiteful Evelyn. It will be interesting to hear what Tiernay has to say about May's fall."

Anna shook her head. "One thing I don't understand. If you didn't want Sherman to be alone, why did you seem to disapprove when May told us at the séance that Sherman was going to stay with her?"

Erna smiled. "That was just a ruse, dear. If I had told May to invite Sherman to move in, she would have balked at the idea. Haven't you noticed that she doesn't like being told what to do? Fortunately, May has always had a soft spot for Sherman, compounded, no doubt, by her animosity toward Evelyn, so it seemed likely that she would make the offer on her own. Plus, I didn't want Tiernay to guess that I suspected her and wanted Sherman safely out of her reach. But I underestimated Tiernay. I shall ask Steven to redouble his efforts to keep his eye on the Raes."

"You've talked to Steve about them already?"

"Certainly. I also asked him to check into their backgrounds."

"And has he found anything yet?"

"No, but you know how slow bureaucracy can be. I'm hopeful that he'll find something soon to confirm my suspicions." She pointed at the clock on the car console. "It's getting late, and you have to get up for work in the morning. Why don't we talk again tomorrow, after we've heard how May's doing? I'll telephone Gerry and call you at work. You should go home and get some sleep." She climbed nimbly out of the car and turned to wave at Anna from the sidewalk.

Anna waved back, and waited until Erna had let herself into the house before heading for home. Erna's suspicions of

Tiernay seemed far-fetched. Sure, she didn't like the young woman, but that was because she thought Tiernay was vain and wanted to draw attention to herself. You didn't have to look any further than the way she dressed and her flaming-red hair to see that. And she talked about having special powers and belonging to covens, too. But maybe Steve was right, and it was all just an act to bring business into the store.

Anna parked her car in the driveway and got out. On the way to her front door, she thought about Greg. She liked him, even though he was a playboy. Greg could probably charm a girl straight into bed, if he wanted to. But there was a mischievous quality about him that seemed as good as a wink, as if to say, "We both know what we're doing here, and no one is pulling the wool over anyone's eyes." She'd hate to think that Erna was right, and that he and Tiernay were scheming to cheat grieving widows and widowers of their life savings.

Her train of thought was disturbed by Wendy's whine on the other side of the door. "Hi, girl," she said, getting down on one knee and hugging the dog after letting herself inside. "You must be wondering what I was doing, charging around in the middle of the night and leaving you here all alone."

Wendy licked her cheek, and Anna laughed and scratched behind the dog's ear. Climbing wearily to her feet, she looked at her watch and groaned; it was 12:42 a.m. The alarm would be ringing in less than six hours. She hung her jacket in the closet and trudged down the hallway to bed with Wendy padding after her. The dog settled on the floor of the bedroom with a sigh as Anna slid back under the covers.

"I'm too tired to worry about it tonight. It's a big, confusing mess, but it's just going to have to wait until tomorrow. Night Wendy." The dog's tail beat a steady response on the floor, and that was the last thing Anna heard until the alarm went off in the morning.

12

Anna rushed home from work on Friday to have supper with her son before going to see May in the hospital. Erna had called late that morning to report that May had just come out of surgery. An orthopaedic surgeon had repaired a break in her tibia with a rod and screws, and put her leg in a plaster cast. May had also suffered a blow to the head, but the extent of the injury was unknown. For now, the staff was running more tests and would keep her in the hospital a couple more days for observation. Erna and Anna planned to meet at the hospital during visiting hours that evening. Gerry was bringing Erna out that afternoon as soon as he could get away from the store, and Erna was going to stay with May until Anna could give her a lift home that night.

After Ben had left, Anna made a pit stop at May's store to buy her friend some flowers. She had wrapped one of her own vases in a towel and slid it into a plastic bag before leaving home so that she wouldn't have to hunt for a vase at the hospital. Once inside, she saw Sherman working behind the till with four customers waiting in line to pay for their groceries. He was too busy to notice her as she headed to the produce section where bouquets were displayed in two large buckets. Finding a nice bouquet of red and yellow daisies and chrysanthemums, she helped herself to a floral liner and headed for the checkout. Greg stood just in front of her in line, and she hesitated before greeting him, remembering Erna's suspicions. But she couldn't just ignore him, so she said hello.

Greg cradled a bunch of bananas, a bag of coffee, and a small carton of premium ice cream against his chest as he leaned back to say, "It's sad, isn't it?"

"What is?"

He nodded at Sherman, who was frowning as he pulled a woman's debit card from the payment machine and re-inserted it. The woman glanced over her shoulder at the line-up; Anna recognized Cindy from the liquor store.

"He used to be a bank manager, but now he can't seem to get the hang of a debit machine," Greg said.

As everyone watched, Sherman handed the machine to Cindy, who studied the display for a few seconds. "Okay, try voiding the transaction," she suggested. Sherman nodded and pressed a couple of buttons.

"Now put in the amount again." Sherman did as she instructed. Cindy pushed a button, waited for the response, and entered more information until the transaction was completed.

"Thank you for your help," Sherman said, red-faced. "I think I know what I did wrong this time." He handed Cindy her bag of groceries, but she leaned against the counter for a little conversation rather than leaving right away.

The middle-aged woman in front of Greg rolled her eyes and said in a not-so-quiet voice, "They shouldn't have left him alone to run the store even if May's in the hospital. Obviously, he doesn't know what he's doing." She stepped up to the counter and plunked her groceries down, squeezing in beside Cindy, who picked up her shopping and left.

"I heard about the accident. How's May doing?" Greg asked. Anna studied his face, wondering if he really cared, but his concern seemed genuine enough.

"She's doing okay. I'm just on my way to see her in the hospital," Anna said, indicating the flowers in her arms.

"Tell her that Tiernay and I hope she's feeling better soon." Greg was about to say more when a can clattered onto the floor and rolled toward them.

"Excuse me," Sherman said, hobbling around the counter to chase after the can while the impatient customer sighed and put her hands on her well-padded hips.

Greg bent quickly and caught the can with his free hand, passing it back to Sherman with a short bow.

"Thanks," Sherman muttered.

"My pleasure."

The woman looked grim as she handed her debit card to Sherman. He accepted it with a polite, "thank you," and inserted it into the machine. The transaction proceeded smoothly, and the woman took her grocery bag and stalked out of the store, cheated of the opportunity for further complaint.

Greg stepped forward with a pleasant smile as a harried mother and small child joined the line behind Anna. "Just a few things tonight," he said, placing his items beside the scanner.

Sherman weighed the fruit and scanned the items. "That'll be $17.59, please."

Greg leaned forward with two bills protruding from his fingers. "I even have cash," he said with a smile. Sherman reached for the money and somehow managed to knock the cardboard lottery sign off its stand.

"Whoops," Greg said. "I'll get it." He picked the sign up off the floor and replaced it while Sherman fumbled for his change in the till. Avoiding Greg's eyes, Sherman handed the money back to him.

"A pleasure doing business with you, sir," Greg said with a pleasant smile. He waved at Anna and left.

"How're you doing?" she asked Sherman as she placed the flowers beside the scanner.

"Do you want those wrapped?" he asked, pointing toward a roll of florist's paper on the counter behind him.

"No thanks. Just put them in a bag so they won't drip. They're for May. I'm on my way to see her now."

Sherman nodded without looking up and scanned the flowers. "That will be $18.98, please."

"I've got cash, too," Anna said, handing him a fifty.

"Thanks," he said, taking the money. "Listen, tell May not to worry about the store, and tell her that I'm sorry about last night." His face was blank as he gave Anna her change.

"I will," Anna said, picking up her purchase. She hesitated, and the woman behind her sighed. "Look, about last night. I want to apologize for the remarks I made about May's accident. Her fall had nothing to do with you, and I was upset when I said them. I didn't mean to imply that you were to blame in any way."

Sherman glanced up at Anna's face. He looked both bone-weary and tense at the same time, but there was a softening of the reserve in his eyes.

"I understand, Anna. Thanks."

She nodded. "See you later, Sherman," she added before hurrying out of the store for the parking lot.

When she arrived at the door to May's hospital room, Anna found her friend propped up on pillows having a quiet conversation with Erna. It was a semi-private room, and the curtain surrounding the other bed was closed. Erna looked around and smiled as Anna slipped into the room.

"Look who's here to see you," she said as Anna circled to the other side of the bed. May's face looked drawn and colourless as Anna bent to kiss her cheek.

"Hi, doll," May croaked, her glazed eyes drifting up to Anna's face.

"I brought you some flowers," Anna replied. She spent the next few minutes filling the vase with water from the bathroom and arranging the flowers. "Here they are," she said, placing them on the shelf next to May's window.

May smiled. "Hey, they're from my store."

"Where else would I shop?" Anna asked, sitting in the other visitor's chair beside Erna.

"The nurse just gave May some pain medication, so she's feeling a little groggy," Erna explained.

"Good stuff. I'm pretty high," May mumbled.

"Gerry just left to get some supper. We've been chatting about last night," Erna said. "May's having trouble remembering, but that's to be expected, poor dear." She gently squeezed her friend's hand where it rested on the blanket.

"I remember the ghost," May said, her bottom lip jutting out.

"Ye-es," Erna said. She turned so that May couldn't see her and raised her eyebrows at Anna.

"You said something about a ghost when I found you," Anna said.

"Uh huh. A big, black ghost." May nodded her head up and down and giggled. "In a big, black dress."

"Where did you see the ghost?" Anna asked.

"On my stairs. Couldn't see him, but he was there. Made me fall." May swivelled to look at her two friends, and frowned. "Call Father Winfield. Tell him to make the ghost go away."

"I will, dear," Erna soothed. "Anna and I will take care of the ghost for you."

"Good. Scared me. Don't want to see it again." She sighed and closed her eyes. "Tired. Going to sleep now." Seconds later, she was snoring.

"What do you think?" Anna whispered to Erna. "For not remembering much about last night, she seems pretty sure that she saw a ghost."

"I think that someone was trying to frighten her, or Sherman."

Anna shrugged. "So, what are we going to do about it? We can't go to the police with a ghost story."

"No, but I will drop by the RCMP station to talk to John Fox Child. Perhaps I can convince him that something criminal is going on in town, and the police will be more vigilant. I haven't seen Steven lately, but I believe that he's had a few days off."

"What about May? What's she going to do when she gets out of the hospital? She can't manage the stairs to her apartment like this." Anna gestured toward May's cast.

"I should think not. I've been talking to Gerry about it. He'd like to take his mother home, but the bedrooms in his house are on the second floor, and May can't sleep on the couch until the cast comes off. I've told him that she can stay with me. She won't have to worry about stairs at my bungalow. It will be nice to have some company for a change, and I can look after her until she's mobile again."

"That's a great solution, Erna. I could have put her up in Ben's old room, but she'd have been alone while I was at work."

"Exactly. My house is best."

They turned to look at their friend, who was sleeping peacefully.

"There doesn't seem to be anything we can do but wait to see what happens next," Anna said. "Maybe whoever is responsible for this didn't intend to hurt anyone, and things will calm down on their own."

"Maybe," Erna said in a doubtful tone.

13

The following morning was cool and overcast as Anna walked downtown for her Saturday breakfast at The Diner. She had had a troubled night's sleep full of dreams of ghosts and falling down stairs, and had slept in later than usual. It was almost eleven, and her stomach was grumbling with hunger. She had a utility bill to pay, however, and the bank was only open until noon on Saturdays, so she would have to postpone breakfast until after a stop at the bank. That wouldn't be too much of a hardship, however, since the bank was right next door to The Diner.

There were three customers ahead of her when she joined the line-up to wait for one of the two tellers. When it was her turn, Shirley, the friendly middle-aged teller who had been at the bank since Anna had first moved to Crane, waved her forward.

"Hi Anna. How're you today?" Shirley asked, her smile extending to her crinkly blue eyes.

"Just fine, thanks. I've got a bill to pay," Anna said, plunking her purse down in front of the teller's wicket and taking out the paperwork. She handed over her debit card and waited for Shirley to process the transaction.

"Anything else I can do for you?" Shirley asked after stamping the invoice and returning it to Anna.

"Yes. I need change for the vending machines at work this week. Can you break a ten for me?" she asked, handing over the bill.

"Sure," Shirley said. "Toonies okay?"

Anna nodded. "Please."

Shirley paused, studying the bill, and frowned.

"Something wrong?" Anna asked.

Shirley looked up and smiled. "Just hang on a second, Anna. I'll be right back." She locked her drawer and headed for an office next to the customer service desk. Anna looked at the man in line behind her and shrugged apologetically. He rolled his eyes and looked away. It was a few minutes before Shirley returned, stepping back behind the wicket and leaning toward Anna.

"Would you mind coming with me for a moment?" she asked with a polite smile that didn't reach her eyes this time.

"Is something wrong?" Anna asked again.

"It won't take long," Shirley said, putting up a sign saying that her wicket was closed. Another teller opened the station next to hers, and the man in line behind her stepped forward as Anna followed Shirley to the office that she had just left. A young man in a grey suit and blue tie stood up as she entered the room.

"This is Anna Nolan, Jim," Shirley said. "Anna, this is Jim Cheong, the assistant bank manager." Anna and Jim nodded at each other. There were two chairs facing his desk, and Jim indicated that she should take one of them. Anna sat down as Shirley left the room, closing the door behind her. There was a ten dollar bill on the desk in front of Jim, and Anna pointed to it.

"Is that my ten?" she asked. "Is there something wrong with it?"

"I'm afraid so," Jim said, picking it up and rubbing it between his fingers. "There are a few abnormalities, I'm afraid. Shirley was on-the-ball to have noticed them. It's definitely a counterfeit."

"Counterfeit?" Anna repeated, perching forward on her chair. "I can't believe it. Nothing like this has ever happened to me before."

Jim dropped the bill back onto his desk and leaned forward on his elbows, clasping his hands together. "Shirley tells me that you've been a regular customer for four years."

"That's right," Anna said, her voice a little higher than normal. "You don't think that I'm a counterfeiter, do you?"

"We'd like to know where the bill came from," he said, gazing into her eyes.

"Just a minute," Anna said, fumbling for her purse. She drew out her wallet and opened the billfold, checking the bills within. "I had a fifty last night when I went to the store, and Sherman gave me back a ten and a twenty in the change. See, here's the twenty," she said, holding up the bill.

"May I?" Jim asked, reaching across the desk for it. He studied the front carefully before turning the twenty over. "You mentioned a store. What store was that?"

"May's Groceries and More," Anna said, watching his face.

"You said that Sherman gave it to you. Sherman Mason?"

"That's right. May had an accident, so Sherman was filling in for her last night."

"I see," Jim said, gazing up at her with a smile and handing back the twenty. "This bill is fine, but I'm afraid that we'll have to give your ten to the police." He opened the drawer in the top of his desk and withdrew a slim plastic bag. Dropping the ten inside the bag, he sealed it. "It's not the first counterfeit ten we've see this week, either."

"Really?" Anna said, her eyes opening wide.

He slipped the bag into his desk and stood up, offering her his hand and smiling. "Thank you for your cooperation, Anna. We'll let the police take it from here."

"You're welcome," she said, jumping to her feet to shake his hand. It wasn't until she was back on the street that she realized she didn't have the change she needed for work next week, but there was no way she was going back inside the bank. Not having just escaped such an unnerving experience. Instead, she turned next door and headed for the sanctuary of The Diner.

14

Sherman sat on the edge of the chair pulled next to May's hospital bed, his baseball cap dangling between his fingers. He had come in just as the lunch trays were being removed. May's elderly roommate had a visitor, a middle-aged woman who was sharing some photographs with her. May wore a nightgown instead of the hospital gown she had worn the previous evening, and cuddled a bouquet of peach-coloured sweetheart roses in her arms. She beamed at Sherman.

"They're just beautiful. Thanks for bringing them."

"Least I could do, May. I used to buy them for Evie on our anniversary. They were her favourite flower."

"I used to buy Earl beef jerky every year. You might think that doesn't sound very romantic, but he was crazy about the stuff. The company that makes it out in Longview has some pretty great flavours, like barbecue and honey-garlic."

There was a lull in the conversation, and Sherman's eyes roamed around the room while he searched for something to say.

"I'm glad to hear that they're letting you go home tomorrow," he said, his eyes lighting back on May. "I mean, go home to Miss Dombrosky's. She'll take good care of you. Not that I wouldn't be happy to help if you wanted to go back to your place, but I wouldn't make a very good nurse." A rare smile of amusement flitted across his face.

"Yeah, I can't wait to get out of here. Not to complain, they treat me real well, but it's hard to get any sleep when they keep waking you up at night to check on you."

"Things are going well at the store," Sherman said, twirling the cap in his hands. "Your son got some extra staff in to help. Besides me, that is. Things are pretty quiet at the cemetery this time of year, so I'm happy to help."

"So Gerry said. It was nice of you to take over for him yesterday, though."

Sherman nodded. "The least I could do, after you've been so kind to me. It's very convenient, too, living over top of the store. I've been keeping things tidy for when you get back." He glanced up after a few moments when she didn't respond; May was frowning at him.

"Listen, Sherman," she said, leaning in close and lowering her voice. "Did anyone tell you what really happened to me the night I fell? Gerry thinks I'm nuts and should keep this to myself, but I know what I saw. I didn't just trip on those stairs. There was a ghost waiting for me, and I fell trying to get away from it."

Sherman stopped twirling his hat to gawk at her. "No, he didn't tell me. What do you mean, a ghost?"

"I know I already said I don't believe in ghosts," May added, "but what else could it have been? One minute it wasn't there, and the next, it was standing right in front of me, waving its shroud around." May shuddered while Sherman stared at her.

"Did it say anything?"

"Not a thing. It didn't make a sound."

"Then what happened?"

"I don't really remember. I fell down the stairs, and I guess I bumped my head and passed out. When I woke up, it was gone."

Sherman grasped her hand between his callused fingers, his face full of dismay. "May, I'm so sorry. Nobody told me about the ghost. It's all my fault."

"How?" May asked, her face creasing in concern.

"If I hadn't been staying with you, she would never have gone to your apartment."

"Who wouldn't have?"

"Evie. It's me she's after. If I had known that she could leave the house, I would never have stayed at your apartment. I wouldn't put you in any danger. You're such a sweet, generous lady." He bent to kiss her cheek, and stumbled to his feet. "I've got to go."

"Go where?"

"I don't have many things at your apartment. I can clear them out right away and leave the key at the store."

May reached for his hand and missed it as he set his cap back on his head. "But Sherman, where will you go?"

"I don't know. I'll figure that out later. I've got to stop Evie before she hurts anyone else."

"Sherman!" May called after him as he ran from the room.

15

Anna glanced around the restaurant, hoping that she hadn't missed Erna. She wanted to talk to her privately about the counterfeit money episode at the bank. She had a bad feeling that Sherman was somehow involved, but she didn't want to air her suspicions in front of everyone else at The Diner. It would be all over town by the end of the day if she did, and that wouldn't be fair to Sherman.

The stools at the front counter were empty. Mr. Andrews was reading his paper at one of the back tables, and the other tables were occupied by out-of-towners. No sign of Erna.

Anna sat down at the counter and watched Mary fill a teapot with boiling water. After a moment, she cleared her throat to catch the waitress's attention.

Mary glanced over her shoulder. "Hi, Anna. You're late. Sleep in this morning?"

"Yes. Have you seen Erna?"

"Been and gone." Picking up the teapot and a mug, Mary paused at the counter for a moment. "Erna said that a friend was taking her to Calgary this morning to buy some new linens and things for May. I'll be back in a second," she said as she hurried past.

Judy backed out of the kitchen, letting the door swing shut behind her, and turned to rest four bottles of ketchup on the counter. Her face lit up as she spotted Anna.

"Hey, Anna. Frank and I were just talking about you. Frank, Anna's here," she called through the kitchen window. "We were so sorry to hear about May's fall," she added, the smile fading. "Erna was telling us earlier that you were the first one to get to her that night."

"Yeah," Frank said, following Judy through the door and leaning against the counter. "I hate to think of May lying on the ground in the dark all that time, poor lady. Erna said she's doing better today, though."

"Is she? That's good. I haven't talked to May since visiting her at the hospital last night. She was pretty much out of it with all the pain medication." Mary came back and sat down on a stool beside Anna.

"Pretty weird, the bulb missing from the light over her stairs," Judy said, resting her hip against the counter. "Erna said that May thought she saw someone on the stairs before she fell."

Anna shrugged. "Who can tell what she really saw."

"It must have been awfully dark without her outside light on. How could she have seen anyone?" Frank asked.

"And she bumped her head and all," Mary added, raising her eyebrows. "Maybe she was delusional."

Judy shook her head. "Maybe, but it's been pretty creepy around here ever since Henry went missing. The Calgary police still haven't found him, you know."

"Honey, you don't have to worry about Henry anymore," Frank said, hugging her with one arm. "What's he going to do, sneak back into town and break into our house?"

"I wouldn't put it past that psycho!" Judy said. She leaned toward Anna. "Don't laugh, but last week, after Henry threatened Frank, I hid our knife block at home inside one of the kitchen cupboards."

Frank sighed. "Makes it pretty hard to cook with all the knives shut away." Judy frowned at him. "Whatever makes you feel safe, honey," he added hastily.

Judy turned back to Anna. "Well, first Henry, and now May. Something weird's going on in town, you can bet on it.

And have you noticed that we haven't seen Steve for a few days? It's like he disappeared or something. What happened to Steve?"

Steve opened his fridge door and stared inside at the meager contents. It was almost noon, and he was starving. He pulled out a carton of eggs, a block of butter, and a jug of milk, and set them down on the counter beside the stove.

"I'm going to make us some eggs, okay?" he shouted.

Tiernay sauntered into the kitchen wearing nothing but a black towel, her hair damp from the shower. She came up behind him as he broke six eggs into a bowl and wrapped her arms around his bare chest. He hadn't bothered with a shirt when he got out of bed this morning; just threw on a pair of jeans. He leaned back and rubbed his cheek against hers.

"Ouch. Time for a shave, handsome," she said, pulling away from him and walking toward the fridge.

"Sorry." He whisked the eggs and milk with a fork, and then set a frying pan on the burner, plopping a spoonful of butter into it.

"I could kill for some orange juice," Tiernay said, rummaging in the fridge.

"We're out. I was going to pick up some things for breakfast last night, but you wouldn't let me leave, remember?"

"Doesn't matter," she said, taking a seat at his pine table-for-two. There was a single red apple left in the wicker basket on top of the table, and she picked it up and bit into it, licking the juice from the corner of her mouth.

"I've got to go into work tonight," he said, tilting the pan to let the melted butter ooze over the bottom before pouring the egg mixture into it. While the eggs sizzled, he dropped two slices of whole wheat bread into the toaster.

"Okay," she said, munching the fruit. "I should check in at the store to see how Greg's making out anyway."

Steve stirred the eggs with a wooden spoon. "Won't he mind you leaving him in charge of the store all this time?"

"It's only been a couple of days. He's been back-up for me before."

"You go AWOL like this often?" Steve switched the heat off under the eggs to let them set and grabbed the toast as it popped up. Tiernay rose from her chair and strolled over to him. She draped an arm over his shoulder and watched him spread butter on the toast. When he was finished, he turned toward her, and she pressed the apple to his lips.

"It's almost gone. Here, have a bite."

He bit into the apple, gazing down into her uncanny, pale eyes as he chewed. But before he could swallow the mouthful, she pulled his head down and kissed him.

"Yum, your lips taste sweet," she said with a smile. She snuggled against his warm chest, and he buried his face into her soft, tousled hair. It smelt faintly of cinnamon, and he wondered where the scent came from. Not from his shampoo. There was something crazy and mysterious about Tiernay, and being with her made him feel off-balance. Satiated, but off-balance. He wrapped his arms around her and kissed the top of her head.

"Happy?" she asked, her lips tickling his chest.

He stopped to think about the past two tumultuous days. Tiernay was beautiful and sexy as all get-out, but she was also demanding and needy.

"Hell, no," he replied, crushing her against him so that she wouldn't get the wrong idea.

"Perfect," she said.

16

The following morning, Anna left home early to catch Erna before mass. Gerry would be bringing May over from the hospital just before lunch, so there wouldn't be time for a private chat with Erna after service. Her friend was just shaking out the front hall mat when Anna arrived, and asked her inside.

"There, everything's ready for May," Erna said, leading her into the living room. Anna peered around the room, catching a whiff of furniture polish. It was a sunny, cheerful space with pale lemon walls, a wood-burning fireplace surmounted by a white mantel, a blue-and-white-striped couch, and a blue upholstered recliner. Erna patted the couch beside her, inviting Anna to sit down.

"What brings you out so early today? I didn't expect to see you before church."

"I wanted to talk to you before Gerry brings May. Something happened at the bank yesterday that's been worrying me, something that might have to do with Sherman. I wanted to warn you to be careful with him."

"What do you mean?" Erna said with a frown.

Anna explained about the problem that she had had with the counterfeit money. "Don't you think it's strange, counterfeit money turning up at the store the week that Sherman starts working there?"

Erna sighed. "You're thinking about the scandal at the bank while Sherman was manager."

Anna nodded. "Maybe you're wrong to suspect that Tiernay was responsible for May's fall. First the counterfeit money, and now another woman gets hurt falling down the stairs. Maybe it's not a coincidence. Maybe Sherman pushed them both."

"But why would Sherman hurt May? She was just trying to help him."

"Who knows what goes on in his mind? I think there's something seriously wrong with him."

Erna shook her head. "I don't believe it."

"Maybe not, but I think that we should warn May to stay away from him. I can come back this afternoon after she's settled so that we can both talk to her, if you like."

Erna clasped her hands together in her lap. "I don't wish to sound harsh, Anna, but sometimes you are a bit impetuous. Perhaps you should think things through more before you share your opinions, or act upon them. Like the time you broke into the Primos' house and removed their gun because you suspected it might be the weapon that killed your ex-husband."

"Technically, I didn't break into their house – Amy snuck me in."

"And then you suspected Jessie Wick of murdering your ex-husband. As I recall, Charles was injured while you were snooping on her."

"That was an accident," Anna said, her face growing warm.

"And this feeling you have about Sherman. Upon what do you base that?"

Anna perched on the edge of the couch. She felt anxious, like one of Erna's slower-witted history students who couldn't recite the causes of the First World War.

Counting on her fingers, she said, "First, he heard Evelyn calling to him in the cemetery. What sane person hears dead spirits calling to him? Second, he's an alcoholic. Third, he's very suggestible. Look how easily he swallowed everything

Tiernay told him at the séance. Now he's convinced that someone killed his wife, and is still on the loose." She held up both hands. "I just don't trust him."

Erna leaned back on the couch and crossed her ankles together. "Yes, Sherman has a drinking problem, but he's held the caretaker's job for four years, and that shows that he's managing his dependency. As to hearing Evelyn's voice in the cemetery, sometimes the wind can play tricks on people's hearing, especially when they are under the influence. That's perfectly understandable. As to having anything to do with his wife's death, I've known Sherman for thirteen years, and I don't believe that he would raise his hand to a woman." Erna paused, pursing her lips as she considered Anna. "You criticize Sherman for so readily believing that Evelyn was murdered and that her killer is still at large. If he is convinced of that, he can hardly have killed Evelyn himself, can he? Which is it, dear?"

Anna's face fell. "Uh, no, I guess that doesn't make sense."

"No. You really must try to be more disciplined in your reasoning. So you see, May is in no danger from Sherman, and there's no reason to upset her with your suspicions." She glanced at her watch. "Look at the time. It's 10:15. Mass will be starting in fifteen minutes. Shall we be going?"

Anna shook her head. "You go ahead, Erna. I need to do some thinking. Maybe I'll take Wendy for a walk instead."

Erna rose to her feet and patted Anna's shoulder. "Don't be too hard on yourself. You don't known Sherman as well as May and I do. If you knew what a fine man he was, you wouldn't suspect him, either."

Anna climbed to her feet. Despite her friend's placatory words, she was still perturbed with Erna for suggesting that her thinking was undisciplined.

"I was thinking of dropping by to see May tomorrow night after supper, if that's all right with you?"

Erna smiled. "Yes, why don't you do that? I'll tell May to expect you. We'll both look forward to it," she said, picking up her cardigan and purse from the coffee table and ushering Anna to the door. They parted on the sidewalk, Erna walking briskly toward the church, and Anna heading slowly for home.

17

The morning had started out with near-freezing temperatures, but it was shaping up to be sunny and warm by the time that Anna retrieved Wendy and was leading her into the countryside. Halloween was only a week and a half away, and many of the leaves had already fallen, making a lovely gold and brown blanket that spread over the fields and drifted onto the road.

She was feeling dejected about her conversation with Erna. Anna had always considered herself to be a practical, no-nonsense kind of person who had worked hard to build a new life for her son and herself after her marriage had broken up. It hurt to hear that Erna saw her as someone who made wild, unfounded assumptions. What kind of a person was she, really? A flake? Paranoid and suspicious, from everything Erna had said. Maybe she spent too much time alone, brooding over problems that didn't really exist. Was she going to end up as the town's crazy lady?

She bent to give Wendy a hug. "Thank God I've got you, girl. At least I won't turn into one of those old biddies who lives alone with her twenty-six cats."

The dog grinned and panted a little in the warm sunshine. Anna patted her head and tossed the stick Wendy had been carrying, and she darted after it. Anna followed, trying to enjoy the sunshine and fresh air while the good weather lasted. Pretty soon it would be November with the possibility of snow and below-freezing temperatures. She rounded a bend in the road and spotted Greg Rae sitting on a stool in the shade of a tree with a sketch pad on his knee. Wendy reached him first, and he looked up in surprise as the dog dropped her stick at his feet.

Anna waved and called, "Hi Greg. Beautiful day, isn't it?"

Greg waved back and rose to his feet. "Anna, what an unexpected pleasure," he said as she caught up to him. "I was just sketching that house over there."

Anna looked down at his pad. Greg had done a beautiful job of rendering the ranch house and barn nestled half-way up the tawny hillside across the field from them.

"My landscapes have been selling nicely with the tourists who stop by the store. Do you like it?"

"It's lovely. You have real talent."

"It's yours," he said, removing a pen from his shirt pocket and signing the drawing.

"Oh, Greg, I can't accept it. You could make some money selling it in the store." But he reached inside his leather pouch and pulled out a matte knife, using it to cut the page away from its binding. Rolling the paper into a telescope, he stood up and handed it to her with a short bow.

"Nonsense. Art is good for the soul, and I like to give it away from time to time to remove the dull tarnish of mercantilism. I only wish that the picture were framed."

"Oh no, I'll take care of that. Thank you so much," Anna said, stretching upward to kiss his cheek.

"There, I have my payment," he replied, cupping his face with his hand and smiling. "Will you walk back with me? I was just getting hungry, and it's close enough to lunch time to eat."

"Sure," Anna said. "Can I carry your stool for you?"

"No need, it's collapsible." He flattened the stool and inserted it into his pouch. Slinging the strap over his shoulder, he crooked his arm at Anna, who smiled and slipped her hand into his arm. Together they turned and retraced their steps toward town, Wendy following behind them.

"So, Greg, I don't know very much about you. Do you make a living selling your sketches?"

"No, that's just one of my many sidelines. Most of my income comes from being a freelance graphic artist. I love it – I'm my own boss, and I can work anywhere with a wireless connection. But working with pen and ink is more tactile, and gets me away from the computer."

"Where do you hail from? Tiernay told me that she's French-Canadian, so I take it that you're not originally from Alberta?"

"No, we're from Montreal, although we haven't lived there for years. I moved to BC, and Tiernay followed to get her massage therapy licence. We opened the first Healing Hands store in Vancouver, as a matter of fact, and lived there for a couple of years before Tiernay decided she wanted to live somewhere with more wide-open spaces. I'm afraid we both have a highly-advanced case of wanderlust. That's how we came to live in Alberta."

"Have the two of you always lived together?"

"Not for years, not before Vancouver. She had had a nasty break-up with a member of her coven, so I came to lend my moral support. Then she wanted to open the store, so I stayed on to help. Like I said, I can work anywhere."

"Oh," Anna said, her eyes widening. She hadn't realized that Tiernay was a lesbian. "I noticed that Steve is interested in Tiernay – romantically, I mean. I wonder if he knows?"

"Knows what? Not everyone in a coven is a woman," he said as if reading her mind, "but in this case, her ex was a female. Tiernay has some pretty liberal ideas about her sexuality, however, so Constable Walker doesn't have anything to worry about. Besides, I'm sure he knows all he needs to by now. They've been holed up in his house for the last three days." He smiled, and Anna felt her cheeks colour.

"Okey-dokey then," she said.

"Now me, I'm more of an old-fashioned guy in the romance department," he added, sliding his arm around her shoulders.

But Anna felt uncomfortable with the gesture and pulled away. "Have you ever been married?" she asked to cover her emotions.

"Not since I was sixteen."

"What?" she sputtered, half-laughing. "You were married at sixteen?"

"And that was only because my girlfriend's parents insisted that the baby have my name. Don't know why they'd want to burden their own grandchild with it. It's not like my family's reputation was any good, what with my mother being in jail at the time."

Anna stopped to stare at him. "I don't know what to say."

Greg grinned. "But that marriage hardly counts since it lasted less than a year."

Anna grinned back. "Are you telling me the truth, Gregory Rae?"

He raised two fingers. "Scout's honour."

Anna shook her head at him. "You were never a scout."

He laughed. "You got me there. But I was an altar boy, once."

Wendy ran past them, chasing a butterfly. They followed behind walking in companionable silence, Anna keeping an eye on Wendy since they were close to the town limits, and Greg admiring the view.

"You know, there is a favour you can do for me in exchange for the picture, Anna."

"What's that?" she replied, patting her leg so that Wendy would heel beside her.

"Join me at home for a bite of lunch, and let me sketch you this afternoon."

"Oh, not the sketching thing again."

He paused, forcing her to stop by placing his hands on her shoulders. Wendy sat at her feet as Greg stared straight into Anna's eyes.

"I have only the most honourable of attentions, Anna. I really must draw you. Why are you being so shy about it?"

She put her hands on her hips. "Come on, Greg, I'm a middle-aged mother, not a beautiful young thing like your sister. I just can't imagine my picture hanging side-by-side in the store with Tiernay's."

Greg wrapped his arms around her and kissed her. Anna froze, and then he released her and was grinning down into her eyes.

"Oddly enough, I'm not usually moved to do that by your average, middle-aged mother."

He bent to pick up his pouch, which had slipped off his shoulder and fallen onto the road, drew her hand back into his arm, and continued with their walk as if nothing had happened. Anna looked away, her cheeks blazing.

"Cat got your tongue?"

"Uh . . ."

"At least you didn't do anything as clichéd as slapping me."

"Give me time, I'm thinking about it."

"Come on, I was just making a point. You've got to get over this modesty about your appearance. You're a real beauty. I'd have thought your sergeant would have convinced you of that by now."

Anna cringed, suddenly remembering Charlie. What would he say if he knew about the kiss?

As if reading her thoughts again, Greg said, "Don't be so middle-class, Anna. It was a kiss, not an affair. You've done nothing to be ashamed of, so don't give it a second thought. You should be thinking about how you want to pose for me instead."

"With my clothes on!"

"Are you so sure?" he asked, one eyebrow arching. "Think what a lovely gift a ravishing portrait of you 'au naturel' would make for your boyfriend this Christmas."

"Greg!" she wailed, becoming more and more flustered.

He laughed and patted her hand. "I'm just toying with you, darling. I wouldn't ask you to do anything that would make you uncomfortable, but what else have you got to do this afternoon? A load of laundry? Make a casserole? Come on, do me this one great favour and pose for me."

Anna glanced at him sideways. He was right, she has been planning to make a pot of chili so that she'd have leftovers for later in the week. But Greg was a lot of fun to be with, and the prospect of spending a beautiful Sunday afternoon without him suddenly seemed rather dull.

"What about Wendy?"

"Bring her along, if you like."

"Okay, but let me duck into the house to drop off your drawing and grab Wendy's leash first," she said as they drew near to her cottage.

Greg nodded and waited outside while Anna rushed into the house, taking a moment to brush her hair and apply some powder and lipstick before hurrying back out with her dog. She found Greg chatting with Betty Hiller. Betty turned to greet her, the dimples flashing in her face.

"Hi, Anna. Greg was just showing me some of his sketches. You're a lucky girl to be drawn by him!"

Anna frowned. Betty was a sweet lady and a good neighbour, but it would have been better to keep the portrait private. Betty was bound to say something about it at The Diner, and soon or later everyone in town would hear about it. And with the nude drawings of Tiernay on display at her store, Anna was sure to get plenty of ribbing. She decided to put a brave face on it, however, and smiled brightly.

"I know! I'm thrilled that Greg wants to sketch me." She turned to include him in the conversation. "Maybe this could be a new sideline for you, Greg. All the ladies in town would line up to have you draw them."

"Not me," Betty was quick to say. "I'm too old and fat." She pointed to the open page in Greg's pad, and Anna sighed as her eyes were drawn to another nude portrait of Tiernay.

"I don't draw every lady in the nude," Greg said. "With my sister, it's impossible not to. There's something so primal in her spirit. I like to reveal both the inner and outer woman."

"There you go," Anna said, shooting him a grateful smile. "Greg's not going to sketch me in the buff. Of course not. That would be silly."

"We'll see," Greg said with a wicked smile that made her want to kick him.

"Well, I mustn't keep you," Betty said. "Greg said he wanted to pose you outdoors in this gorgeous sunlight, so you probably want to get going."

"Just chomping at the bit," Greg replied, closing his sketch pad and dropping it into his bag. He took Betty's hand and raised it to his lips. "Lovely to meet you, Betty."

She giggled and dropped him a short curtsy. "Have a fun afternoon, Anna," she said with a wink before turning and trotting up the road to her driveway. Probably in a hurry to tell her husband all about it, Anna thought.

"Shall we?" Greg said, offering her his arm as they began to walk again. "I'm glad we're spending the afternoon together – there's something I want to talk to you about."

"Oh? What's that?" Anna asked, suddenly wary.

"Tiernay told me about the conversation you and your friends had with her earlier this week. She was pretty disappointed when you didn't want to hold another séance, and she's been feeling anxious about Evelyn ever since, especially after May's accident. Or was it an accident? A little birdie told me that May thought she saw a ghost on her apartment stairs just before she fell."

He looked at her, waiting for a response, but Wendy was stalking a cat, and Anna used the diversion to stall. Pulling sharply on the leash, she called, "Wendy! Leave that cat alone." The dog dropped back to heel beside her, and the cat continued washing its face from the end of its driveway.

"Cats! They have so much more attitude than dogs," Anna said with a smile. "Do you have any pets, Greg?"

"Not at the moment," he replied, an expectant expression still on his face. Anna could see that she would not be able to evade his question, and took a moment to grope for a politic response. She shrugged.

"You heard right – May thought she saw a ghost on her apartment stairs. She tripped trying to get away from it."

Greg nodded. "Just as Tiernay suspected. Evelyn's unhappy that her death still hasn't been avenged, so she's beginning to take it out on the people who held the séance. The question is, what are you ladies going to do about it?"

Anna shook her head. "Be reasonable. What can we do about it? Even if Evelyn were murdered, how are we supposed to find out who killed her?"

"By holding another séance and asking Evelyn."

"And if Evelyn, speaking through Tiernay, told us who her murderer was, what then? Are we supposed to kill for her?"

"Of course not. Evelyn would probably want you to go to the police."

"As if that would get us anywhere!" Anna replied, throwing up her hands. They were walking down Main Street, and Anna nodded to someone she knew exiting the post office.

She turned back to Greg. "I'm sorry to say this, but I'm still not convinced that there is a ghost. I don't mean any disrespect to your sister, but there's absolutely no proof that Evelyn was murdered, or that her ghost is haunting the town. May thought she saw something on her stairs that night, but it was pitch black, and she fell and hit her head. We can't put much weight in what she thinks she saw."

"What about what Sherman heard in the cemetery?" Greg asked as they crossed the street toward Healing Hands. Tiernay was inside, and they waved at her. The young woman's eyes followed them as they continued their walk past the store and up the street.

"That's the crux of it, isn't it, Greg? It all started with Sherman hearing someone calling to him in the cemetery."

"Yes. What's your point?"

"Look, try to listen to me without any bias, okay?"

"I'll try. Go ahead."

"First of all, Sherman might have been drunk and imagined the whole thing."

Greg shrugged. "That's always been a possibility, if you discount what Tiernay felt at the séance. Anything else?"

Anna spoke slowly, trying to sort through her thoughts. "Maybe there was something going on in the cemetery that night, and Sherman interrupted it. Everyone knows Sherman, so calling his name and pretending to be a ghost to scare him away wouldn't have been so difficult."

Greg glanced at her sideways. "What do you think might have been going on?"

"Well, maybe some kids were smoking pot and didn't want to get caught. The cemetery's just down the street from the school, so it would be a pretty convenient place for them to meet. Heaven knows, kids get up to stuff, even in small towns. Maybe especially in small towns. Or, someone might be using the cemetery to sell drugs. It's nice and private in there, especially at night."

Greg was silent beside her, pondering what she had said. "That's interesting," he said after a moment. "I wonder if the police check the cemetery at night. Maybe I should ask Tiernay to talk to Steve about it."

"Good idea. That would be one less thing for me to worry about."

"I should hope so," Greg said, grabbing her elbow. "Don't go getting any daft notions about visiting the cemetery alone at night. If there is something going on in there, I don't want you getting hurt and ending up in the hospital, too." They were on the sidewalk outside his house, and Greg waited for her response as Wendy stuck her nose between them.

"Of course not," Anna said, smiling to reassure him. "Even I wouldn't be that stupid."

"All right," Greg said, calming down. "Sorry about that, Wendy," he added, looking down and patting her head.

Anna looked away and noticed a man sitting on the front porch. The stranger rose from his chair as they made eye contact.

"Greg," she said, nudging him, "there's someone waiting for you."

"Huh? Emmanuel! What a pleasant surprise," he replied, towing Anna and Wendy across the lawn.

"Surprise?" the man said, sunlight glinting off his bald head as they climbed the stairs to meet him. He was short, broad, and muscular, dressed in a jacket and tie with jeans. "Did you forget our appointment?"

Greg's eyes widened. "I'm such an idiot! I did forget. I'm sorry. I hope I didn't keep you waiting long."

Greg's friend nodded. "About twenty minutes. I was just about to leave."

"How stupid of me. Please accept my apology."

The man smiled at Anna, the folds of his swarthy face lifting. "You must have been distracted by your lady friend."

Greg turned to her with a smile. "Of course. This is a business associate of mine. Emmanuel Cabrero."

"Pleased to meet you, Anna," Cabrero said, holding out his hand. Anna smiled and shook it. His grasp was warm and strong.

"I'm so sorry, Anna," Greg said, taking her hand when Cabrero released it. "Emmanuel commissioned some artwork for a catalogue he's producing, and we were going to go over the proofs this afternoon. We'll have to reschedule our sitting. You will forgive me, won't you?" He looked genuinely disappointed, and Anna felt touched that the sitting meant so much to him.

"Sure, not a problem. We can do it any time."

"Thanks for understanding," Greg said, kissing her hand.

"Nice dog you got there," Cabrero said. Anna turned to notice her dog sniffing the man's crotch.

"Wendy, stop that!" she commanded, tugging at the leash and pulling her pet away. "Sorry," she added to Cabrero.

He shrugged and clasped his hands together. Anna noticed how thick and meaty they appeared. "What can you do? Dogs will be dogs."

"Thanks for understanding," she said with a smile. He nodded. "I'll see you later, Greg. Nice meeting you, Emmanuel."

"Bye," Greg called after her as she and Wendy climbed down the stairs and cut across the yard toward the sidewalk.

Anna sighed. It looked like she was going to spend the afternoon making chili after all.

18

Anna drowsily half-opened her eyes. Something had woken her, but she couldn't remember what it was. The room was dark; it was the middle of the night. She could hear Wendy's gentle breathing coming from the floor beside the bed, so whatever it was that had woken her hadn't disturbed the dog. She turned her head to glance at the green display on the clock radio: 2:47 a.m. She sighed and rolled over, hoping to drop off again quickly. A flash of lightning brightened the room, however, and the curtains fluttered in the breeze. She had left the window open a couple of inches to let in some fresh air. Was a storm brewing? Too groggy to get up and close the window, Anna decided to ignore it and shut her eyes.

She was drifting off to sleep again when she heard a noise, a high-pitched sound just loud enough to be annoying. Must be the wind rising. She sighed and snuggled down under the covers, cozy in her little cocoon. But the noise grew louder, and Anna stiffened, suddenly wide awake. It wasn't the wind she had heard; it was that song again. The same creepy old tune that she had heard on the night of the séance. Anna sat up in bed with the sheet wrapped around her waist, her eyes fixed on the window. The music was coming from outside.

With her heart rate accelerating, she swung her legs over the side of the bed and stood up. Wendy, immediately awake, got up from her pillow and shuffled over. Anna stroked the dog's sleek head before forcing herself to creep across the room to the window. Reaching for the curtain, she flicked it aside and peered out at the front lawn.

Half-way up the grass, a woman stood, motionless. A fork of lightning streaked across the sky, illuminating her and making Anna squint. The woman was draped from head to toe in a shapeless black dress that billowed in the wind, her face covered by a hood, her arms hanging loosely by her sides. What had summoned her to Anna's front yard in the middle of the night?

As Anna stared, the woman lifted her arms and began to move in time to the music, revolving in the slow circles of a ghastly waltz. There was something odd about the way she moved, and Anna strained to see better in the darkness. The graceful creature swirled up her lawn, and as she drew nearer, Anna suddenly saw what was wrong. She moaned in fear. The woman's feet hovered an inch or so above the ground, treading on air.

Abruptly, the woman stopped in mid-turn, even though the tinkling music played on. She had seemed oblivious to Anna's incredulous eyes, but now she swivelled to face her. Slowly reaching up, she pulled the hood down from her head, and Anna's mouth dropped open. Where there should have been a face, there were only smooth waves of silvery hair tossing in the wind. The creature revolved once more, turning her back as if to spite Anna, and a bone-white, gleaming face appeared, the neck twisted brokenly over the back.

Anna gasped and covered her mouth in horror. The woman's unblinking eyes gazed at her from her awkwardly-angled head, her mouth gaping open as if to speak. While Anna watched, the ghost raised her arms and started drifting up the yard toward her.

Anna shrieked and dropped the curtain. She grabbed the telephone from her table and scrambled over the bed, putting it between her and the window. Her trembling fingers scrabbled over the number pad, trying to find the right buttons in the dark. Finally, she managed to punch in "911."

"Fire, police, or medical emergency?" a calm voice inquired.

"Police!" Anna shouted. "It's Anna Nolan at 84 Wistler Road. There's this thing out on my front lawn. She's headed straight for the house. Please, send someone over right away."

As she paused to listen, something scratched on her window screen, and a voice whispered, "Anna . . ."

She screamed and dropped the phone while Wendy erupted into a frenzy of barking. Bolting from the room, Anna tore across the hallway for the bathroom, where she slammed and locked the door. She fumbled for the wall switch. The lights blazed on, blinding her. Bursting into tears, she grabbed a towel from the rack and pressed it against her mouth, stifling her sobs. She collapsed onto the toilet and began to rock back and forth, terrified of that appalling thing with the broken neck and staring eyes. She paused, shivering. What about Wendy? What if that horrible creature came through the window and got Wendy?

Clutching the towel to her chest, Anna rose and pressed her ear to the door. She tried to listen, but all she could hear was Wendy's barking and the sound of her own breath rasping in her throat. Reaching for the knob with trembling fingers, she unlocked the door and pulled it open a few inches. The hallway was empty. Taking a deep breath, she stuck her head through the opening and croaked, "Wendy!"

Fear had strangled her vocal cords, making her inaudible. Anna swallowed the lump in her throat and tried again. "Wendy!" she managed to shout. "Wendy, come here!"

Miraculously, the dog stopped barking and trotted out of the bedroom. Anna nabbed her by the collar and hauled Wendy inside, slamming and locking the door once more.

"Good girl," she whimpered, squatting down on the cold tiles and cradling her pet. Wendy squirmed in her arms and tried to lick her face, her nails accidentally scratching Anna's foot.

"Lie down," she ordered, pushing her pet onto the floor. The dog settled beside her and panted, her warm body snuggled up close. Anna tried to calm down enough to listen. The dreadful music seemed to have stopped, thank God, but maybe she just couldn't hear it over her chattering teeth?

Wendy cocked her head and clambered to her feet, breaking Anna's hold. Had she heard something? Dear God, please don't let that thing be in the house! But then Anna heard someone pounding on the front door and shouting her name.

She jumped to her feet and opened the bathroom door. The dog burst through the opening, barking, and Anna raced down the hallway after her. Reaching the front door, she peered through the peephole, slammed back the dead bolt, and flung the door open.

"Steve!" she shouted, throwing herself into his arms and bursting into tears.

She clung to him as Steve rubbed her back and murmured, "It's all right, Anna. Don't cry. Everything's all right."

19

Attracted by the cruiser's dazzling lights, Betty and Jeff appeared at Anna's door and waited in the living room with her, huddled in a blanket, while Steve searched the house and checked the property in the driving rain. When he couldn't find any trace of the intruder, her neighbours took Anna and Wendy home for the rest of the night. Jeff even plied Anna with brandy to help her sleep, and she managed a few sips before shutting herself in their guest bedroom and lying awake for hours with Wendy nestled on the bed beside her.

Anna made it to work on time the following morning, but she acted like a zombie all day, still consumed by her nightmarish memory of the night before and trying to make sense of what had happened to her. The problem was, she couldn't make any sense out of it at all.

In the evening, she called Charlie. He was in his third week of a murder case in Swift Current, Saskatchewan, where he hoped to wrap things up soon so that they could see each other again, or at least before Christmas. Anna didn't like to disturb him during an investigation because she knew what long hours he put in, but tonight she simply needed to hear his voice. He was so calm and brave and sane, plus he had a deep baritone voice and a posh British accent that she always found sexy.

She tried him at the station first; he had given her the number to his direct line. He answered on the second ring.

"Tremaine."

"How's it going, hot stuff?"

"Anna!" he said, dropping his official tone. "What an unexpected pleasure. I was just thinking of you."

"You were?"

"Yes. I had to arrest a minor today, and his mother hit me over the head with her purse." He chuckled, and Anna's face broke into a smile for the first time that day.

"Very funny. How's the investigation going?"

"Not too badly. I don't think that there'll be any surprises. But with the murder victim being a retired army general, the press are ready to pounce on us, so we're dotting the i's and crossing the t's. How are you doing, my darling girl? You sound tired tonight."

"I am, Charlie. There was a ghost on my lawn last night, and it woke me up."

"I beg your pardon?"

Anna started her story at the beginning, telling Charlie all about Sherman Mason and his wife, the séance, the attack on May, and the ghost dancing on her lawn the night before.

"Did Steve Walker examine your yard in the light of day?"

"He told me that he would, and that he'd call me at work if he found anything. I haven't heard from him, so I guess that he didn't."

"No, probably not. Whoever did this to you had plenty of time to remove the evidence and get away while you were locked in the bathroom."

"So, you don't believe that this had anything to do with supernatural forces?"

"No, of course not." He paused before asking, "Do you?"

"I didn't before last night. I was sure that Tiernay and Greg had faked the séance. The attack on poor May wouldn't have been difficult to pull off, but that thing on my lawn last night seemed so real. I'm just not sure anymore," she said, her voice trailing off.

"I'm sure that it must have seemed real, darling. It woke you from a sound sleep, after all. You must have been groggy. I'd have loved if you had been able to turn on the outside lights and sic Wendy on the so-called ghost. I've seen you in action with a bat. You can be pretty terrifying, too."

"I wasn't in any shape to do that last night."

"No, of course not, love. I hate to think of you all alone in your house with this nonsense going on. Is that where you are now?"

"Yes."

"You're not going to stay there alone tonight, are you? There's not much the police can do. They won't put a car out front and just wait for something to happen. You've had your scare – hopefully the lunatic behind these pranks will move onto someone else. Meanwhile, why don't you stay next door with the Hillers for a couple of nights? I know you – you won't be able to sleep for worry tonight."

"I like the Hillers, but I think Betty would drive me crazy if I stayed another night with them."

"Right, she is a bit of a chatterbox. How about asking Ben to sleep in for a couple of days? He could commute back and forth to school with you."

"I don't want to put him out, Charlie. He's got mid-terms. But don't worry, I'll figure something out."

"If I weren't in the middle of a case I'd come myself. Promise me you won't stay alone for the next few days. Even if you have to check into a hotel."

"I promise, Charlie, and I'll stay in touch and let you know what's happening."

"Good. Even if you can't reach me on the cell, I always check my e-mail."

"I know. Don't worry about me, hot stuff. I was nervous before, but I feel better just talking to you. Go catch some bad guys so I can see you again soon."

"I will. I love you, Batwoman."

"Me too, Charlie. See you."

"Bye."

There was a knock on Erna's door. When she opened it, she discovered Anna and Wendy on her doorstep. Anna had an overnight case and a heaping shopping bag full of dog paraphernalia at her feet.

"Can we stay with you?" she asked.

"What happened? Of course you can. Come in, come in," her friend replied, and Anna kicked the shopping bag into the foyer and shut the door behind her. A few minutes later, she was sitting on the floor with her back propped against the couch May lay upon, telling them the whole story. Erna sat on the recliner beside them, while Wendy lay on the floor next to Anna.

"I've had a talk with Charlie, so I feel better now, but I still can't get that thing's face out of my mind," she murmured, staring straight ahead. "It was all bony, and the eyes were sunken. It stared at me sideways, like this," she said, demonstrating. "It had to, because the head was on backwards, and the neck was broken. But it was Evelyn. I recognized her from the family portrait in Sherman's living room. Not as she was then, but the way she must have looked when they found her." Anna shuddered, and Erna and May exchanged a worried glance over her head.

"And the music – that horrible music we heard at the séance. Remember?" Anna hummed the two lines. There was silence in the room when she finished. "Someone did a really good number on me. But enough of that," she said, changing the subject. "What exactly did you see on the stairs the night you fell, May?"

May sighed. "I'm not sure. It was dark. I couldn't see very well. I remember the shroud going into my mouth, though – that was terrifying – and the horrible smell. Like something rotting."

"Do you believe that it was a ghost?" Anna asked.

"Yeah. The way it suddenly appeared out of nowhere. The terrible smell. It was too real to be a trick."

Anna nodded and looked at Erna. "What do you believe?"

"I think that something truly evil frightened the two of you."

Anna held her gaze for a long moment. "What do you think we should do?"

"I don't know," Erna replied.

"I do," May said. "We're going to swallow our pride and ask Tiernay for help. It's all happening like she said it would, isn't it? Evelyn wants us to avenge her death, but we don't know how. Sherman doesn't know how, either, and now he's disappeared, and we don't know where he is." She told Anna about her conversation with Sherman in the hospital.

"And he hasn't contacted you since?"

"No. I called Gerry this morning to see if Sherman had been by the store, but he hasn't seen him."

"Maybe Sherman's gone to stay with one of his sons," Anna suggested.

May threw up her hands. "I don't know, and I'm worried about him, but it looks like we're going to have to do something about Evelyn without his help. I don't want to wait for her to show up here."

Anna groaned involuntarily, and Erna murmured, "May!"

"Sorry, sorry. Didn't mean to upset you, Anna. I'm sure nothing bad is going to happen to us here. We just won't let Evelyn inside. We'll sprinkle some herbs around the house or something. Plus, Wendy will protect us." The dog thumped her tail, and Anna petted her. "So, are the two of you going to go talk to Tiernay, or what? I can't go like this." May held up one of her crutches to remind them of her infirmity.

"I still don't believe that you and Anna encountered a real ghost, but. . ." Erna said, holding up a finger to ward off May's interruption, "I don't think that we should wait for another attack, either. It's time we took the initiative, and I'm willing to try anything. Let's talk to Tiernay and see what she suggests. May, don't open the door to anyone while we're gone."

May shook her head. "Don't worry, I won't even get up off the couch. Just give me the TV remote and the phone, and I'll be fine."

"Good." Erna checked her watch. "It's almost seven thirty. If Tiernay has a massage tonight, she'll still be at the store. We'll try there first. If she's not there, we'll try her house. Let's take your car, Anna."

When they arrived at the store, however, it was locked and the lights were out, so Anna drove them to the Raes' house. The porch light was turned off as they made their way up the lawn, but they rang the doorbell and waited for a response, anyway. Anna took that moment to tell Erna that Tiernay and Steve were seeing each other.

"Oh dear," was all Erna had time to say before the front door opened.

"Anna! Erna! How nice of you to drop by. To what do I owe the honour, ladies?" Greg asked, a smile of welcome on his face. "Don't tell me that you're both here to pose for me?"

Anna snorted, and Erna said, "Actually, Greg, we'd like to see your sister."

The smile instantly evaporated from his face, and he looked worried. "Is something wrong?"

"We need her help," Anna said.

"Come in," he replied, swinging the door wider for them to enter.

The women preceded him down the hallway to a small living room. "Have a seat in here, and I'll go find Tiernay," Greg said, motioning them toward the couch. He hurried down the hallway and called Tiernay's name before bounding up the stairs to the second floor.

Erna and Anna gazed about the room. There was a fire crackling in the hearth, a wooden mantelpiece with framed pictures of a younger Greg and Tiernay displayed on top. The walls were painted a serene sage green, and an area carpet in squares of cream, brown and red lay on the floor before an L-shaped couch. A cushioned rocking chair, complete with footstool, was pulled up next to the fireplace with a book lying face down on the seat.

"Wonder where Tiernay does the human sacrifices?" Anna asked.

Erna shook her head. "Don't do anything to antagonize her," she said, taking a seat in the middle of the couch.

Anna sat down beside her, folding her hands in her lap. "I'll be on my best behaviour."

They heard footsteps coming down the stairs, and Tiernay entered the room with Greg right behind her. She paused to fold her arms over her chest, gazing down at them with a haughty expression as Greg sidled past and sat in the rocking chair.

"Ladies," Tiernay said with a nod. "You wanted to see me?"

Erna gestured at the couch. "Please sit beside me."

Tiernay sat down and crossed her legs, her long skirt falling open to display two bare legs tucked into thigh-high leather boots.

"We have a situation that needs your help," Erna began. "We need you to prevent Evelyn's ghost from breaking into my house."

20

On hearing Anna's story and a description of what had befallen May, Tiernay became all business, insisting on following the women back to Erna's house in her car. She showed up thirty minutes later, and spent the next hour burning candles and herbs while strolling around the house mumbling warding incantations. She also brought the stones she had given to the women on the night of the séance, insisting that they keep them on their persons until the trouble with Evelyn was resolved.

"We're going to have to hold another séance," she declared, sitting on the recliner sipping green tea while Erna sat on a dining room chair and Anna sat on the floor. May, still on the sofa, had kept a respectful silence during these proceedings, but now she piped up.

"Where?"

"In the graveyard."

"I'd hoped you weren't serious when you suggested that before," Anna exclaimed. It seemed like such a cheesy cliché, holding a séance in a graveyard. But then she remembered not to antagonize Tiernay, and pretended to look concerned instead.

"Well, I was," Tiernay said, returning her cup and saucer to the coffee table. "I'm not going to take a chance on Evelyn possessing me in her house again. We're going to summon her spirit this time, and the graveyard is the ideal place for that. Not only will we be invading her resting place, but I'll have the forces of nature around me to draw upon with you ladies amplifying my powers. Maybe you can arrange a wheel chair for May," she added, studying the older woman as she lay upon the couch. "She won't be able to stand on crutches for long enough."

May shrugged. "Shouldn't be a problem. I know someone I can borrow a chair from."

"I'll ask Greg to join us," Tiernay added. "I like to have a masculine presence in my coven, particularly when we have to face Evelyn's unquiet spirit. A coven should be thirteen, and it takes a lot of power to summon a spirit, so we're on the light side. What about Sherman? Is he going to be there?"

"I have no idea," May said, explaining Sherman's disappearance.

Tiernay frowned. "I would have preferred to have him with us, but we'll have to manage. I'm not worried about Evelyn manifesting herself without him. She's shown a particular connection to both May and Anna, so it shouldn't be a problem." Both women frowned, neither particularly pleased to hear that.

"When do you plan to hold the séance?" Erna asked.

"Tomorrow would be too soon. I have preparations to make." Tiernay thought for a moment. "I should be ready the night after tomorrow."

"Night?" May said in a shaky voice. "Does it have to be at night?"

"I prefer to commune with psychic forces at night," Tiernay said. "It's the best time, when the line that separates the physical and spiritual worlds is at its thinnest. Besides, Anna works during the day, don't you?"

"Yes," she answered.

"Well then, it will have to be at night, unless Anna wants to take the day off. Besides, I don't want to close the store, and Greg will be with us, so he can't cover for me. Don't worry, May," Tiernay said, noting her worried expression. "We'll have more control over Evelyn by summoning her than we had at the séance. She won't be able to hurt anyone this time." Erna leaned over to squeeze her friend's shoulder, and May tried to smile.

"We're very grateful for your assistance, Tiernay," Erna said. "Things seem to be getting out of hand, and we'd like to lay Evelyn's spirit to rest."

"I agree. There has been an imbalance in the spiritual dimension from the day I first sensed an evil presence following Anna, and it just hasn't felt right since. We should have dealt with it then, but you ladies have taken some convincing, and I couldn't have managed it on my own. No one is powerful enough to do that." Tiernay stood. "I've got to go. We'll meet at the cemetery entrance at 8 p.m. on Wednesday night."

"What if the gate is locked?" Anna asked. "If Sherman hasn't shown up by then, we won't be able to get inside."

"Not a problem," Tiernay said. "I've broken into the cemetery before. There's a hill beside the back entrance that makes it easy to climb over the wall. I'll meet you at the front gate and unbolt it from inside."

"I hate to ask, but why did you break into the cemetery before?" May said.

"I like to walk around graveyards at night. The psychic energy from all those souls is pretty wild," Tiernay said with a glint in her eyes. May's mouth opened, but Anna shook her head not to pursue it.

"Thank you," Erna said, rising to show Tiernay out. "You've been very helpful. I'm sure we all feel more secure now that you've safeguarded the house."

The young woman nodded. "Maybe you ladies can repay me when I need your help in the future. There's a lot of energy in this room. I can't wait to channel it when I call upon our powers Wednesday night."

"Yes," Erna said, looking over her shoulder at her friends' unhappy faces. "I'm sure that we all can't wait."

21

Anna spent Monday and Tuesday nights on Erna's couch, plagued by nightmares of Evelyn's ghost trying to claw her way into the house. It seemed that Anna's rational mind couldn't control the fear that the dreadful visit had impressed upon her subconscious. She was anxious to get the séance over with, hoping that somehow life would return to normal once Tiernay had her way.

She drove May and Erna to the cemetery Wednesday night, parking in the driveway close to the gate. They had arrived early to have time to settle May into a wheelchair before Tiernay and Greg arrived. The brother and sister were late, however, and the three women had to wait in a light drizzle on the cool, moonless night, armed with umbrellas and flashlights.

"Sorry we're late," Tiernay said, hurrying to the gate from inside the cemetery when she and Greg arrived five minutes later. "Greg has this deadline for a catalogue he's working on with Emmanuel Cabrero, and he had to do some last minute work before we could leave the house." The gate rattled as she slid the bolt back and pulled the door open. "Come in."

Tiernay was dressed in an ankle-length navy cloak with the hood pulled over her hair, while Greg wore his black coat and watchman's cap. Anna felt underdressed in sweat pants, a hoodie, and a waterproof jacket as she wheeled May through the entrance, but at least she was warm.

"Here, let me take her," Greg said, scrambling to get behind the wheelchair. "How're you doing, May?"

"Never better," she chirped. "Let's get this show on the road. It's about time we got some of our own back on Evelyn." Anna shook her head, knowing that May had a rosary tucked in her pants pocket beneath the rain poncho, even if she did sound confident and jaunty.

The group was just turning on their flashlights, ready to venture beyond the light of the security lamp, when a cruiser pulled into the driveway behind them.

"Now what?" Anna asked.

The car parked behind hers, and Steve got out, in uniform.

"Wait for me," he called, jogging over to the gate.

"Steve, I told you not to come," Tiernay said, rushing to meet him. She unbolted the gate and swung it open.

"I had to see this for myself. It's not every day a ghost gives a command performance," he said, slipping past Tiernay and joining the others. She sighed and clanged the door shut behind him.

"All right, all I ask is that you keep quiet during the ritual. I don't want any distractions from unbelievers."

"I'll be good," he responded with a twinkle in his eye. "Ladies," he said, touching the brim of his hat. "Greg."

Anna was glad to see that Steve looked his usual self, afraid that succumbing to Tiernay's charms might have changed him somehow. Not that she expected the young woman to have drained his soul and turned him into a zombie, but something.

"So, where are we headed?" she asked.

"To the older part of the graveyard at the back," Tiernay replied. "I've already prepared the site. Unfortunately, it's not that easy to get to."

Erna nodded. "That part of the cemetery was mostly full when the town built the addition with the ring road. Since many of the people who were buried in the old part died over fifty years or more ago, the council thought their graves wouldn't attract many visitors, and didn't bother with road access."

Tiernay sighed, impatient with Erna's explanation. "Follow me," she commanded, striding down the pavement beside Steve, Greg following behind with May, and Anna and Erna, arm and arm, in the rear.

"Are we walking too fast for you?" Anna asked a minute later as Erna's breathing became audible. "I can ask Tiernay to slow down."

"Oh no, I'm fine, dear," Erna said, flashing a smile. She was bundled up in a coat and scarf with a vinyl rain bonnet tied firmly over her hair. "This is exciting, isn't it? Tramping through a cemetery in the middle of the night."

Anna smiled fondly at her. "I hope that I'm half as game as you are when I'm you're age."

Tiernay and Steve halted, waiting for the others to catch up. "It's time to leave the road. We're headed through there," Tiernay said, pointing toward some plots. "Do you think you'll be able to manage with May and the wheelchair, Greg?"

"Not a problem. You just leave it to me, darling," he added, smiling down at May.

"Go for it, kid," she replied with a flourish of her hand.

"Stick together and don't get lost," Tiernay said, leading the way.

The light rain had become a murky mist, making it difficult to see very far even with the flashlights. They moved at a slower pace, navigating around tombstones and statuary, and sometimes through slippery layers of damp leaves. Despite his bravado, Greg was having trouble with May, and Steve had to help him clear soggy handfuls of leaves from the wheels whenever the chair bogged down.

It was quiet except for the scampering of inconspicuous animals and the occasional howls of coyotes in the countryside beyond. Anna concentrated on keeping her footing and helping Erna. She tried not to feel nervous as they worked their way deeper into the cemetery. It was irrational to give way to fears of the dark and the dead, and Erna's admonishments about her undisciplined mind had spurred Anna into trying to think more logically.

At last Tiernay pointed with her light and said, "It's right over there, on the other side of those trees." They followed her around a stand of evergreens and emerged beside a bench.

"Good," Erna said, limping a bit on her way to sit down. "I was hoping for a rest." She pulled a wad of tissues from her pocket and wiped the bench dry before taking a seat. "Are you all right, May?"

"Sure. He did all the work," May replied, pointing over her shoulder at Greg, who was puffing and leaning on the wheelchair. "Thanks, kid."

"My pleasure," he replied between gasps.

"Greg, help me with the lamps," Tiernay said, shining her light on a Coleman lamp set on the ground a short distance away.

"Coming," he responded, crossing to another lamp. Steve followed Tiernay, leaving the three friends to watch them from the bench.

"Where are we?" Anna asked, looking around.

"I'm afraid I have no idea," Erna replied. "My family is buried in a different section."

Curious as to why this particular location had been chosen for the séance, Anna flicked her flashlight on and stood up. There was a tombstone directly in front of her, and she wandered over to read the inscription. Pausing to study the stone, she inhaled sharply and rushed back to Erna and May.

"It's Evelyn's grave," she said in a loud whisper, pointing at the stone with her flashlight. "I can't believe it!"

"Where else would we hold the ceremony?" Tiernay asked, suddenly appearing at her side.

"I don't know. I didn't think. Somewhere in the open, I guess. Isn't this disrespectful, holding the séance on her grave?"

"Anna, I don't think you understand what we're doing here tonight," the young woman replied. "We're summoning Evelyn's spirit. That means that we're forcing her to appear before us to answer our questions. It's not a matter of respect. We're here to gain control over Evelyn's ghost."

"I don't think that's a good idea," Anna said, suddenly apprehensive. Tiernay looked amused, however, and her expression irritated Anna enough to calm down. She decided to lay it on thick for the younger woman's benefit. "Evelyn's very powerful, isn't she? Won't this make her angry?" she asked with a tremor in her voice.

Tiernay shrugged. "Maybe, but together we're much stronger than she is. Don't worry, Anna, just do what I tell you, and everything will be fine. Let's get started, everyone," she called in a louder voice. "It's not getting any warmer. As you'll notice, I've painted a white circle on the ground." They all looked to where Tiernay pointed, the circle illuminated by the three Coleman lamps the Raes had lit outside the line.

"Oh my gosh, she spray-painted Evelyn's grave," Anna said, collapsing onto the bench beside Erna. Her friend patted her arm absent-mindedly as Tiernay continued.

"After we summon her, Evelyn's spirit will be contained by the circle as long as we stand on the perimeter and don't let her past us. So, remember everyone, stand on the white line. Do not leave the white line. Understand?" She looked around the group, their faces dimly lit in the lamplight, and nodded. "Okay, places everyone. Greg, please push May onto the circle."

Greg manoeuvred the wheelchair-bound woman into position while the others took up spots on the white line. Tiernay studied their formation, her head to one side and her hands on her hips.

"I'm thinking that our power grid will be at its optimum if we anchor the circle with each of the ladies between Steve, Greg, and myself. I'll stand here at the foot of the grave with May to my right and Erna to my left. Greg, you stand beside Erna, and Anna, you stand across from me in front of the headstone. Steve, you're between Anna and May. Let's go, everyone." They reassembled themselves according to Tiernay's directions, and the young woman smiled at the result.

"That's better. Now, listen closely. The most important part of the ritual is to state our intention that Evelyn must appear before us. We're going to say the same thing, all together, over and over again until I tell you to stop. So, repeat this sentence after me: 'Evelyn, departed from the earthly plane, appear to us this night, we command you.' All together now . . ."

Anna repeated the line with the others, peering about as she did so. She felt unreasonably uncomfortable with her back to the stone, as if Evelyn's ghost might creep up behind her.

"Okay, let's get started. Say the sentence with me, everyone," Tiernay ordered.

"Evelyn, departed from the earthly plane, appear to us this night, we command you," they chanted.

Tiernay nodded. "Again," she said, raising her arms over her head.

"Evelyn, departed from the earthly plane, appear to us this night, we command you."

Anna's eyes darted to the others, their faces shadowy with the lamps behind them. Greg's eyes were closed in concentration, while both Erna and Steve looked alert and watchful. May's eyes were wide, and she had something clutched against her chest, probably her rosary. Anna wished that she had brought one herself, irrational or not.

"Louder!" Tiernay said, shaking the hood from her hair and closing her eyes.

"Evelyn, departed from the earthly plane, appear to us this night, we command you."

"Once more!" Tiernay shouted.

"Evelyn, departed from the earthly plane, appear to us this night, we command you."

"Enough!" Tiernay shrieked, flailing her arms over her head and lowering them to point into the circle.

Anna stared. Within the line, just above the grass, she could see a faint pool of silvery-blue light. She rubbed her eyes and looked again. Yes, the eerie light was definitely there, growing stronger all the time. As she watched, the light began to stretch upward. It became a column of blue sparkles glowing in a swirling white mist. The core of the column began to darken, and, after a minute, the outline of a woman appeared. Anna's breath caught in her throat. It's not real, she told herself. It's a trick. She glanced at the trees and along the ground, hoping to find cables or other electrical equipment, but it was too dark and misty to see clearly.

"Who summons me?" the figure trapped within the column said in a hoarse whisper. Anna's eyes darted back to the circle.

"We did," Tiernay said in a commanding voice. "We are the friends of Sherman Mason."

"What do you want of me?" the spectre croaked, seeming to become more and more solid before their eyes. Anna could make out a seamless shroud encompassing the figure, covering it from head to foot.

"You have upset and frightened people, Evelyn," Tiernay said. "Sherman, who has run away, May, and Anna. If you promise to stop, we will help you. You spoke of revenge at our séance. Who are we to take your revenge upon?"

From far away, the tinkling notes of music began to play, the same terrible melody that had haunted Anna's dreams. She cringed. The figure seemed to hear the music, too. It extended its arms and began to revolve once again in the same bobbing waltz. Anna clasped her hand over her mouth, afraid that she was going to be sick. It's not real, it's not real, she told herself again and again.

"I want revenge on everyone!" the ghost shrieked. Anna jumped. "Everyone who mocked me, everyone who wished me harm, everyone who laughed at my downfall. And, especially, on the monster who did this to me!" The apparition stopped right in front of Anna. Tremulous, bony fingers reached up to pluck the shroud from its head. Anna cried aloud as a tumble of white-blond hair fell down upon its shoulders while Evelyn's lifeless blue eyes stared at her. Abruptly, the spectre's head fell to one shoulder at a sick, twisted angle. It was too much for Anna. Instinct took hold of her and she sprinted away, trying to escape the horrific apparition.

"Anna!" Steve hollered after her.

She glanced over her shoulder and saw the thing chasing her. Yelping, she veered around a stone cross and blundered into the dark. A low tombstone appeared out of nowhere, and Anna slammed, face-first, into the ground. Wiggling onto her back, she gasped, seeing the ghost gliding toward her. But Steve was right behind it, his flashlight trained upon the apparition.

As if sensing the constable's presence, the ghost stopped, turned, and pointed at him. As Anna watched in horror, Steve stumbled and catapulted headlong into a tree.

There was shouting from the others. Greg came sprinting out of the gloom, closing in on the ghost. It waited, motionless except for its fluttering garment, raised its arm, and pointed at Greg. His feet flew out from under him, and he crashed into a heap on the ground.

Anna jumped to her feet, her courage returning now that the others needed her. But where was Evelyn? Anna looked everywhere, her eyes darting around the tombstones, but the apparition had vanished. Turning back to her friends, she saw Tiernay dash up to Greg with Erna jogging behind her.

Anna ran to Steve lying crumpled on the ground. He was unconscious, and as she caught up his flashlight and shone it in his face, she saw blood dripping down his forehead. Pulling a handful of tissues from her pocket, she cradled his head in her lap and pressed the wad against the wound. She felt for a pulse in his throat with her free hand, and felt it throbbing beneath her fingers. Thank heavens, he was still alive. She patted at his cheek.

"Wake up, Steve!" she urged.

He mumbled incoherently.

"What?" she asked, bending closer. He was silent, but his eyes fluttered open.

Tears of relief welled in her eyes. "How are you feeling?" she asked, stroking his cheek. He tried to sit up, but Anna pressed him back down again.

"Whoa, don't try to get up yet."

"What happened?" he asked, collapsing back into her arms and staring up at her.

"You were chasing Evelyn's ghost, but she knocked you down somehow. You were running so fast that you hit a tree."

Twenty feet away, Anna could hear Tiernay's frantic voice calling, "Greg, wake up!" She turned and saw Tiernay rocking Greg in her arms. Erna was leaning over them, dialing her cell phone.

"It's a police *and* a medical emergency," her friend said. Glancing over, Erna caught Anna's eye. "Send two ambulances."

22

An hour and a half later, there was a rap on the door, and Erna rose to answer it. Anna heard her say, "Come in, John," and then her friend ushered the corporal into the living room. May was ensconced in the recliner with a blanket and a hot water bottle to ward off the cemetery chill, while Anna sat on the couch with Wendy at her feet.

"May, Anna," John said, acknowledging them in turn with a stiff nod. He removed his hat and tucked it under his arm.

"Please take a seat," Erna said, indicating the couch. "Can I get you a cup of tea?"

"No thanks, Miss Dombrosky," he said, removing a notebook from his back pocket and opening it. "I just had a coffee at the hospital while I was checking in on Steve and Greg." He glanced at May and Anna before settling his gaze back on Erna. "Now, do you want to tell me what six supposedly sane people were doing running around the cemetery in the middle of the night?"

His question was met by silence. Erna perched on the couch.

"How is Steve doing, John?" she asked.

"They've put ten stitches into his head."

"And how about Greg?" Anna asked.

He turned his leaden gaze upon her. "He's still not conscious." She felt uncomfortable and looked away. "There doesn't seem anything particularly wrong with him, except some bruising and abrasions. He just doesn't wake up. His sister is still with him. The doctor told her that talking to Greg might help him regain consciousness."

Anna nodded and let out a deep breath. "It's my fault, John. I got really spooked at Evelyn's grave when her head collapsed over her shoulder, just the way it did when she haunted my front lawn Sunday night, so I ran. Evelyn chased me, and Steve and Greg chased Evelyn. Then she lifted her arm and shot some sort of invisible ray at them that knocked them down. Poor Steve slid into a tree and got hurt even worse. I don't know what she did to Greg."

John paused, his face immobile, and plunked down upon the couch. "Okay, you want to take that from the top?"

The three women interrupted each other over the next half hour as they tried to explain the events leading up to the cemetery ceremony. John listened patiently, jotting down notes and asking for clarification when necessary. When the friends had finished, he snapped the notebook shut and slid his pen into its binding.

"To sum up, someone's been playing tricks on May and Anna, and Sherman has disappeared. Is that about it?" he asked in an exasperated voice.

"I think that the situation is a little more serious than that," Erna murmured.

"I'll say. We've got two men in the hospital because of tonight's little escapade."

"What about Sherman?" May asked from the recliner.

John turned to her. "I would have expected more sense out of you, May. You just checked out of the hospital Sunday morning. It took two constables to haul you and your wheelchair out of the cemetery tonight. That's a pretty big waste of the taxpayers' money."

May's face turned pink as she sputtered, "Yeah, well, I'm one of those taxpayers, and I've been paying my taxes for years, so don't you talk to me like that, John Fox Child!"

John stared at her for a long time before shaking his head. "Listen, May, Sherman told you that he was clearing out, so there doesn't appear to be any foul play in his disappearance. As it so happens, we've been trying to talk to him ourselves, but we weren't been able to find him, either at his house or at your apartment. Now we know why. We'll try contacting his children – maybe he's staying with one of them."

"Will you call me if you find him?" May asked in a meek voice.

John nodded and stood up. "Will do. Well, ladies, if you don't have any further information, I'm going back to the station."

Erna rose to show him out. "I know that this all sounds foolish to you, but I think that there is malicious intent behind the events involving May and Anna, not to mention the attacks upon Steven and Gregory tonight."

John paused at the entrance to the living room and sighed. "We're a week away from Halloween. What happened to May and Anna might be some elaborate prank gone wrong. I'll ask our people to keep their eyes open for anything unusual, but that's about all I can do. As for Steve and Greg, people running around a cemetery in the dark are bound to get hurt."

"John," Anna said, "what about Henry? Have the police found him yet?"

"As a matter of fact, Henry walked into a Calgary police station yesterday morning to turn himself in. I was over telling Frank and Judy about it this evening, but I guess there hasn't been time for word to spread around town yet. So, if you were thinking that these pranks were pulled by Henry, you can count him out. He's been staying with a friend in Calgary all this time, and we've still got his car in the impound, so he can't have driven back."

Anna's face fell in disappointment. "Thanks. Just a thought."

John nodded. "You three try to stay out of trouble, will you? Good night."

"Night, John," Anna and May replied as Erna followed him from the room.

"We came off sounding like a bunch of idiots," May said. "Looks like the police aren't going to be of any use."

"Come on, Wendy," Anna said, climbing to her feet. "It's time to go home."

"What?" May asked in surprise as Anna and Wendy left the room. Erna returned a minute later to find her friend frowning. "Anna's leaving," May said.

"What did you say to upset her?"

"Nothing!"

"Why is she leaving, then?"

"She didn't say."

Anna re-appeared in the doorway carrying Wendy's dishes and the sack of dog kibble. The dog padded into the room to sit down beside the recliner.

"Erna, thanks so much, but it's time for me to go home," she said. "John just put this whole thing into perspective for me. I'm a grown woman. I can't hide out here forever."

"Do you think that's wise?" Erna asked.

"Don't let what John said bother you," May said. "Sure, we may look like fools for believing in ghosts, but what do we care? Better safe than sorry. You'd better stay here with us."

"May's right. You're too vulnerable at your house, whether there's a ghost behind all this or not," Erna added.

"Look, I really don't think that there's a ghost," Anna said. "And who's to say where it's safe or not. Don't worry, I'll lock my doors and windows and sleep in Ben's room, in case anyone tries to wake me up with more fun and games on the front lawn." May frowned as Anna turned to Erna. "I really appreciate you letting me stay here the past couple of days, but it's time I went home."

Erna laid her hand on Anna's shoulder. "Are you leaving because you're embarrassed about what happened in the cemetery tonight?" she asked.

Anna forced herself to meet Erna's gaze. "If I had stayed in the circle like Tiernay told us, that 'thing' wouldn't have chased me, and Steve and Greg wouldn't be in the hospital. It's time I started reacting more logically, wouldn't you say?"

"There was no shame in running, dear. You were deliberately singled out for special attention by the apparition. Anyone in your situation would have run."

"It sure scared me," May said from her chair. "If I hadn't already been sitting down, I would have collapsed."

Anna smiled. "Thanks for trying to make me feel better, you two. And maybe you're right. But if someone tries to scare me a third time, I just won't let it happen." They looked at her doubtfully. "Don't worry, if I see another ghost, I won't go near it. I saw what it did to Steve and Greg tonight."

Erna frowned. "Yes, I wish that we had an explanation for what happened to them. That worries me most of all."

Anna glanced at her watch. "Wow, it's going on eleven! I've got work in the morning." She kissed Erna's cheek and hurried over to hug May. "Oops, almost forgot my overnight bag," she said, snatching it up from where it rested beside the couch. She smiled at her friends. "Don't look so worried. I'll be just fine."

"Call us if anything happens," Erna said as Anna left the room.

"Will do," Anna called from the front door. "Come on, Wendy, let's go home!" The dog sprang up from the living room floor and trotted after her.

When the door shut behind them, May said, "Better start praying."

23

When Anna pulled into her driveway, she let the car idle for a few moments, using her headlights to scan the front of the house. Everything seemed fine, so she turned off the engine and nudged the car door open. Wendy jumped over her lap to relieve herself on the lawn, while Anna gathered up their things and jogged to the front door. She unlocked it quickly, glancing over her shoulder as she did, and pushed the door open before calling for Wendy to come. The dog galloped up the yard and into the house, with Anna slamming and bolting the door behind them. After putting away the dog's things, she walked reluctantly to her room. The bed was still unmade from Sunday night, but Steve had locked the window for her. Taking a moment to throw two days' worth of dirty laundry into the clothes hamper, Anna grabbed a clean nightshirt from her bureau and changed out of her clothes in record time. Performing the sparest of evening ablutions, she left the bathroom light on to go next door to Ben's room.

The room looked as if Ben still lived there. His books were in the bookcase, his concert posters were tacked on the bulletin board over the desk, and a shabby teddy bear that had accompanied him on all their cross-country moves leaned against the headboard. Fortunately, the bed was made up with fresh linens, and Anna had only to set the alarm on the clock radio before crawling inside. Wendy sat in the doorway, confused by the change in sleeping arrangements.

"Here, Wendy," Anna said, patting the quilt beside her. "You always sleep on the bed when Ben's home, anyway."

The dog loped into the room and sprang onto the bed beside her, turning around once before hunkering down. Anna switched off the bedside light, nestled under the covers, and stared into the darkness. She lay still for all of ten seconds before groping for the clock radio. It was too quiet, and she could hear the creepy music box tune in her head. If someone or something started playing it for real outside, she didn't want to hear it. She hit the snooze button, and late night jazz from a Calgary FM station drifted out of the speaker. Anna sighed and settled down to sleep.

She slept soundly and smiled when the alarm woke her in the morning. Nothing had disturbed her after all. She climbed out of bed and attended to the usual morning chores before saying goodbye to Wendy and leaving the house with time to spare. The clouds were tinted a soft gold and pink as she enjoyed a leisurely drive through the countryside. Traffic was sparse when she reached the city limits, and the lights were green all the way to the university. It was shaping up to be a wonderful day. At noon, she called Erna for news of the invalids in the hospital.

"Steven went home this morning, and Gregory's conscious and doing fine. They ran additional tests, but they couldn't find anything wrong with him, so he's being released this afternoon."

"I'm so glad to hear it. I was afraid that whatever had happened to him had damaged his brain."

"No. Just a minute, Anna." There was talking in the background. "May wants to know if the ghost showed up last night."

"No, everything was fine. Didn't see or hear a trace of it."

"I'm glad, dear. I had trouble sleeping last night for worrying about you."

"I'm sorry that you were worried about me, but nothing happened."

"She says she's fine, May."

"By the way, I'm thinking about dropping by the Raes' to talk to Greg after supper. I want to hear what happened to him in the cemetery."

"Good idea. If I weren't looking after May, I'd come with you. Give me a call when you get home and let us know what he says."

"Will do. Give May my best."

"Goodbye."

It was eight o'clock when Anna climbed into her car to drive over to the Raes' house. The sky was clear, and the air was cool and fresh. Anna was cheered by the sight of light spilling from Jeff and Betty's windows as she drove by their house. Many of the other houses she passed on the way through town also had on lights, as if everyone had decided to stay home that night. Even Greg and Tiernay's barren front lawn looked cozy under a blanket of dry leaves that crunched as she made her way to the door. The drapes were drawn, but she could hear the murmur of conversation within, and only had to wait a few seconds before someone responded to her knock.

"Anna," Tiernay said, her face flinty as she gripped the door, "I had a feeling that we'd see you tonight. Come in."

"Thanks," Anna said, skirting around her. "I wanted to see how Greg was doing." The scent of sandalwood smoke drifted down the dark hallway as she followed Tiernay to the living room.

"Anna's here," Tiernay announced, standing aside to let her guest enter. Anna blinked in the lights.

"Anna!" Greg said. "Just the tonic I needed. Come and sit beside me, lovely lady." He waved at her from his rocking chair next to the hearth, where a cozy fire burned. Dressed in a robe and pyjamas, he even had a blanket on his lap. "Tiernay's playing nurse tonight."

"I'm not surprised. You just got home from the hospital."

"Hi, Anna," a thin voice piped from across the room. She turned to see Steve lying on the couch, a white bandage covering part of his head and his face looking pale and drawn. Smoke rose from a brass incense burner on the table beside him, while soothing classical music played in the background.

"I didn't know you'd be here, too," Anna said, taking two steps toward him, but Tiernay cut in front of her and sank down onto the carpet beside him.

"Makes it easier for Tiernay to look after us both," Greg said, attempting to rise, but pausing half-way to clutch the arm of his chair. "Just a little dizzy spell. It will pass in a second. Let me get you a chair."

"No, don't get up," Anna said, hastening to him. "I'm a floor person anyway." She picked up the blanket that had fallen from his lap and tucked it back over him before sitting on the carpet at his feet.

Greg smiled and rested his hand on her shoulder. "Isn't this nice, all of us here together? To what do we owe the pleasure?"

Anna hesitated, but she wanted to get her unpleasant business out of the way. "Well, there are two reasons for my visit." She turned to include Steve and Tiernay in the conversation. "First, I didn't get a chance to apologize for breaking the circle last night. I feel like it's my fault that you and Steve got hurt."

"It was. Why did you do such a dangerous thing when I specifically told everyone to stay put?" Tiernay asked in a strident voice. "I didn't get a chance to do anything with Evelyn, either."

"Now Tiernay, don't start again," Greg said. "That spectre was truly appalling. Did you see how it stared at Anna? I was scared, and it wasn't even looking at me."

Anna was grateful for Greg's support, but his words didn't remove the scowl from Tiernay's face. "Second," she said, "I wanted to ask what happened to you last night. Since Steve is here, I can ask you both. What did Evelyn's ghost do to you?"

"I've been trying to explain it to Tiernay," Greg replied. "It was the damnedest thing. One minute Steve was chasing Evelyn's ghost, and the next, he was down. I had my flashlight pointing at Evelyn at the time, so I could see her face when it happened. She was laughing at us. And it wasn't happy laughter, either. I could see that she hated us. I've never seen such a look of pure evil on anyone's face before. Ugh, it gives me the willies just thinking about it." Anna felt him shudder, and his words brought back her own terrifying memories.

"Then Evelyn raised her arm and pointed at me. I wanted to get out of the way, but I couldn't move fast enough. This thing that I can only describe as a bolt of pure energy hit me. It felt like cold fire zapping through my body, and then my muscles locked and I was paralyzed. That's when I hit the ground and blacked out. I don't remember anything after that, until I heard Tiernay's voice calling to me, begging me to wake up. Poor dear, you sounded frantic," Greg said, looking at his sister. She grimaced. "It bothered me to hear how upset you were, so I struggled to find my way back to you. I'm fine now, but I still feel as if I've been to hell and back."

Anna was appalled by his words. "I'm so sorry, Greg. I feel like I brought this upon you," she said.

He shrugged. "It's over, and I'm fine. The doctor said there's nothing wrong with me." He reached for her hand. "Try not to let it bother you, darling."

She smiled, grateful for his comforting words, before looking at Steve. "What about you, Steve? Is that what happened to you?"

"I don't remember anything after I left the circle to chase after you."

"Nothing?"

He shook his head.

"The doctor said he had a concussion," Tiernay said, her eyes still angry as she glared at Anna. "It's probably the reason for his memory loss." She turned back to Steve, and her eyes softened. "You look tired, honey. Is your headache still bad?" He nodded. "Why don't I make you some more of that tea while you go up to bed? You look exhausted."

"Yeah," he said. "I think I will. Sorry, Anna, but I'm all done in."

Tiernay rose from the floor while Steve sat up. Climbing to his feet, he paused to grab hold of the back of the couch and closed his eyes.

"Dizzy?" Tiernay asked, taking his arm.

He opened his eyes and shook off her hand. "I'm okay. Night Anna. Night Greg."

"Steve, I'm so sorry," Anna said, clambering to her feet. She stood awkwardly by while Steve shuffled from the room with Tiernay at his elbow. She listened to them mount the stairs before turning back to Greg.

"I feel terrible," she said.

"Don't. Evelyn's to blame, not you."

"But what are we going to do?" she asked. He reached for her and pulled her back to the chair when she took his hand. She knelt so that their heads were on the same level.

"It's going to be okay. I promise," he said, kissing her hand.

"What do you mean? How is everything going to be okay?"

He put an arm around her waist. "Tiernay e-mailed her old coven while Steve and I were in the hospital. The group is run by a powerful witch, someone who's been practising magic all her life. Tiernay explained what's been happening here, and now she's just waiting for the witch to reply. I'm sure that the two of them will get Evelyn sorted out between them. Meanwhile, you stick close to home and don't go for any long walks with your dog, right? Are you still wearing the stone Tiernay gave you?"

Anna nodded, fingering the stone in her jacket pocket. She had stuffed it in there on the night of the séance and hadn't removed it since.

"Good. That will protect you." He smiled and tapped her nose. "I don't want anything to happen to you. I still want to sketch you, remember?" Anna nodded and smiled.

"That's better. You have such a pretty smile." Releasing her waist, he cupped the back of her head and kissed her. His mouth was warm and tender against hers, and Anna lingered there for a second before turning her face. Greg sighed, his breath warming her ear.

She pulled away and rested her hands on his shoulders. "Look, Greg, I think you've got the wrong impression. You're a great guy, and you're very attractive, but I'm in love with Charlie."

"So you keep saying," he said, drawing his finger across her lips. "I'm starting to feel discouraged."

Anna snorted. "Well you should," she said, climbing to her feet. He rose beside her, dropping the blanket onto the floor and stepping over it.

"Go on. Go home. We all need our rest," he said, turning her around and pushing her gently toward the hallway. "I'll watch to make sure that you get safely to your car."

"Thanks Greg. You're a dear," Anna said over her shoulder on her way to the door.

After opening it, she glanced quickly around the porch, ensuring that no one was waiting in the shadows. Better safe than sorry. The porch was empty, so she scooted down the stairs and was in her car with the door locked and the engine started seconds later. Her headlights flashed on, and Greg waved before she pulled away from the curb.

Anna felt a little better as she drove the few blocks to Main Street and turned onto it. Greg seemed fine, and Steve was on the mend. At least the nutcase behind all these pranks hadn't done any permanent damage. And Tiernay was getting help from a more experienced witch. Did two witches outrank a ghost? She smiled and shook her head; what a ridiculous thought. She had witchcraft and ghosts on the brain.

Three blocks later, she turned left. Halfway down the street, her headlights picked out a man striding down the sidewalk, his pony tail swinging like a pendulum over his back and his thick arms pumping like pistons. She caught a glint of metal in his hand and squinted. It was Frank, and he was carrying a tire iron. She pulled up beside him and rolled down the passenger-side window.

"Frank, what are you doing?" she called to him. He paused, and turned to look at Anna.

"I'm hunting a ghost."

24

An hour and a half earlier

Judy hurried into the garage, smacking the door opener on the wall and climbing into the car. It was ten to seven, and she only had ten minutes to make it to church before the Catholic Women's League meeting began. She started the engine and waited for the door to finish lifting.

The second Thursday night of the month was always such a rush, dashing home from her secretarial job with the Foothills Premium Real Estate Agency and hurrying to get to the church on time. Thank heaven Frank always had supper waiting on the table so that they could spend half an hour together before she had to run out again. She smiled; Frank was such a sweetheart. Her ex-husband had always grumbled when supper had been late getting on the table. There were benefits to living with a chef.

When the door finished opening, she turned to look over the seat, and began backing out of the garage. Judy frowned; who was that coming up from the bottom of the driveway? The red glow from her brake lights illuminated a woman in a long cloak with a hood pulled low over her face. The woman paused halfway up the drive and pulled the hood down. A mess of blond hair tumbled onto her shoulders. Judy recognized the woman, her eyes starting from her head. It was Evelyn Mason. Her neck was broken and twisted, just the way she must have looked after her fall down the town office stairs.

Judy shrieked. Evelyn just stood there staring at her with cold, dead eyes. Out of nowhere, Evelyn pulled an axe from behind her cloak, swung it over her head, and started for the garage. Judy screamed, hit the remote to close the garage door, and jumped out of the car with the motor still running. In her panic, she tripped over a rake leaning against the wall and collided into the car. Gasping, Judy looked over her shoulder and saw that Evelyn was about to duck under the door before it could close. She screamed again, shoved the rake out of the way, and raced for the door into the house. Terrified that Evelyn was in the garage behind her, Judy flung the door open and screamed Frank's name. He met her half-way down the hallway, where she threw herself, sobbing and shaking, into his arms.

"Judy, what's wrong?" he asked, trying to peer into her face, but she was staring over her shoulder.

"It's Evelyn! She's coming after me with an axe. Did she get inside?" she asked, turning fear-crazed eyes at Frank.

"What are you talking about?" he demanded. Instead of replying, she broke out of his arms to hit the hallway light switch. The fluorescent tubes blinked twice before staying on, revealing the empty corridor behind them.

"Let me see," he said, taking a step toward the garage, but Judy grabbed his shoulder and dug in her heels.

"No, Frank! Don't go in there. She'll kill you!"

"Now calm down, honey," he said, holding the hysterical woman in his arms. He sniffed. "I smell gas. Did you leave the engine running?"

"No, Frank!" Judy shrieked as he pulled away.

He strode the last few steps to the door and opened it gingerly, peeking into the garage. The fumes belching from the car made him gag. Covering his mouth with one hand, he smacked the door opener and ran into the garage, jumping into the car to turn off the motor. Twisting in the seat, he watched the door rumble upward. It cleared the first two feet from the floor before clanking to a stop, the machinery clicking twice before failing. Frank climbed out of the car, the cool, fresh air blowing around his legs, and turned to investigate what was wrong. His mouth gaped open. Three feet from the top, an axe blade pierced the garage door.

Anna convinced Frank to climb into the front seat beside her. He closed the door, and she saw the tire iron in his right hand.

"What are you talking about?" she asked. "What ghost?" He swivelled to look at her, and Anna saw that his face was white with anger.

"Someone scared the hell out of Judy tonight."

"What happened?"

Frank told her.

"Oh my lord," Anna said. "How's Judy?"

"She's terrified. I couldn't leave her alone, so I dropped her at Erna's before I came out again." Anna shook her head in sympathy. "Anyway, after I found the axe stuck in the door, I got Judy calmed down enough to tell me what happened. She didn't even remember screaming."

"Oh Frank, how horrible. Poor Judy."

He nodded. "It was like a freaking horror movie. Judy couldn't let go of me, so we went to the front door together to have a look outside. The porch light was on, and we could see that there was no one out there. Once we stepped out on the porch, though, we could see the axe handle sticking out of the garage door, and Judy started screaming again. It took me a long time to get her calmed down enough to walk over to Erna's. My car's still stuck in the garage."

"Did you call the police?"

"Not yet. I want to have a look on my own first. There's a lunatic running around town, and I want to find him before the police do."

"Him?"

"Yeah. When you ladies started talking about a ghost on May's stairs, I thought that it was Henry. It was just the fruitcake kind of thing he would do. Then someone scared you, and there was all that trouble in the cemetery last night with Steve and Greg. Only, John came by last night to tell us that Henry is under arrest in Calgary, so it couldn't have been him. But Sherman Mason is missing, and he's four quarters short of a dollar. I don't know what the hell is going on, but it's time someone found out who's behind it and stopped him. Me." He opened the door to climb out, but Anna grabbed his arm.

"Don't, Frank. Leave it alone"

Frank glanced at her impatiently. "Don't worry, I can look after myself."

"Sure you can, but I think you should stay out of it. Whoever's behind this, he's got some way of hurting people. Look at what he did to Steve and Greg. Let the police take the risk. That's what they're paid for."

Frank tugged his arm out from under her hand. "Go home, Anna. I'll see you later." He got out of the car and slammed the door behind him.

"Frank!" Anna shouted, but he jogged down a driveway and disappeared between two houses. She watched for a moment in case he re-appeared, then put her car in gear and drove straight to Erna's house.

25

Anna parked on the street and rushed to ring Erna's doorbell. She jittered back and forth on her feet, shivering with nerves in the chilly night air.

"Anna," Erna said in surprise when she opened the door.

"I just saw Frank. He told me what happened. Where's Judy?"

"In the living room," Erna said, stepping back to let her inside. Anna hurried to the living room, where Judy, wrapped in a blanket with a mug clasped between her hands, was sitting in the middle of the couch. May was on the recliner next to her, both women looking up in surprise.

"You've got to stop Frank, Judy. He doesn't know what he's up against," Anna said.

"I can't," Judy wailed, breaking into sobs. Anna sat down beside her, hugging her close as Judy's shoulders shook, while Erna circled the couch and sat down on her other side.

"We've got to call the police," Anna said. "If we tell them that Frank's out looking for the person responsible for leaving an axe in his garage door, they'll take us seriously. They'll find him before he gets hurt."

Judy stopped crying, her eyes widening. "You want to get Frank into trouble?"

"Of course not, but it's better than letting him tangle with someone crazy enough to come after you with an axe."

Judy stared in disbelief from one friend to another. May slowly nodded her agreement, while Erna frowned.

"You don't think it was Evelyn's ghost?" Judy asked.

"You bet," May said, while Anna said, "Don't be ridiculous."

"This is getting out of hand," Erna said, rising to her feet. "Anna's right. I'm calling the police."

The night did not end well for Frank. A half hour after speaking with Anna, he was peering into Sherman's front windows when a police car pulled up on the street and flashed its lights at him. Frank dropped his tire iron in the bushes and sprinted for the side of the house, but the constable chasing him was twenty-four, athletic, and tackled him with ease. He took Frank to the station for questioning, where John Fox Child gave him a good talking to and told him to go home. When the constable dropped him off at Erna's house, Frank was limping.

"Come on," he said to Judy when Erna fetched her, "let's get out of here." Anna and May were watching from the living room entrance, May on crutches.

"I'm sorry, Frank, but it was for your own good," Erna said. Anna didn't dare say anything.

Frank shot Erna an angry look, but kept his mouth shut. He took Judy's hand, and they walked out the door without saying a word. Erna closed it behind them and turned to look at her friends.

"I haven't made myself popular with either one of them tonight," she said.

"At least Frank's safe. You did the right thing," Anna said, bending to kiss Erna's powdery cheek. "But it's almost midnight, and I have to go to work tomorrow. I'm going home." She shrugged her arms into the jacket she was carrying and patted her pockets for the car keys.

"So, we're agreed, right?" May said. "Tiernay's going to take care of this ghost business with her witch friend, and we're going to keep our noses out of it from now on. Unless they need our help."

"Or the police do," Anna said. "Things are getting too dangerous, and we don't want anyone else getting hurt – or killed."

"Agreed," Erna said. "Good night and try to sleep, Anna. I'll call you at work tomorrow if we hear anything."

The next day was Friday, and when Anna got home from work, her son was waiting for her. Ben set the table and fed Wendy while Anna heated some defrosted turkey soup made from Thanksgiving leftovers and set out a loaf of crusty bread. She had already told Ben about the séance at Sherman's house and May's fall, and brought him up to speed on what had happened since last Friday. He frowned when Anna described the ghostly visitor on her front lawn, shook his head when she talked about being chased in the cemetery, and stared at her wide-eyed as she described Judy's scare and the axe in Frank's garage door.

"I can't believe you didn't call me, Mom. I could have come out and stayed with you," he protested.

"I know, but you had mid-terms, and I didn't want to bother you."

"That's crazy! Who cares about school when some psycho is running around town with an axe?" He got up from his chair to fetch another bowl of soup from the pot on the stove. "What did the police have to say when they came to Erna's house after she called the police on Frank?"

"Not much. They listened to Judy's story and left to check out the garage door."

"Well, you haven't been taking Wendy for any bedtime walks, have you? Just out into the backyard to let her do her business and back in again?" He straddled the chair and sat down again with his full bowl.

"I sure didn't take her for a walk last night when I finally got home."

Ben sighed. "I wish that you'd move further into town. I don't like you being so isolated out here."

"That's just what Erna and May said when I stayed with them this past week. Don't worry, honey, I'll be extra careful until this business gets sorted out. I'm glad you're home tonight, though. Wendy hasn't had a decent walk for days. We can take her together after we're done eating." The dog sighed from where she lay beside Ben, and he reached down to ruffle her fur.

"Poor girl, we'll take you for a walk right after supper," he said. Wendy lifted her head, suddenly alert. "Right after dessert," Ben added, eyeing the pan of brownies that Anna had also defrosted.

A half hour later, Ben waited while his mother slipped the cell phone and flashlight she always carried at night into her coat pocket and pulled on her gloves. Wendy sat at her feet, coiled to spring as soon as Anna made a move for the door.

"Ready for your walk?" Anna asked, attaching the leash to the dog's collar. Wendy bounced to her feet and trotted beside Anna as she flicked on the porch light and followed Ben from the house.

They turned right at the bottom of the driveway and headed for the old part of town. It was an overcast night with banks of white cloud masking the moon. Dry leaves skittered ahead of them as they strolled down the sidewalk. Anna shivered in the frosty air and pulled her hood up over her head.

"You warm enough?" she asked Ben. He was hatless, and his hands were inside his coat pockets.

"Sure. I'm never as cold as you are." Striding along beside him, Anna tucked her hand into his arm. Funny; their roles were reversed now. She was looking to Ben for support and protection when, not so long ago, she had been the one watching out for him. Anna sighed. The days of leading Ben by the hand were gone.

They paused mid-block to allow Wendy to relieve herself. As they waited, something rustled in the bushes beside them, and Anna jumped. Ben grinned at her.

"Nervous?"

"A little. It's probably just the wind or a squirrel or something." Only the intersections had street lights, so the stretches of sidewalk between the corners were pitch black unless someone had their outside lights on. Wendy finished her business, and they continued up the street.

Halloween was only three days away, and many of the front porches boasted pumpkins, straw bales, corn stalks, and even more elaborate decorations. Anna loved Halloween. She had been shy as an only child, but something about wearing a costume and racing around in the dark had emboldened her. One year, her neighbourhood had even closed the street to host a bonfire. Anna and the other kids had danced around the fire and played blind man's bluff until they were exhausted and cold. Then they and their parents had toasted marshmallows over the embers and drunk hot chocolate out of thermoses. To this day, the scent of wood smoke and the sight of children dashing up and down the street on Halloween night always brought happy memories back to her.

Rambling down the sidewalk, Anna noticed that one house had gone all out with its ghoulish decorations. The owners had erected a mini-cemetery on the lawn complete with gravestones and wooden coffins, green lighting adding to the spooky atmosphere. A dark figure hanging from a tree twisted back and forth in the wind, while another figure lay in an open coffin with a knife handle protruding from its gruesome chest. Anna grimaced.

"Looks more like *Nightmare on Elm Street* than Halloween to me," she said. "We used to go in for scary stuff when I was a kid, not gore."

"Yeah, well there were only Frankenstein and Wolf Man movies when you were young, right?"

"Not quite," Anna said. "We even had colour TV back then, smart-ass." Ben grinned, and she smiled back at him.

They passed Erna's house and St. Bernadette's Church. Not surprisingly, the street outside the cemetery was deserted and the gate was closed, not that Anna fancied another stroll among the tombstones.

"How far are we walking?" Ben asked. "I'm surprised you want to go anywhere near the cemetery after what happened to you on Wednesday night."

"Do you mind if we walk by Sherman's house? No one's seen him for six days, and May's worried. I want to see if there are any lights on inside the house."

Ben looked at her out of the corner of his eye. "I wondered why we were headed this way. I don't mind, if you're not scared, but it's pretty creepy out here, especially with no moonlight. Who knows what disgusting things might come slithering out of the graveyard." He chortled, crooking his fingers as if he were going to attack her, but Anna smacked him in the shoulder.

"Cut it out, okay? I'm not crazy about being here, either, but I'm doing it for May's sake."

"Okay," Ben said, sobering and looking suitably chagrined.

Two-thirds of the way past the cemetery, Anna could see that there were no lights on in Sherman's house and the front yard was dark. Either he was in bed, or Sherman was holed up somewhere else. Her curiosity unsatisfied, she was about to suggest they turn back when Wendy growled. Anna slowed, looking down at her pet.

"What's the matter, girl?" she asked. But the dog was ignoring her, staring straight ahead at the caretaker's house. Wendy's growl increased to a deep-throated, threatening rumble.

"What's got into her?" Ben asked. Anna peered at the house, but there wasn't anything out of the ordinary. All the same, Wendy strained forward on her leash. Anna slipped the flashlight from her pocket and flicked it on.

"Come on," she said.

"You've got to be kidding," Ben said, trailing after her.

They stopped on the sidewalk out front of the house, Wendy stiff-legged and alert. Anna trained her flashlight over the yard, past the two big trees and into the bushes encircling the front windows. Nothing there, as far as she could see. She tried shining her flashlight along the side of the house, but there wasn't anything there, either. Abruptly, Wendy threw back her head and howled.

Anna froze, her breath catching in her throat. Wendy had howled like that on only one other occasion, and things had turned out very badly afterward.

"What do you think it is, Mom?" Ben whispered, his fingers digging into her arm.

"Shhh," she said, her eyes swivelling over the house. She strained to listen. The leaves were shimmering in the wind, sounding just like rain, and the tossing tree limbs made a rhythmical creaking noise.

Anna exchanged a look with Ben, and they began inching their way up the leaf-strewn lawn. Wendy tried to scramble ahead, but Anna hauled her back on the leash. They circled the two trees and came to a stop outside the windows. Anna shone her light inside, but it reflected back, preventing them from seeing. She pressed her nose against the glass and cupped her hands. All she could see was the outline of the living room furniture.

Anna suddenly sensed something moving behind her and ducked. She pivoted; there was nothing there. She glanced at Ben. His eyes were huge as he stared back at her. Slowly, Anna trained her flashlight up into the tree.

A dark figure hung from a branch, its head lolling forward on its chest. The body swayed on its rope, moving back and forth, back and forth, creak . . . creak . . .

There was a sign hanging from its neck. One word was written in bold, black, capital letters on crude cardboard.

"MURDERER."

Anna screamed.

26

Anna stood behind the ambulance wrapped in a quilt. Ben stood beside her with his arm around her shoulders. Two cruisers were parked behind them, their red and blue lights rhythmically sweeping the street.

"Here," a paramedic said, handing them each a paper cup containing hot fluid. Anna gripped hers with both hands and raised it to her lips. It was tea loaded with lots of sugar. She didn't like tea, but she sipped at it anyway to ward off the after-effects of shock. Wendy lay at her feet, her eyes fixed on the police personnel cordoning off the caretaker's yard with yellow tape.

John Fox Child was busy by the tree where the body had been taken down. Anna looked away, not wanting to know what he was doing. A third cruiser pulled up behind the others, and Steve clambered out from behind the wheel. He looked much better than he had the night before, his hat covering the bandage she knew lay beneath. Steve opened the back door, and Anna's eyes popped wide as Sherman climbed out onto the sidewalk. He limped around the back of the cruiser to the other side and opened the door, removing two crutches. Leaning them against the car, he extended his hand inside, and May emerged. As Sherman helped her out of the car, the front passenger door swung open, and Erna slid out. John walked over to join the group, with Steve leaning against the car.

"Thanks for coming, Sherman," John said. "I'd like you to have a look at the crime scene, see if you notice anything. I'll warn you, the body's not pretty. Ladies, why not join

Anna and her son over by the ambulance?" He pointed in their direction, and May and Erna turned to look at them. John took Sherman's arm, Steve lifted the tape, and they led Sherman up the lawn toward the trees.

Erna helped May hobble down the sidewalk as Anna hurried forward to meet them, Ben and Wendy following close behind.

"You found Sherman," Anna said, catching up to them. "How?" As she looked from May to Erna, Ben took May's other arm, and they all walked slowly toward the ambulance.

"Sherman called us," May said with a shrug. "He's been staying at the parish house with Father Winfield all this time. He tried going back to his own house, but he just couldn't stay. Too rattled. Plus, he found a message from the police on his voice mail saying they wanted to talk to him. Something about counterfeit money being passed at the store. There's still a lot of suspicion over why he was let go from the bank, and Sherman couldn't deal with that and Evelyn, so he asked Father Winfield to hide him for a while. But things changed when you found the body tonight. The police called Father because the caretaker's house belongs to the parish, and Father told Sherman that he had to cooperate with the police. Sherman agreed, but he wanted to talk it over with us first. You could have knocked me down with a feather when he walked into Erna's living room, I'll tell you. But we all agreed with Father that Sherman should cooperate with the police, so he called them from Erna's. They wanted him to have a look at the crime scene, but he refused to come without us." Reaching the ambulance, May collapsed onto the tailgate with a heavy sigh.

Now that her arm was free, Erna hugged Anna. "What a terrible thing to have happened to you. I'm so sorry that you had to go through this again," she said, patting Anna's back.

Erna turned to look at Ben. "I'm so glad that you were here with your mother," she added. He nodded, looking grim.

"How're you holding up, doll? You have the worst luck for finding bodies," May said.

Anna shuddered, remembering the previous spring when she had found her ex-husband's body on a country road while on a bed-time walk with Wendy. "It's Henry Fellows this time."

"So Steve told us," Erna said.

"What's Henry doing here? I thought he was still in jail in Calgary," Anna said.

"Steve told us about that, too," May replied. "Our boys called the Calgary police after identifying Henry's body, and they said that Henry had been bailed out of jail the day after he turned himself in, apparently by the friend he was staying with. The friend said that Henry's been missing for two days, though."

"You'd think the Calgary police would have contacted our guys about that," Anna said.

Erna shrugged. "Apparently not."

"Did you hear about the sign?" Anna asked, her eyes straying for a second toward the three men standing beside Henry's body.

"No. What sign?" May asked.

"There was a sign hanging around Henry's neck." It said 'murderer.'"

"Murderer? Is that all?" Erna asked with a frown. Anna nodded.

"What's that supposed to mean?" May asked. "That Henry was a murderer?"

"I guess so," Anna said, sitting down on the tailgate beside her. Wendy stuck her head into Anna's lap, and she absent-mindedly patted the dog.

A small crowd had gathered across the street, attracted by the cruiser lights and all the activity at the crime scene. The observers wore hats and coats over their nightclothes, chatting and watching the police go about their grim business as if they were at a football game. Occasionally, newcomers arrived, and their neighbours filled them in on what was happening.

"Who is Henry supposed to have murdered?" Erna asked.

Anna shook her head, distracted by the crowd. Someone had caught her eye, a woman dressed in a long cloak pushing her way to the front. The hood covering her head did not quite mask the bright red hair. It was Tiernay. The young woman turned, as if feeling Anna's gaze, and stared back. They looked at each other for a moment until Tiernay nodded and disappeared back into the crowd.

Anna frowned. Tiernay didn't live anywhere near the cemetery. How had she found out about the death so quickly?

"A suicide note? Kind of short for a suicide note," May was saying.

"What?" Anna asked, turning back to her friends.

"Don't forget what Henry said at The Diner," Erna added. "He accused Frank of ruining his life. What if Henry felt that he couldn't go through the disgrace of another trial? He might have decided to end it all, and put that sign around his neck as a final accusation against Frank."

"You mean that Henry was calling Frank a murderer?" May paused to consider. "I suppose it's possible, but Henry should have written, 'Frank murdered me,' if that's what he meant to say. Why be so ambiguous?" She glanced up at Anna. "What do you think?"

Anna shook her head. "The thought never occurred to me. I've been so worried about Evelyn's ghost and all the pranks lately that Henry's death just hasn't sunk in yet.

Speaking about Evelyn, remember Sherman saying that Henry had been giving Evelyn trouble about the bylaws?"

"Yes," Erna said. "Sherman said that there was a bylaw preventing Henry from putting in his drive-through window."

"Well," Anna said, trying to piece her thoughts together, "what if Henry came back to talk to Evelyn about his drive-through on the day she died?"

"Surely someone would have seen him at the office," Erna said.

"Evelyn was the last to leave that day. What if Henry came in just as she was getting ready to go? They could have quarrelled, and Henry might have pushed her down the stairs in a fit of temper. Or he might have killed Evelyn to keep her quiet about the bylaw."

"I don't know," Erna said slowly, pursing her lips together. "I'm reluctant to think that Henry would have murdered Evelyn over a drive-through window. Besides, that theory only works if no one else at the town office knew about the bylaw."

Anna pushed on, too muddled to worry if her reasoning was sound or not. "But Sherman said Evelyn had re-organized the files. Maybe it was some obscure ordinance she had come across that no one else remembered. There's not much call for a drive-through window in this town."

"Wait a minute," May said. "I hate to burst your balloon, Anna, but if Evelyn had turned down Henry's application, wouldn't there have been a paper trail citing the bylaw?"

"And we still have no evidence that Evelyn was murdered. As far as the police investigation went, her death was an accident," Erna added.

Ben stared at the three women. "You're making me dizzy just listening to you," he said.

Erna laughed. "Poor Ben. You're not used to hearing us speculate."

Anna rubbed her eyes. It was late, and she felt wrung-out from discovering Henry. "You two could be right – Evelyn's death may have just been an accident."

"Maybe. And Henry's death was probably a suicide," May said.

"Otherwise," Erna added, "who murdered Henry?"

"Yes," Anna said as all three women turned to look at John and Steve deep in conversation with Sherman. "Who could have murdered Henry?"

27

Steve dropped Anna, Ben, and Wendy home later that night after they had signed their statements, and Anna had a terrible sense of déjà vu as she unlocked the front door and went to bed, remembering her ex-husband's murder investigation. She woke Ben at eight the following morning so that he could make it to his part-time job in Calgary by nine. Going back to bed to snooze for another half hour, she got up, smoothed on some moisturizer and lipstick, and was at The Diner for breakfast by nine. Mr. Andrews was seated at the end of the counter next to Erna and May with no newspaper in sight, wonder of wonders. Anna collapsed onto an empty stool beside them, still feeling exhausted.

"I was going to pick you two up if you weren't here," she said, speaking to May. "How'd you get in this morning?"

"Tom gave us a lift," May said, nodding toward the retired rancher. He saluted Anna with his cup of coffee, and she gave him a weak smile.

"Any news?" she asked, turning back to May.

"Some. We got here at seven thirty just as Frank was opening. Steve turned up about twenty minutes later."

"He looked worn out, poor boy," Erna added. "He must have had quite a night."

"Yeah, he was bushed. Anyway, he said that it looked like Henry hadn't been dead too long when you found him, but they'll have to wait for the autopsy to be sure. And there wasn't much damage done to him, other than – well, you know. Nothing to indicate he'd been in a fight, or tied up, or anything. So, it still looks like suicide."

"Wouldn't be too hard to imagine Henry getting himself murdered," Mr. Andrews said. "There were times I wanted to get my hands around his throat myself."

"Shame on you, Tom Andrews," Erna said. "Speaking ill of the dead."

He shrugged. "Hell, I'm not the only one who felt that way."

"Just don't say it out loud," May whispered. "Not with the police as edgy as they are."

"I'm not surprised," Erna said. "One murder and another suspicious death all in the same year. That's unprecedented in Crane history."

"Hi, Anna," Mary said, bustling around the counter to pick up a pot of coffee. With four tables occupied, another couple coming through the door, and no sign of Judy yet, she was in a hurry. "Looks like you're getting all the news. Do you want the usual?"

"Please," Anna said.

"Frank, Anna wants the usual," Mary called through the pass-through before rushing away.

Anna turned back to Erna. "How was Frank when you showed up this morning? Did he still seem angry for calling the police on him the other night?"

"No, he said 'Morning' the same as usual."

"Good. At least things are okay with Frank." Anna turned to May. "How about Sherman? Have you heard from him?"

"Yeah. He's a basket case. Thank God he's staying with Father Winfield. Imagine how he would have felt opening his curtains this morning to discover Henry's body swinging from a tree. If it had been me, I'd have had a stroke for sure."

The door opened as another customer arrived.

"Now what are we going to do?" Anna asked.

"Nothing. It's over," a husky voice said from behind them. Anna whirled to see who had spoken. Tiernay stood just inside the door wearing the same cloak Anna had seen her in the night before. There was mascara smeared under her eyes and her hair was flattened. Most of her make-up was worn off, too. Anna had never seen the young woman looking so unglamorous before.

"I've been up all night taking readings around Sherman's house and consulting the cards. Evelyn's murderer is dead, and she's finally at peace. I knew I'd find you all here this morning, so I came to tell you."

"Do you mean that Henry killed Evelyn?" Anna asked.

"Yes, and now that he's dead, the balance is restored. Evelyn can deal with Henry in the afterlife." Greg pushed through the door behind her with his hair tousled and damp and his coat flapping open.

"There you are. I told you to wait for me." He took his sister's hand. "Come on, let's go sit down and order some food. Morning, everyone," he added, nodding to the group at the counter. Tiernay followed Greg to a table while Anna and her friends watched.

"Don't look so worried, ladies. Didn't you hear the young woman? Everything's taken care of," Mr. Andrews said with a chuckle. He picked up his coffee and ambled over to his usual table where the newspaper was open and waiting for him.

"I'm not so sure," Anna said, leaning toward Erna and May. "Of course, I don't believe that Evelyn's ghost killed Henry, but we can't be sure that his death was a suicide, either."

"Morning everyone," Judy said, pushing through the kitchen door with a sunny smile on her face. "It's a beautiful day, isn't it? I sure slept well last night. Even slept in a little this morning." Frank rang the bell, and she walked over to check the food orders while the three women glanced at each other.

"No way," Anna whispered.

"I don't know. Is she strong enough to lynch someone?" May asked. They watched Judy as she sauntered by with three heaping plates of food balanced on her arms and a coffee pot.

"Does it take strength? What if Judy had a gun?" Anna asked. "She might have forced Henry to climb up on a chair, and then kicked it out from under him."

"What about motive?" May asked. "Why would Judy kill Henry?"

After considering for a moment, Erna whispered, "Well, Henry must have returned to Crane for a reason. What if it were to take revenge on Frank? It might have been Henry masquerading as Evelyn who threatened Judy with the axe. Frank might have discovered his ruse, and either one of them, or both, could have killed Henry in self-defence."

The pass-through bell rang again. Anna glanced up quickly and caught Frank's eye. He nodded at her before disappearing back into the kitchen.

"I don't believe it," Anna said. "If anything, Frank might have beaten Henry black-and-blue for coming after Judy, but I don't believe Frank would have strung Henry up."

Judy sauntered to the pass-through, picked up a plate of pancakes and bacon, and set it down before Anna. "I'll get your apple juice," she said, turning to retrieve the carton from the cooler. "You must be talking about Henry. Pretty shocking news, but I'm glad it's finally over." She placed the glass in front of Anna, pausing for a chat.

"Over? The police have just opened their investigation," Erna said.

"Well, there is that, but I haven't been able to sleep since that fruit loop tried to kill Frank two weeks ago. Now that I know Henry's about to be buried six feet under, I'm sleeping like a baby. But I've got to go. Time for Mary's break. Catch you later, ladies." Judy winked, pulled a pencil from behind her ear, and hummed as she strolled away. May arched her eyebrows at Anna.

"Oh, come on, you're not really thinking that either of them had anything to do with Henry's death?" Anna said.

"It's all conjecture at this stage. We're just toying with possibilities," Erna replied. "We mustn't let our emotions prevent us from examining the case from all angles."

"Well, if we're going to toy with possible suspects, I've thought of someone no one else had mentioned yet," May said.

"Who?" Anna asked.

"Tiernay."

"Tiernay? How do you figure that?" Anna replied. "She hasn't lived here long enough to murder Henry. She barely knew him."

"Yeah, but just think," May said. "She's been worried about Evelyn's ghost wanting revenge, right? And she thinks she was possessed. What if she thinks Evelyn told her to murder Henry, so she did?"

"That would mean . . ." Anna began.

"That Tiernay is seriously looney tunes, just like I said."

"What are you three whispering about?" Judy asked, returning to the counter. The women jumped. "You look like a pack of magpies sitting on a wire. Anna, you haven't even touched your food yet."

Judy made another pot of coffee while Anna poured syrup over her pancakes and cut into them. Picking up the spare pot, Judy asked, "Can I get anyone a warmer?"

"Thanks," May said, shoving her cup forward. They sat in silence as Judy refilled May and Erna's coffees before strolling away with another order.

"We're too conspicuous here," Anna murmured. Peering nonchalantly over her shoulder, she glanced around the restaurant. Greg was watching her with a frown on his face and a slice of toast mid-way to his mouth. He put it down and nodded at her, and Anna smiled before returning to her plate.

"Look, we're wasting time," she said in a low voice. "We don't know anything for sure. We've got to get some solid facts before we can come up with a theory. I'm going to start by returning to Sherman's house to have a look around in broad daylight. If I see anything interesting, I'll stop by your house on the way home to let you know." She nabbed a fat forkful of pancake and chewed vigorously while fumbling for her wallet.

"Good idea," Erna said. "But call May's store if you have anything to report. May and I are dropping by to see if anyone wants to talk about Henry's murder. We still don't know where he hid when he came back to town. Maybe someone saw him."

"That's right. We've got to retrace his steps," May added. "We'll ask Gerry for a lift back to Erna's when we're done."

"Good, looks like we've all got something worthwhile to investigate," Anna said, plunking money down on the counter and snatching up two strips of bacon from her plate. "See you later," she added, saluting her friends with the bacon and then making a beeline for the door.

28

Anna had company when she arrived at the caretaker's house, however; a cruiser was parked out front, and John was sitting on the porch steps, wearing a pair of sunglasses. She waved at him from the sidewalk, and he beckoned for her to join him. Stepping over the crime scene tape, Anna trotted across the lawn, noticing that the leaves had been removed.

"Have a seat," John said when she reached him. She climbed up the steps and sat down beside him. John was still in uniform with his hat pushed back on his forehead and his tie loosened inside his jacket. With his eyes hidden by the glasses and his face expressionless, Anna wasn't sure if she were intruding.

"You been here all night?" she asked.

"No, I just came back an hour ago. The forensics unit finally packed up and left, and I wanted to have a look at the place in daylight. What are you doing here?"

"Same thing." She looked over at the tree that Henry had been hanging from and shivered, pulling her feet onto a higher step and hugging her knees. Even with the blue sky and sunshine, it was hard to get the picture of Henry's body hanging from the tree out of her mind.

John glanced at her. "Cold, or does this place give you the creeps?"

"Both." Anna frowned. "Turning around and seeing Henry's body swinging there was one of the scariest moments of my life. And I've had a few."

John nodded. "Dead bodies take some getting used to."

"I don't ever plan to get used to them," she said. He smiled at her small joke, and Anna relaxed a little. "So, since I'm here, do you mind my asking what the forensics team discovered?"

"Kind of hard for them to find anything with all the leaves. Sherman wasn't keeping up with the raking, so our team had to bag a lot of them to sift through later. It will be a while before they can make a report."

"I see," Anna said. "How about the time of death, then? When did Henry actually die?"

"We won't know until after the autopsy," John replied, taking off his hat and rubbing the red mark on his forehead.

"Hmm. Well, how about the sign around Henry's neck? 'MURDERER.' What do you make of that?"

"Hard to say. Could mean a lot of things."

"That's fair," Anna said, flicking a piece of lint from her pant leg. She wasn't getting anywhere using the direct approach, so she decided to try a different tack. "You know, Erna and May were just saying that Henry seemed to disappear right after he attacked Frank at The Diner. You guys never found him here afterward, right?" John nodded, watching a crow fly over the street. "Pretty clever of him, don't you think? I mean, if it were me, I'd probably have panicked and driven straight to Calgary. Probably would have got picked up for speeding. You found his car – what – two days later?" John nodded again, his face still inscrutable. "So, where do you think Henry was before he turned himself in?"

"That's currently under investigation."

Anna frowned and folded her arms over her chest. "I'm beginning to catch your drift here, John. You're not going to tell me anything, are you?" John frowned, slapped his hat back on his head, and rose wearily to his feet.

"Death is about as serious as it gets in a police investigation, Anna. I heard about your involvement with your ex-husband's case. I don't want it happening again here. You can pass that information along to Miss Dombrosky and May, too." He nodded and climbed down the steps, headed for his car.

Anna jumped up and followed him, kicking at the leaves when she reached the boulevard. "Last time was different," she said to his back. "I was the prime suspect. I couldn't just sit back and do nothing."

"Okay," he said, leaning against the cruiser, "what's your excuse for sticking your nose in this time?"

"I found Henry's body, so I have a stake in this. Besides, I've been involved ever since the first séance. All May, Erna, and I want to do is help Sherman."

John studied her for a moment before saying, "I wouldn't worry too much about helping Sherman if I were you."

"Why?" she asked, suddenly worried.

John shook his head, climbed into his car, and shut the door. The engine started up, and he powered down the window. "See you around, Anna," he called, waving before pulling away from the curb.

Anna stared after him, her lips pressed together, wondering just what he meant by his comment. Why shouldn't she help Sherman? Did John think Sherman was involved with Henry's death, or was he referring to the counterfeit money issue? After a moment of unfruitful contemplation, however, she decided to ignore the comment and have a look at the tree.

The rope was gone from around the trunk, of course, but she could see where it had scored the bark. Leaning her hand against it, she peered up into the branches. That was the limb Henry had been hanging from, right? Or was it the one beside it? Anna sighed. Some sleuth she was. She couldn't even remember an important detail like that.

She circled around the tree, her eyes searching the ground. The grass was brown and damp from its recent blanket of leaves, but she couldn't see any marks on it. What had the forensics team seen? She sighed. She didn't have any forensics training, so she couldn't read the crime scene from a scientific point of view. What she needed was a different angle; something more intuitive. She closed her eyes and tried to picture Henry standing under the tree. What had he been feeling last night?

She remembered how angry he had looked when he stormed into The Diner two Saturdays ago. She had never seen Henry like that before. Sure, he'd been a complainer, always ready to bend your ear with his latest injustice, but she'd never thought of him as the violent type. The way he'd shoved Judy into the cash register was so unlike him. And trying to stab Frank! Well, it was obvious he'd been deranged. Yet somehow he had managed to evade the police for two days until disappearing into Calgary, and then he'd vanished again after his friend had bailed him out of jail. How long had he been back in Crane before he died, and where had he been hiding?

He wouldn't have risked staying at his house, no matter how cold it got at night. If a neighbour had spotted him, it would have been all over. Maybe he'd lived rough, hiding in different garden sheds or garages to stay out of sight. Poor Henry, he had always been so fastidious; she couldn't imagine him surviving without clean clothes and a daily shower.

Maybe someone had helped him – but who? Prior to the attack, she might have imagined Frank or even Erna helping him, but no one afterward.

Still, he must have foraged in someone's garage for the stuff to make the sign. A piece of cardboard, a brush, some paint, and a piece of string to hang the sign around his neck. And the rope. She mustn't forget the rope.

Okay, time to concentrate. After making the sign, he'd come here to kill himself. But why here? If "MURDERER" was an accusation against Frank, why hadn't he hanged himself on Frank's lawn? Or, even more poetic, in front of The Diner, since he blamed Frank's business for ruining him. Dying here on Sherman's lawn just didn't make sense.

Wait a minute! Anna stared up at the tree again. How had Henry got up there? He certainly wasn't the athletic type. There was no way he could have climbed the tree, especially carrying a rope and the sign. He'd have needed a ladder for sure. And she and Ben would have seen it if there'd been one propped up against the tree or kicked over onto the ground. For heaven's sake, they'd have fallen over it in the dark!

Anna shook her head. She should have thought of that before, but the shock of finding Henry's body must have affected her thinking. Okay, there was no ladder, so it seemed highly improbable that Henry had committed suicide. He had been murdered.

She frowned. It was easy for her to imagine poor Henry standing here on a chair last night, trembling, waiting for his murderer to kick it out from under him. Now came the hard part: imagining the face of the murderer.

Well, they had shared all kinds of theories at the restaurant. Personally, she didn't believe that Tiernay was the murderer. She might be vain and selfish, and she might have a grossly exaggerated belief in her own abilities, but she wasn't criminally insane. And Frank or Judy just couldn't have killed Henry. They might be capable of killing in self-defence in the heat of the moment, but not in cold blood, and not by lynching.

So, she was back to Sherman again. Her gut told her that he was still the best bet. If Sherman had got it into his head that Henry had killed Evelyn, then killing him here and labelling him a murderer made a lot of sense, at least to someone mentally unstable. And despite what Erna thought, Anna still considered Sherman to be mentally and emotionally unstable.

She kicked at a tree root. She and her friends hadn't done him any favours, had they? They should never have let Tiernay mess with his head, not when he was already delusional about his wife calling to him from beyond the grave. But guilt would have to wait until her next visit to the confessional. For now, what mattered was protecting her friends from Sherman.

Her mind made up that Sherman was the most likely suspect, Anna strode across the lawn, heading toward Erna's house. It was time for a talk. She had to convince Erna and May that Henry hadn't committed suicide, and – and what?

Reaching the sidewalk, Anna paused, stuffing her hands in her pockets. There was no way that she could persuade May of Sherman's guilt unless she had some bona fide evidence. And Erna had already said that her ideas were half-baked when it came to Sherman. If she weren't careful, she'd end up estranging both her friends, and then what help would she be?

Anna started down the sidewalk; she always thought better on the move. If Erna were here, she'd tell her to use logic and emotional detachment to solve the problem, but if there was one thing Anna had learned over the past week, it was that she and her friend approached problem-solving differently. Maybe she was impetuous; didn't that mean she was good at thinking outside the box? And what she needed was to come up with a fresh approach.

So, to reiterate her dilemma, Henry had been murdered, and she was afraid that Sherman had killed him. And why was that a problem? Because she was afraid that he might hurt May and Erna. Fair enough, but was that likely? Sherman was still staying with Father Winfield, and with May housebound, she and Sherman hardly saw each other anymore. There was another thing: the police already had their doubts about Sherman because of the counterfeit money, and with Henry being hanged on Sherman's lawn, there was plenty to keep them interested in him.

So, even if Sherman were a murderer, all she had to do was keep her mouth shut and wait for the police to arrest him. If she were wrong about him, well, there was nothing that she could do to help the investigation, was there? John had just told her to keep her nose out of police business, hadn't he? So, not doing anything was a win/win solution to the Sherman problem.

Anna walked past Erna's house and smiled, feeling like a new woman. She was going to turn over a new leaf – no more sticking her nose into other people's business. From now on, Anna Nolan was going to play it safe!

29

Feeling as if she deserved a little self-indulgence after her hard work, Anna decided to have a Saturday night in with a bowl of popcorn and a new mystery novel. Erna had called during the afternoon to report that no one at the store had any inkling as to Henry's whereabouts once he was back in town, or even a guess as to where he had been hiding. She had also come up with the theory that Henry must have committed suicide due to the absence of a stool or ladder at the crime scene, and they had congratulated each other on their mental acuity.

"But we're no closer to divining poor Henry's killer," Erna had said.

"No, afraid not," Anna replied, sticking to her resolution not to repeat her concerns about Sherman. "Give it some time, though. I bet you'll figure it out before the police do."

Erna had laughed and said, "Thank you for your faith in me." Their conversation had ended on a high note, and Anna was pleased that their earlier discord seemed to be healed.

Ben had also called to check up on her when he had finished work. "Are you scared being by yourself, Mom? Do you want me to come stay with you tonight?" he had asked.

"No, that's okay. I'm actually feeling pretty good. I had a talk with John Fox Child this morning, and he seems to have more up his sleeve than he's letting on. I'm sure that the police are on top of things. If I were scared, I could sleep on Erna's couch again tonight, but that's not necessary. I'm going to start a new book and go to bed early. How about you? You put in a full day of work after finding Henry's body last night. You must be exhausted."

"Yeah, I am a little tired, but I'm planning to meet up with some friends at a club later, so I wanted to call you first to see how you were doing."

"You're going out?"

"Sure."

Anna had chuckled. "The resilience of youth, taking death in its stride."

"Yeah, well, what am I supposed to do?"

"Nothing, honey. You have a good time, and I'll call you if anything happens before I see you again next Friday."

"Okay, Mom. Sleep well."

"Night."

Anna had just pulled the popcorn out of her microwave and had settled down on the couch when someone knocked on her front door. Sighing, she shuffled to the foyer with Wendy trailing behind her, pausing to check the peephole before opening the door.

"Hi, Anna," Steve said, pulling off his hat. The bandage had been removed, and she could see where his hair had been shaved for the stitches.

"Oh, look at your poor head!" she exclaimed.

He touched it self-consciously. "Can I come in?"

"Sure." She shut the door behind him, and he followed her into the living room. "Have a seat," she said, indicating the recliner. "Can I get you something to drink?"

He checked his watch. "No thanks, I have to be on duty in twenty minutes. I just wanted to talk to you first."

"All right," she said, sitting down on the couch. "What's up?"

He sat down beside her. "I wanted to warn you to be careful. We don't have the autopsy report on Henry back yet, but the preliminary findings show that he was murdered."

Anna paused before saying, "I sort of guessed that already."

"You did? How?"

"There was no ladder on Sherman's yard, so how did Henry hang himself?" Steve nodded. "What did the preliminary findings show?"

"That he was garrotted. The mark was still visible on his throat when the rope was removed. Someone garrotted him first, and then hanged him."

"Yuck," Anna said, touching her own throat. "That's horrible."

"The murderer must have thought that the rope would obliterate the signs of the garrotting, but it didn't work. The coroner still found them."

Anna remained silent, her hand still at her throat.

"You okay?" Steve asked, touching her arm. "I don't want to scare you, but I want you to be careful with a murderer on the loose. Don't worry, though, we're investigating a very strong lead with the Calgary police. The friend Henry was staying with and who posted his bail is definitely a person of interest."

She nodded. "Thanks for telling me, Steve. You always look out for me."

He gazed into her eyes until Anna felt uncomfortable and glanced away. Did he still harbour feelings for her even though he was seeing Tiernay? "How are you feeling?" she asked aloud. "Tiernay seems to be taking good care of you."

Steve snorted. "I felt better after I went home yesterday morning. Turns out the tea she was giving me was made from valerian root. It's used for pain relief, but also to treat insomnia. Between that and the pain meds I had from the doctor, it was no wonder I was feeling wobbly." He stood up. "I've got to be going."

"I'm sure that she was just trying to help. She seems to really care about you," Anna said, rising and following him from the room.

"Yeah, she and I got pretty close this past week," he replied, pausing by the door.

"Um, it's none of my business, Steve, but isn't she kind of . . ?" Anna paused, searching for the right word.

"Wacko?" he added with a sudden grin.

"Not quite the way I was going to put it," Anna said with an answering smile. She opened the door.

Steve shrugged. "She's got some pretty different notions about how the world works, and she can be a lot of work herself, but we're having a good time. We'll see how things go."

Anna laid her hand on his shoulder. "I'm glad you're taking your time with her, Steve. I worry about you too, you know. You're a good guy."

"Thanks, Anna."

She stretched to kiss his cheek. "Be careful out there, all right?"

"Always am."

She smiled and pushed the screen door open, glancing outside. A hooded figure in a long robe waited in the moonlight upon her lawn. As Anna gasped, the creature came floating up the yard toward her.

30

Steve reached past Anna to switch on the porch light. The figure stopped at the bottom of the porch stairs and threw back its hood. Tiernay's hair blazed in the light, and her eyes flashed with anger.

"Were you following me?" Steve demanded.

"No. I was coming to see Anna. I sure didn't expect to see you here. I saw her kissing you!" the young woman sputtered.

"It wasn't anything, Tiernay. I've only been here for five minutes. Anna and I are just friends," he responded.

Tiernay glared at him. "I haven't seen you since yesterday morning, since before Henry's body was discovered. How come, as soon as there's any trouble, you come looking for Anna and not me? Are you sure that's all she is to you – just a friend?"

"Sure." He climbed down the stairs to close the distance between them. "Just friends," he repeated, resting his hands on her shoulders. Tiernay slipped her arms around his neck and pulled him in for a kiss. The kiss mounted in intensity as it continued for several long seconds. Anna looked away, and when she looked back again, Tiernay was glowering at her over Steve's shoulder.

"I've got to go to work now, honey. Everything okay here?" Steve asked. Tiernay raised her eyes to study his face before smiling and relaxing.

"Everything's okay. I can read you like a book, you know." She stroked the side of his cheek and kissed him again. "Have a good night at work. I'll see you later."

Breaking away from Steve, Tiernay sauntered up the stairs to the porch. Steve looked at Anna from behind his girlfriend's back, his eyebrows raised inquiringly. Anna grimaced back at him. Great, he was leaving her alone with Tiernay. The young woman paused beside Anna, waiting to be invited inside.

"Bye, Steve," Anna said in a resigned tone. "Come on in, Tiernay." She held the door open for her unwelcome guest and followed her into the house. Shutting the door, she was about to lead Tiernay into the living room when the young woman turned and seized her arm. Wendy, who had been watching everything from inside the house, growled a warning.

Ignoring the animal, Tiernay said, "I need your help."

"With what?" Anna asked in alarm.

Tiernay released Anna's arm and reached deep into her cloak pocket to remove a black wooden box.

"What's that?" Anna asked, her eyes drawn to it. The box was about five inches wide with glossy pink and white roses painted on its lid.

Tiernay opened it, and music began to play. Anna inhaled sharply; the song was "Lara's Theme." "Where did you get that?" she stammered.

"I found it in Greg's studio among his drawing things. I was looking for my pen, and I thought he had taken it. I didn't realize what the box was until I opened it. It must be Evelyn's."

"What was Greg doing with it?"

"How should I know?" The two women looked up from the box; Tiernay's eyes were troubled. "I'm going back to Sherman's house to have a look around. I want you to come with me."

Anna frowned. "Why me?"

"Who else can I ask? You want to know the truth about Evelyn's ghost, don't you?"

"Why don't you just ask Greg about the music box?"

Tiernay shook her head, her lips pressed together.

"Why not?"

"Don't you see? If Greg has had this all along, he's been using it to enhance Evelyn's psychic manifestations without telling me. What else has he been up to? We've always told each other everything. All of a sudden, I feel like I can't trust him anymore. I have to go back to the beginning to figure out what he's been hiding from me. If I find something at Sherman's house, I want you to witness it so that you can back me up when I confront Greg."

Anna shook her head. "I don't want to be put in the middle of your problems with your brother. The two of you have to work this out together."

Tiernay took a step closer to Anna and stared down at her with steely-eyed determination. "You want me to fix this problem with Evelyn's ghost, don't you? Well, I have to know what I'm dealing with. Help me. Come with me to Sherman's house."

Anna studied the young woman's face for a long moment before sighing. "I'm going to regret this, aren't I?" Tiernay's smile was triumphant as Anna said, "All right, let's get this over with."

31

The two women paused on Sherman's porch, Anna glancing over her shoulder to make sure that no one saw them. She tried turning the knob, but, just as she expected, the door was locked.

"How're we going to get inside?" she whispered.

"Where's your flashlight?" Tiernay asked. Anna removed it from her pocket and switched it on. "Shine it on the lock." Tiernay pulled a crochet hook and a slender metal tool from her pocket and began fiddling with the lock. A minute later, the door clicked open.

"After you," the young woman said with a lofty smile. Anna passed into the house with a cool, appraising glance at Tiernay. What other tricks did she know?

The living room smelled musty. "Don't turn on the lights," Tiernay warned.

Anna nodded and swept her flashlight around the room. The light caught the dreary furniture and the family portrait. Anna didn't let the light linger on the portrait for long; Evelyn's blue eyes seem to be watching them. "What are we looking for?" she asked.

"Wires. Speakers. Anything Greg might have used to fake the music. I haven't been back in here since the séance, but Greg has. Let's see if he left anything behind."

The women searched the house, starting with the cabinet in the dining room where the fog machine had been secreted, and continuing room by room through the first and second floors, but there was no sign of anything that indicated how the music had been faked. Anna paused in Sherman's bedroom to note the meagre collection of clothing and personal items inside the closet and the bureau. She saw a framed picture of Evelyn on the bedside table and picked it up. The photograph captured Evelyn as a beautiful young teenager with a carefree expression on her face. That expression had vanished by the time she was photographed for the family portrait.

"She was a knock-out," Anna murmured.

Tiernay glanced at the picture over Anna's shoulder. "Yeah, not at all like a murdering, soul-sucking harpy." She took the frame from Anna's hands and set it back on the table. "Come on, Greg said there's an attic upstairs."

They found a door opening onto a steep flight of wooden stairs leading to the attic. Anna took her time climbing them, trying not to inhale the stale, dusty air too deeply, and hesitated at the top to shine her light around the room. The roof slanted down to the floor on the outer edges, but the ceiling was high enough to stand up in in the middle. A jumble of cardboard boxes was piled against the exterior wall.

It was chilly, and Anna shivered. "No insulation in these old houses. It must be freezing in the winter," she said. There were no windows, either, but a string hung down from a solitary light bulb in the middle of the room. Tiernay brushed past her to turn it on.

"Wait a minute," Anna said. Tiernay paused to look at her over her shoulder. Anna gestured at the floor with her flashlight. "See those footprints in the dust? Someone's been up here recently."

Tiernay nodded. "It was probably Greg," she said, switching on the light. "Let's look for clues in those boxes."

They crouched down beside the pile. The boxes were folded shut and had no markings to identify what they contained. One small box sat on its own beside the pile; Tiernay opened it and peeked inside. She pulled out a wicker basket and unfastened the lid. "Sewing kit," she said, showing Anna spools of thread, a package of needles, and a scissors. Placing the basket on the floor, Tiernay reached back inside and pulled out a silver comb and matching hair brush with long, blond hairs still attached. They exchanged a glance. "Evelyn's," Tiernay said.

They examined the rest of the boxes and discovered a jumble of feminine items, including clothing and shoes. Some of the items were worn-out and should have been discarded. One heavy box contained a collection of well-thumbed cookbooks, romance novels, and magazines. At the bottom of the box lay the family bible. Anna opened it and studied the front pages. Sherman and Evelyn's birth and marriage dates, and their sons' birth and baptismal dates, were inscribed within in a fine, cursive script. Anna closed it and lay it carefully back inside the box on top of the other books.

Finally, there was nothing left but a rectangular white box with a lid. Anna opened it and dropped the box with a start. The inner lining was clear plastic, and through it she saw what appeared to be half a female torso. Tiernay picked up the box and inspected the contents more closely.

"It's just a wedding gown," she said, smirking at Anna.

"Evelyn's," Anna said, straightening from her cramped position and dusting her hands off on her pants. "It looks like everything Evelyn ever owned has been boxed and dumped up here without sorting through it first. It's pretty sad to think that this is all that's left to show of Evelyn's time on earth."

"The music box was probably in one of these boxes," Tiernay said. "Greg could have found it on the day he was supposed to be helping me to prepare for the séance. I was in the dining room all afternoon casting purification and protection spells, but he could have been doing anything in the rest of the house."

"So, just to reiterate, Greg rigged the fog machine and the music?"

Tiernay nodded. "I was supposed to knock on the table and turn on the fog."

Anna folded her arms over her chest and leaned against the wall. "What about the trance, Tiernay, and the things you said to Sherman? Did you and Greg plan what you were going to say ahead of time?"

Tiernay shook her head. "Erna came to the store to ask me to tell Sherman that Evelyn loved him and that everything was fine. I asked for some background information about the two of them so that I would know how to say it, and she told Greg and me how unhappy their marriage had been. After Erna left, Greg and I agreed that if Evelyn's spirit was disturbed, it had to be something to do with her death. That she hadn't died accidentally, and that she needed Sherman to find out what had really happened. I could feel her presence in the room during the séance, and I knew that she was angry. The trance was real, and so were the things I said."

"You were possessed?" Anna persisted.

"For sure," the young woman said, her bobbed hair swinging as she nodded her head.

"Then what are we doing here?" Anna asked, stepping into the middle of the room. "So what if Greg rigged the music? It was just to make the séance more credible for the rest of us." She noted the glum expression on Tiernay's face. "Except that Greg didn't tell you about the music," she added, pointing at the box in the young woman's hand.

"Yeah."

"And he faked the music again at the cemetery." The young woman nodded. Anna paused, wondering how far to push Tiernay. "Did it ever occur to you maybe he's faked

207

other things, too? That maybe Greg doesn't believe that you're the real deal?"

Tiernay's head shot up and her eyes flared with anger. "You're wrong. He does believe in me. He's always been my biggest supporter." She stalked toward Anna, and Anna remembered that she was alone in the house with this mercurial-tempered woman, and that no one knew where she was.

"Okay, calm down," she said, taking a step back toward the stairs. "You came to me for help, remember?"

"Fine, but don't get insulting," Tiernay muttered.

"Look, it's really stuffy in here, and I'm thirsty. Let's go down to the kitchen and get a glass of water," Anna said, edging around Tiernay and hurrying toward the stairs. "Don't forget to turn off the light."

Anna clicked on her flashlight and clambered down the steps while Tiernay turned back toward the string. Safely back on the second floor, Anna felt in her pocket for her cell phone. Only, it wasn't there. Of course not. She had put it in her purse before leaving for The Diner this morning, but she hadn't brought it along with her tonight. She heard Tiernay clattering down the steps behind her, and hurried down the hallway for the stairs leading to the first floor.

"Hey, wait for me. It's dark in here," the young woman protested.

Anna hesitated. What was she going to do, abandon Tiernay to run out of the house? The young woman hadn't done anything to warrant that kind of behaviour, and Anna didn't want to feel like an idiot. She slowed down, allowing Tiernay to catch up with her.

"Come on, let's see what Sherman has to drink. I'm thirsty, too," the young woman said. They climbed downstairs together. "The kitchen's at the back," she added, letting Anna light the way.

Once in the kitchen, Tiernay headed straight for the fridge. The light flashed on as she opened the door and had a quick look inside before opening the freezer door, too.

"Bingo!" she said with a grin, pulling out the vodka bottle. "Good old Sherman. Let's have a couple of shots."

"You go ahead. I'm just going to have some water," Anna said, opening the cupboard doors to look for glasses.

Tiernay shrugged. "More for me."

Anna handed her a juice glass and went to the sink. Turning on the faucet, she let the water run cold for several seconds before filling her glass. She glanced out the window while raising it to her lips.

The moonlight had disappeared, replaced by a black, overcast sky that threatened rain. The wind had come up, too; she could hear it howling outside the window. The trees were thrashing in the cemetery, and Anna thought she could see a light glimmering between them.

Tiernay walked up behind her. "Can I have some water, too?"

"Hey, look over there," Anna said, pointing out the window. "Through the trees on the right. Do you see a light?"

"Yeah."

"What do you suppose is going on in there?" Anna asked, exchanging an apprehensive glance with Tiernay.

32

They clambered down the slope toward the cemetery wall with the wind snatching at their clothes.

"Get out your tools," Anna said when they reached the gate and discovered that it was locked. She waited while Tiernay fiddled with the mechanism, and winced when the young woman shoved the gate open and the hinges shrieked.

"Sorry," Tiernay whispered. Anna rolled her eyes; too late for whispers now. They snuck through the gate and paused to get their bearings on the cemetery road.

"I think the light was coming from this direction," Anna said with a nod, clicking off her flashlight and pocketing it. Tiernay nodded back, and they followed the ring road as silently as possible, aiming for the older section of the cemetery.

"Doesn't she look familiar?" Anna whispered a few minutes later while studying the statue of a mourning woman towering four feet above her. "I'm sure I saw her when we were here on Wednesday night."

"Yeah, on the way to Evelyn's grave," Tiernay said. They exchanged an uneasy look.

"Great," Anna said. "Let's hope that Evelyn is otherwise occupied tonight." She noticed Tiernay fingering the silver snake in the neckline of her cloak, and her own fingers reached for the blue obsidian in her jacket pocket. It was ridiculous, she knew. A blue stone wasn't going to protect her from a ghost she was convinced didn't exist, but it was easy to believe in ghosts in the middle of a cemetery on a windy night. If only her gold cross wasn't at home in her jewelry box.

Anna switched her flashlight back on and shone it on the ground where it was less likely to be noticed by anyone else. Together the two women stepped off the road and edged across the grass. Anna's ears were pricked for any sounds beyond the rustling of the trees and the leaves that scattered before them, only to be caught up against the tombstones. The wind gusted against her back, whipping her hair into her face, and Anna set the flashlight on the ground and unzipped her jacket to stuff her hair inside. Bending to retrieve the flashlight, she could smell the decaying leaves and fancied that it was more than leaves that she was smelling. Shivering, she was about to share that observation with Tiernay when she noticed that the young woman was no longer there. Anna turned, shining her light in every direction, but Tiernay had vanished.

"Where are you?" she whispered in a low, urgent voice. "Damn it, you must have eyes like a cat's." She waited, but Tiernay didn't answer.

Anna hesitated, not wanting to go in search of the young woman in case she came back, but too afraid to stay there alone. Where was she? She looked around for a landmark. A tall birch shimmied in the wind beside her, sounding just like whispering. She shifted from foot to foot, unable to hold still. A coyote howled, and Anna started violently. She was panting, for heaven's sake. Enough! Tiernay or not, it was time to get out of here.

Anna had run a few steps back toward the road when she thought she heard voices. Pausing, she held her breath to listen. It was no hallucination; she could definitely hear voices, a man and a woman's. Swallowing to moisten her bone-dry throat, she shone her light on the ground and crept toward them. No one must know that she was there until she found out what was going on.

Raising her head, Anna spotted the same stand of evergreens she had previously seen on the way to Evelyn's grave. One of the trees bent inward in a weird way, as if cradling a weight. Surprised that she was already so close, she sidled around them, intent on hearing what the man and woman were saying.

"I told you, you can't stay. I'm waiting for someone."

"What's that?"

"No!"

Anna heard scuffling noises and dashed forward, snapping off the light as she emerged from the trees. A Coleman lamp was lit on the ground, and Tiernay was clutching Greg's leather satchel to her chest while Greg tried to wrestle it from her. He let go of the satchel and wrapped his arms around Tiernay, jerking her off her feet and throwing her to the ground. She scrambled to her knees and crawled toward the bag, but Greg snagged the strap and swung it out of her reach. The bag burst open, and several bundles flew out. Anna crouched behind the bench as Tiernay pounced on one of them before Greg could snatch it up.

"Give me that," he snarled, advancing toward her, but Tiernay jumped to her feet and danced out of the way. She was tearing a booklet from the bundle and flipping it open, pausing to examine it as Greg caught up with her and snatched it from her hand.

"It's a passport," Tiernay said. "They're all passports," she added, holding up the bundle. "What are you doing with them?"

Brother and sister glared at each other, panting from their struggle. Without saying a word, Greg held out his hand, and Tiernay dropped the rest into it. He turned and hurried back to the lantern beside Evelyn's grave, stuffing the passports back into the satchel as Tiernay trotted after him.

"Greg, what are you doing? What's this all about?"

"Stay out of it, Tiernay. Go home before he gets here."

"Before who gets here?" she asked. She grabbed her brother's arm, forcing him to look at her.

Someone seized Anna from behind and dragged her to her feet. She screamed and struggled to break free, but her assailant wrenched her arm behind her back and she stopped, gasping in pain. Frogmarched into the circle of light on Evelyn's grave, Anna panted as Greg and Tiernay whirled to look at her.

"Too late," her assailant growled.

33

"Emmanuel," Greg said without inflection.

Cabrero shoved Anna toward them, and she fell onto her knees. She scrambled to her feet and turned to look at her assailant. The gun in his hand didn't waiver as he pointed it straight at her head. Anna could feel her heart thumping in her chest as she peered into his small, cold eyes.

"What are your sister and your lady friend doing here, Greg?" the squat, muscular man asked.

"It's a mistake," Greg said, starting forward. The gun swung toward him, and Greg halted, holding up his hands. Anna glanced at him and saw a nervous smile on his face. Greg's eyes didn't waiver from the gunman's.

"You have broken our agreement once again, my friend. Our business was to be conducted in absolute secrecy."

"I know, I know. I can explain."

"If you are going to suggest that these ladies should join in our business, I would urge you to remember how things worked out with Henry Fellows."

"Of course not. I should never have allowed Henry to become involved, but he threatened to tell the police if I didn't."

Cabrero shook his head. "What a waste he was – not only a snivelling coward, but a terrible forger, too. Not an artist like you. Your talent is the only thing keeping you alive right now. But I am running out of time. The Calgary police are asking a lot of questions about Henry. It's getting too dangerous."

"I can appreciate that."

"Where is my merchandise?" Greg eased the satchel from his shoulder and held it out, keeping his other hand in the air.

"Anna, go stand beside Tiernay," Cabrero said. Anna nodded and shifted toward the young woman, her eyes never leaving the gun.

Cabrero tucked the weapon into his belt and pulled a slim, powerful flashlight from his coat pocket, using it to examine each document as Greg passed it to him. While he was distracted, Anna glanced at Tiernay. The young woman's eyes were terrified as she stared at her brother and Cabrero.

"What are we going to do?" Tiernay whispered.

"How well do you know him?" Anna asked, nodding toward Cabrero.

"He's been to the house a couple of times. We had a glass of wine together, once. I had no idea what he and Greg were doing, Anna, I swear it!"

Anna grimaced and muttered, "Keep your voice down!" Tiernay nodded. "I don't like what he said about Henry," she added.

"Do you think Emmanuel killed him?"

"Unless you think it was Greg?"

"No!"

Anna took a step backward.

"What are you doing?" Tiernay whispered, her eyes darting to the men and back again.

"Our only chance is to run for it while they're looking through the stuff."

"No! We don't know what he might do to Greg."

"I'm willing to risk it. He'll keep Greg alive because he's useful, but what good are we to him?"

"No!" Tiernay whispered, grasping Anna's wrist.

"Ladies," Cabrero said as Anna glared at Tiernay. "Time to join us over here."

Anna broke from Tiernay's grasp and looked up. It was too late. The gun was back in Cabrero's hand and pointing straight at them. Sick with dread, Anna headed toward the men with Tiernay shaking at her side.

"We're going for a walk. Greg, you will stay here."

"No!" Greg shouted. Cabrero raised his eyebrows. "No," he said in a lower voice. "There's got to be some way to fix this." He smiled at his partner, but Anna saw his eye twitch. "I swear they'll never say a word." Cabrero glanced at the two women.

"Why would they?" Greg continued. "If they say anything, it would only implicate me. Tiernay is my sister, and Anna is my fiancée. They wouldn't want to do that." Cabrero studied his face while Anna held her breath, praying that the gunman would listen to Greg and let them live.

"I have your assurance?"

"Of course. I swear it on my life."

"Very well," Cabrero said, removing an envelope from his coat pocket. "Here is your money. We'll have to move the operation somewhere else, though. It's not safe here anymore."

"Thank you," Greg said, relief flooding his face. Tiernay's legs gave way, and Anna had to hold her up to prevent her from falling. "Come on, girls," Greg said. He held out his hand, and Tiernay stumbled forward to grasp it. Greg slid his arm around his sister's shoulder and turned to guide them away. As they circled around Cabrero, however, the gunman seized Anna's arm. She stared at him with terrified eyes.

"Not Anna, though. You lied about her. Her boyfriend is a police sergeant. I know all about the people close to you, Greg. A pity," he said, his merciless eyes appraising her.

Anna turned a pleading face to Greg, who stared miserably back at her.

"If you don't go now, I will change my mind about your sister," Cabrero added, pressing the gun to Anna's head. She heard a wheezing noise and realized it was coming from her own throat. There was a pause as she waited for Greg to think of something. His expression was wretched as he looked away.

"I'm so sorry, Anna," he said, taking a stronger hold on his sister's shoulders and dragging her forward. Anna's breath caught in a half-sob.

"Greg!" Tiernay screamed, twisting to look back at Anna as her brother thrust her into the trees.

Anna, rooted to the spot with fear, watched them disappear. She glanced back at Cabrero, only to see his fist flying toward her. Toppling onto Evelyn's grave, she blacked out.

34

Someone slapped her. Anna cringed, trying to raise her hands to protect her face, but they were bound behind her back. Wire was cutting into her wrists, and it hurt. She realized that she was sitting up, leaning against something cold and hard. As her eyes fluttered open, she saw Cabrero's grim face inches from her own.

"That's better," he said with a nasty smile. "Time to get up." Seizing her by the shoulders, he dragged her to her feet. Anna gasped as he wrenched her shoulder, and she staggered forward a step, trying not to fall. Cabrero grabbed her elbow and spun her around.

"This way," he said, shoving her in a different direction. Anna raised her head and realized that she was still at Evelyn's grave; it was Evelyn's stone that she had been leaning against. How long had she been unconscious?

"Come on," he said, taking her arm. He wore Greg's satchel slung over his chest and carried the lantern in his other hand. Anna's eyes were still watering from the slap and she couldn't see very well.

"Wh-where are we going?" she asked, but Cabrero didn't respond. He even hummed as he pulled her along, his fingers squeezing her arm. She had a wild hope that Cabrero wasn't going to kill her after all. If he were, why hadn't he shot her while she lay unconscious, and abandoned her body on Evelyn's grave? Was he taking her hostage?

They were nearing the back of the cemetery; Anna could see the white stone wall through the trees. She had never been this far back before. As they drew closer, she saw a grey-stoned mausoleum, looking forlorn and deserted. It was square, about eight feet wide, with two columns holding up a triangular roof. She could make out a name carved on the lintel: "Beringer." An iron gate barred the door.

As they drew near, Anna was seized with dread and tugged backward, trying to wrench herself from Cabrero's grip. He shoved her forward the last few yards, however, and pushed her hard against the wall beside the door.

Tears welled up in her eyes and streaked down her cheeks. Cabrero pulled metal tools from his pocket and fell to work on the lock.

Anna turned her head to look at him. "What are you going to do to me?" she murmured.

"Huh?" he said, glancing at her in a distracted way.

Anna tried again. "Are you going to shut me in there alive?" she asked, her eyes glittering with fear.

He stared at her for a second before returning to the lock. "What do you take me for, some kind of monster?" he muttered. "I'm going to kill you first and hide your body inside."

Anna's legs gave way, and she slumped to the ground. "Why didn't you kill me before when I couldn't feel it?" she asked, all hope gone.

"What, and carry you all the way here? Do you have any idea how heavy a dead body is?" The lock on the gate clicked open, and he smiled with satisfaction. Dragging the rusty gate open, he pushed the door inward with a resounding crack. Cabrero thrust the lantern inside to have a look around.

This was her last chance. A burst of adrenalin coursed through Anna's body as she clambered to her feet.

"Plenty of room," her captor said, turning to look at her just as she darted away. "Hey!" he shouted, putting down the lantern and racing after her.

He caught up with her in seconds, grabbing her hair from behind. Anna screamed in pain and tried to kick him. Cabrero lugged her off her feet and carried her back under one arm, writhing and kicking, to the mausoleum. He slammed her up against the wall again, trapping her body beneath his own.

"I don't like to shoot people," he said, reaching into his pocket as she squirmed. "It's messy, and it leaves too much evidence for the forensics police. This is much neater."

He pulled a length of wire from his pocket and, kneeing Anna in the back, wrapped it around her throat. Anna gasped as she felt it tighten. She tried to head-butt Cabrero, who jerked backward, tripped, and fell. Anna jumped sideways out of his reach. As Cabrero scrambled to his feet, swearing, Sherman Mason charged out of the darkness. Anna screamed, Cabrero turned, and Sherman bashed him in the head with a shovel. It made a sickening clang. As Anna watched, Cabrero staggered backward and collapsed onto the ground.

There was a moment of silence as Anna became aware of the howling wind. She stared at Cabrero, lying motionless on the ground with his eyes closed, and then at Sherman. He was gasping for breath, his face grey and clammy with sweat.

"Sherman, thank God," she said, but the caretaker groaned, clutched his chest, and tumbled to the ground.

"Sherman!" Anna shouted, dropping to her knees beside him. He was grimacing with pain and his eyes were screwed shut. "Sherman, no!" With her hands tied behind her back, Anna was helpless. She peered around frantically.

"Help!" she screamed. "Can anybody hear me? Help!" But when she looked at Sherman again, he was staring up at her, his eyes glazed with pain.

"Sherman, I'm so sorry," she said. "Can you untie me? Do you have any medication with you?"

"No," he said with a gasp. "It's at home beside my bed."
Overcome with shock and frustration, Anna started to cry, slumping into a sitting position on the ground beside him. "Don't, Anna." His hand fluttered upward and rested on her knee. "I want to die. Maybe Evie will forgive me now."

"Forgive you?" Anna sobbed. "Wh-what for? You're a hero. You saved my life."

"No, I'm not," he said, gazing at her. "I'm a murderer. I killed my Evie." Incredulous, she stopped crying to stare down into his face.

35

Anna was still trying to absorb Sherman's words when she heard someone shouting her name.

"I'm over here!" she screamed, struggling to her knees. Flashes of light came zigzagging toward her through the darkness. She staggered to her feet. "Over here! Hurry!" she screamed, jumping up and down. The light came closer until it blinded her, and she had to close her eyes.

"Anna!" Steve shouted, grabbing her waist and hoisting her off her feet. "You're all right," he said in a hoarse voice, putting her down again and hugging her tightly.

More lights converged, and Anna saw John Fox Child and two other men running toward them. Their guns were drawn, and they were wearing protective vests.

"I-I'm okay," she stuttered as Steve cut the wire from her wrists. "Help Sherman."

"Sherman?"

She turned Steve around and pointed to the caretaker on the grass. Steve knelt beside him and began checking his vital signs.

"Anna!" John shouted, blinding her again with his light. She averted her eyes, shaking with cold and shock, and felt his arms around her shoulders. "Over there," he said with a nod, leading her out of the way while the other men stalked forward, their guns trained on Cabrero's inert form. Anna heard Steve radio that it was all right to send in the paramedics.

"What happened to you?" John asked, lifting her chin to examine the swelling on her face. He inhaled sharply.

"What's this?" His fingers brushed the ugly red line on her throat.

"Cabrero – Greg's partner – tried to strangle me. He's the one on the ground over there," she said through chattering teeth.

"Emmanuel Cabrero. We know him. He was the one Henry was staying with in Calgary, the friend who bailed him out of jail." John drew her back into his arms, and she collapsed against him, his arms feeling so warm and safe.

"How did you find me?" she mumbled.

"Tiernay Rae called us."

"Tiernay called you?" Anna asked, her head jolting up in surprise.

"Yes. She told us Cabrero had you captive in the old part of the cemetery. It just took us a while to find you."

Anna shook her head. "I can't believe that Tiernay did that for me. What about Greg?"

"He's gone. Don't worry, we're looking for him." John turned to speak to his men. "How's Cabrero?" he asked.

"Not good," one of the constables answered. "I haven't got much of a pulse."

"Sherman stopped him. With a shovel," Anna said. John stared at her for a moment before turning to Steve. "How's Sherman doing?" he asked.

The young man looked up. "He's going to need a stretcher." Anna started to cry again, and John rubbed her back.

"I'd be dead if it weren't for Sherman," she moaned.

A team of paramedics converged on the scene and went to work on the two men lying on the ground. They were quick and efficient; one of the teams pushed Sherman out on a gurney a few minutes later. Anna saw him go past with an oxygen mask clamped over his grey face. When the gurney carrying Cabrero left a short time later, however, there was a blanket drawn over his head. Anna stared after him, rubbing her sore shoulder.

John returned to drape a blanket around her. "You look as if you're ready to collapse. I'm going to have Steve take you over to one of the ambulances to check you out. He'll ask you a few questions, and then he'll drive you home, unless you want to stay at a neighbour's house?"

Anna nodded wearily. "I'll think about it. Thanks, John. I really owe you."

He shook his head. "I hate to say it, but maybe you'll listen to me next time I tell you to butt out of an investigation." She stared at him wordlessly, her face dirty and bruised, the angry red mark circling her throat. Steve joined them and glanced from John to Anna.

"Ah, take her to the ambulance," John said, dismissing her with a wave.

"Come on, Anna," Steve said, putting an arm around her shoulders and leading her away.

36

It was late Sunday afternoon. Anna had just arrived at Erna's house and was sitting cross-legged on the couch with a mug of hot chocolate in her hands. Erna sat beside her with one of May's homemade afghans draped over her shoulders and a cup of tea, while May sipped her glass of red wine from the recliner. A fire burned brightly in the hearth, and the house smelled enticingly of beef roasting in the oven. Anna still felt limp from her near-death experience and her muscles ached, but she felt surprisingly well, otherwise.

Erna tsked as she examined Anna's face and throat. "That animal. Look what he did to her, May."

"If he weren't already dead, I'd take my crutch to him," May said, lifting it up from beside her chair. She let it drop back to the floor and took another swallow of wine.

"You look tired, May. How's Sherman doing?" Anna asked.

"Not bad. They only let me see him for five minutes today. He was kind of dopey from the pain killers, but they said the heart attack was mild. He should be out of the hospital in a few days if he behaves himself. No more running around the cemetery at night for him."

"Thank God he did," Erna said. She turned to Anna. "So, you got the rest of the story today from Steve?"

"Yes, when I went to the station to make my statement. I saw Tiernay from a distance. She had been brought in for questioning and was just leaving. She looked like the stuffing had been knocked out of her. Actually, I felt sorry for her."

"Never mind her, start at the beginning," May said. "Greg was a counterfeiter . . ."

"Yes. When he left the cemetery last night with Tiernay, he went straight to the basement of their house. He kept his counterfeiting supplies there, hidden in his art studio. He grabbed them and left – didn't take anything else. He tried to talk Tiernay into leaving with him, but she refused to go. Instead, she called Steve as soon as Greg was gone."

"What was he counterfeiting?" Erna asked.

"Passports, driver's licenses, credit cards, and ten-dollar bills. He told Tiernay that he'd been doing it for eight years, using his graphic design business as a front. He'd had some trouble with a crime gang hassling him when they were living in Vancouver, though, so when he and his sister left, he was finished with big cities. Tiernay wanted to try Alberta, and as it turned out, a contact of Greg's was just finishing his sentence in the same prison as Henry. The contact told Greg that Henry had a storefront for sale in Crane, and Greg thought it was a great opportunity to start over again. That's how he and Tiernay ended up here."

"Did he already know this Emmanuel Cabrero before they came?" Erna asked.

"No. His contact made the introduction. The police already knew about Cabrero – he'd had a record. But Greg didn't have one, and that's why Steve couldn't find anything on him. Greg's been lucky, up until now."

"So, why were he and Cabrero meeting in the cemetery?" May asked.

"Steve said that it was an ideal location. Cabrero could use the back roads to get into the rear entrance of the cemetery and avoid being seen in town altogether. He and Greg met in the old part of the cemetery where it was nice and private, and no one would see their lights."

"Except Sherman," May said.

"Yes." Anna gave her friend a sympathetic look. "The only drawback to the cemetery location was Sherman. Obviously, Greg would have asked Henry about the caretaker living next door to the cemetery, and Henry would have told him all about Sherman and Evelyn. Sherman must have seen Greg and Cabrero's lights when they were meeting on Thanksgiving night, but they must have heard him coming. Tiernay and I opened the side gate last night, and it made a horrible squeak. Greg told his sister that he pretended to be Evelyn to scare Sherman off, and that's how all this business started with Evelyn's ghost coming back. Greg used the séance to frighten Sherman out of his house, and kept up the pressure with the ghost sightings around town."

"That was Greg who frightened me on my apartment stairs?" May asked.

"Yes, but he meant to scare Sherman, not you."

May's face darkened, and Anna couldn't tell if she was angrier about Greg wanting to frighten Sherman, or about the attack on herself.

"Tell us about Henry," Erna coaxed.

"After Henry threatened Frank at The Diner, he ran across the street to his old store, still angry about the cleansing ritual. Tiernay wasn't there – she told Steve that she never knew Greg was helping Henry – but Greg was. Henry told Greg that if he didn't help, he would tell the police about meeting him through his jailbird friend. It might not seem very incriminating to us, but Greg didn't want any attention from the local police. Flying under the radar was critical to his operation. So he agreed to hide Henry in his basement until he could smuggle him out of town and into Calgary. Remember, the police were searching for Henry after he attacked Frank. But then Henry found out about the counterfeiting business and made things worse by wanting to be cut in. Greg kept him happy showing him how to counterfeit ten-dollar bills, but they were unusable, so Greg salted a couple of them at the store to incriminate Sherman. He figured that the police were already suspicious of Sherman with his old trouble at the bank, so if Sherman got arrested, well, that would keep him away from the cemetery permanently."

"Let me get this straight," May said. "Greg was on my stairs hoping to scare Sherman?"

"That's right."

"And on your front lawn?"

"Yes, that was Greg and his computerized special effects. That, and the recorded music from Evelyn's box." Anna shivered, remembering how effective Greg's ghostly show had been.

"You see, Greg and I had just spoken that day concerning how worried Tiernay was over not holding another séance. Stupidly, I told him that I thought the key to the ghost mystery was in the cemetery, that maybe someone was using it to sell drugs and keeping Sherman away by frightening him. Greg offered to talk to Steve about it, but of course he never did. Instead, he decided to keep me away from the cemetery by giving me a healthy fear of ghosts."

"Diabolical," Erna said.

Anna nodded. "By then, Henry had abandoned his car outside of Calgary, and Greg had driven him to Cabrero's house. Cabrero bailed Henry out of jail after he turned himself in, and brought Henry back to Crane in time to help with the summoning ritual in the cemetery."

"That was Henry dressed up as Evelyn's ghost?" May asked.

"Partly. The ghost's appearance on Evelyn's grave was more of Greg's special effects, but the ghost who ran after me was Henry. He was hiding nearby and took off after me when I ran. Everyone was so distracted, they didn't realize that they hadn't seen Evelyn's ghost actually leave the circle."

"How did Henry stop Steve?" May asked.

"Taser. It brought him down when Steve was getting too close, but the blow to his head from falling into the tree was the icing on the cake. It affected Steve's memory enough that he didn't realize he'd been tasered."

"Did Henry taser Greg, too?" Erna asked.

"No, Greg faked his reaction. All he had to do was fall down when Henry pointed at him and pretend to be unconscious. When the doctor couldn't find a medical reason for Greg's condition, we were supposed to chalk it up to Evelyn's evil powers."

"And Tiernay didn't know anything about this?" Erna asked.

Anna shook her head. "No, she thought it was all real. That's why this is so difficult for her to take in. She truly believed that Evelyn's ghost talked to her at the séance, although Greg had her convinced beforehand that Evelyn had been murdered, and that her ghost was looking for revenge. It was all part of his scheme."

Erna shook her head and sighed. "His own sister."

"Hey, what about the attack on Judy?" May asked.

"That was Henry again," Anna replied. "And that was the beginning of the end for him. He enjoyed playing the ghost in the cemetery so much that he took it upon himself to frighten Judy to take his revenge on Frank. But Cabrero thought Henry had gone too far. Up until then, the ghostly scares could pass as Halloween pranks, but going after someone with an axe draws police attention. Plus, Cabrero thought Henry was emotionally unstable and worthless as a counterfeiter, so he decided to get rid of him. Henry came along with Greg for a meeting with Cabrero on Friday night, and Cabrero garrotted him. Greg swore that he didn't know

Cabrero's intentions ahead of time, but who can say?" She shrugged. "But it was Greg's idea to hang the 'murderer' sign on Henry's body afterward to further confuse things. It was all smoke and mirrors with Greg. He saw himself as a gentlemen thief, and counterfeiting as just another art form, but being an accessory to Henry's murder was too real for him. He realized how dangerous Cabrero was, and when things came to a head last night in the cemetery, he decided it was time to get out. But Tiernay wouldn't go with him, so he had to risk her going to the police."

"And Greg left you there to be murdered," Erna said with a forbidding look in her eyes. "Gentleman thief or not, he dammed himself to eternal hellfire when he left you there to die."

Anna looked at her friend and knew that Erna truly believed what she had just said. Erna had a fundamental faith in right versus wrong, good versus evil, and justice for justice's sake, and she was passionate about her values.

The ridiculous thing in all of this was that part of Anna felt sorry for Greg. Greg had some grandiose illusion about himself that didn't include anyone getting hurt, but Cabrero had forced him to leave her in the graveyard to die. On the other hand, Anna vividly remembered her absolute terror as the wire had slipped around her neck and tightened. If it hadn't been for Sherman, she knew that she would not have survived her encounter with Cabrero. Aside from that, there was a callous indifference in Greg's treatment of Sherman, terrifying the poor, tormented soul just so that he wouldn't witness Greg's criminal activities, which was difficult to forgive.

But, maybe Sherman wasn't such an innocent victim after all? Was it true that he had he murdered Evelyn? Since he had been in the middle of a heart attack, his admission in the cemetery was the equivalent of a death-bed confession, wasn't it? She would have to find out the truth before she could close the book on her ordeal.

"What are you thinking, Anna?" Erna asked, studying her friend. "You have the most peculiar expression on your face."

Anna smiled and turned to Erna. "Probably just a trick of the firelight. I'm starving. When will supper be ready?"

37

It was Wednesday, Halloween night. Anna welcomed the trick-or-treaters who arrived at her door at six and handed out candy for a half-hour after that, but she turned out the lights and locked the door at six-thirty. She was going to the hospital for visiting hours. It was time for a talk with Sherman.

After parking her car in the visitor's lot, she hurried down the hospital corridor to his room, wondering what she would do if May were there. Erna had told her that May had visited Sherman every day for the four days he had been in the hospital, but she usually came during the day and was back at Erna's house in time for supper, so it probably wouldn't be a problem. All the same, when Anna rounded the corner and peeked into Sherman's double room, she sighed with relief. Sherman's roommate was engrossed with two little girls in fairy costumes while a young woman, probably their mother, smiled from her chair. The chair beside Sherman's bed was vacant, and he was smiling at his roommate's adorable visitors. The smile faltered when Anna stepped through the door.

"Hi, Sherman," she said, walking up to his bed. "I thought a chrysanthemum might brighten up your room."

"Thanks, Anna. Good of you to come," he responded, taking the yellow-and-orange potted plant from her hand and setting it on his tray. "Have a seat."

Anna set her coat on the back of the chair, dropped her purse onto the floor, and sat down.

"How are you feeling?" she asked with a bright smile.

"Good. I'm going to be discharged on Friday."

"Great. Glad to hear it. What are your plans for after that?"

"I'm going back to my house. May said that she and Erna would look in on me every day."

"Oh, that's good," Anna said, her head bobbing up and down. She glanced at the young family at the next bed, wondering how she was going to introduce the topic she so wanted to discuss. Sherman was watching her warily when she looked back, and she decided that now was as good a time as any to broach it.

"Listen," she said, leaning toward him, "I wanted to tell you how beholden I am for what you did for me in the cemetery. I wouldn't be here if you hadn't saved me." Sherman nodded, a smile of relief flickering across his face. "By the way," she added, "what were you doing in the cemetery that night?

Sherman didn't answer for a long time. Finally, he said, "Look, Anna, would you mind drawing the curtain around the bed? We need to talk in private."

"Sure," Anna said, getting up to do as he requested, but knowing that the flimsy curtain gave only the illusion of privacy.

Sherman waited until she was reseated before he started talking. "I was in the cemetery that night because I knew something was up when they found Henry on my front lawn," he said in a low voice. Anna drew her chair closer, not wanting to miss a single word.

"See, Father Winfield was keeping me up to date with the town news while I was hiding out at the parish house. It made no sense to me. I could understand Evie's ghost looking for me at May's apartment, but why would she come after you at your house? She didn't even know you when she was alive. And taking an axe after Judy? Evie would never have done that – she was too much of a lady. Plus, I knew someone was trying to frame me for the counterfeit money at the store." Sherman shook his head. "Something was up, and it wasn't a ghost. I might have my bad moments, but I'm not stupid."

"How long were you in the cemetery before you found me?" Anna asked.

"Not long. I'd walked the ring road, watching for anything unusual. When I got to the back gate, I found it open with a car parked just inside. I knew someone was up to no good, so I went to the tool shed to get my shovel. I thought I'd better have something with me, just in case. I went to Evie's grave because that's where I'd seen the lights the first night, and then I heard you scream. I ran toward you as fast as I could. That Cabrero fellow was trying to strangle you. It was lucky for me that you broke away from him. Gave me a better shot at hitting him without hurting you."

"Lucky for me, you mean," Anna said, taking his hand and squeezing it. "But Sherman, I've got to ask. What you said to me after your heart attack." She bent down and whispered, "When you said that you'd murdered your wife – was it true?" She tried to look into his eyes, but he turned his face away.

"Yes, it was true," he said, the words dragged from him.

"But how did it happen?" Anna asked, still holding his hand. "You seemed to love your wife so much."

"I did," Sherman said, gazing back at Anna. "I didn't mean to kill her. Evie and I didn't always get along, that was true, but I'd never hurt her. First, there was the trouble at the bank. Things had never been easy for her parents, but Evie thought they could make improvements to the farm and turn it around enough to sell it. Problem was, they didn't have the money. They'd applied for a loan, but the farm already had two mortgages on it. That's when Evie convinced me to falsify their assets and approve the loan. As the manager, I was able to get away with it. But then her parents started missing payments, the loan came due, and they couldn't pay. I changed the term date on the papers, but I was found out. I cashed in all our personal investments to pay off the loan so that her parents wouldn't lose the farm, but the bank still fired me. Evie was so angry when I lost my job, but she couldn't blame it on me." He shrugged. "I started drinking, we lost our house, the kids got upset, and . . ."

Sherman paused, looking away until he could master his emotions. Anna patted his hand and waited.

"We hit rock bottom when we moved into the house next to the cemetery. Evie wanted us to move to Calgary instead, but I just didn't have it in me to start over again. I was in pretty rough shape back then. Anyway, I came home that day to get a sweater, and when I went up to the bedroom, I saw that Evie had cleared her things out of the closet. There was a note taped to the door saying that she couldn't stand it anymore, and that she was leaving me. I went down to the kitchen and had a drink or two to steady myself, and then I decided to try to talk her out of it as soon as she got off work. It was getting late, and I was afraid that Evie might have already left by the time I got there, but the door to the town office was unlocked. I went inside. She wasn't at her desk, but the light was on in the basement, so I went to the top of the stairs to see what was happening. She was coming up, carrying her old suitcase. I asked her what she was doing down there. She said she'd hidden her suitcase in the basement because she didn't want the other ladies to know that she was leaving me. I begged her to give me one last chance, but she said she wouldn't. She tried to push past me, I grabbed her suitcase, we struggled, and she fell."

Sherman paused, covering his face with his hands. Anna heard him sob. She waited a long time for him to regain control, the broken man's breath coming in and out in gasps. Finally, he took a deep breath and laid his hands on top of the bedclothes.

"I ran down to have a look at her, but I knew that she was gone. Her neck . . ." His voice caught, and he hesitated a few more seconds. "I sat there on the steps for a long time. I realized how it would look when the police arrived. My Evie was gone, and there was nothing anyone could do for her. So I took her suitcase and left her lying there. I locked the office door and went home. I hung her things back up in the closet, tore up her goodbye note, and flushed the pieces down the toilet. And then I got well and truly drunk."

Sherman stopped talking. He stared stonily ahead, looking at something only he could see, giving the impression that he had turned to stone himself. Anna reached for his hand on the blanket; it felt cold and dry.

"I'm so sorry, Sherman. Sorry for both you and Evelyn. You were only trying to help her parents, and it ended up finishing the two of you. I know that your wife's death has been eating at you all these months, but it seems to me that you're not the only one who needs forgiveness. I don't want to offend you – I didn't know your wife, after all – but she let a whole lot of worthless things get in the way of her love for you. Maybe she should have begged for your forgiveness before it was too late."

Anna hesitated, waiting for Sherman to say something, but she wasn't even sure that he had heard her. She rested her hand on his shoulder.

"Don't worry, Sherman. I promise that I'll never tell anyone what you told me today." She kissed his cheek, stood up, and walked out of the room with Sherman still locked in his own private hell.

38

By the time Anna had driven home, the trick-or-treaters had abandoned the streets, and the neighbourhood looked deserted. She blew out the candle inside the pumpkin on the front porch and went in to hug Wendy, who waited patiently while the tears coursed down her face. When she had finished crying, Anna sniffled and wiped her eyes with one hand.

"Come on, Wendy. I need a walk," she said, straightening. The dog sprang to her feet and waited for Anna to grab a few things. When Wendy hesitated at the bottom of the drive, wondering which way to go, Anna turned left and headed out Wistler Road for the countryside.

It was chilly but dry with a bright moon shining down upon the sheared fields. Anna strode down the road, driving herself with an animal instinct to escape all of the misery she had endured over the past few weeks. When she got too warm, she stuffed her gloves into her pockets and unbuttoned her coat, enjoying the rush of cold air blowing through her clothes.

Eventually she came to the intersection between the township road and the laneway leading to Clive's farm. She paused in the middle, enjoying the silence and the solitude. Wendy came dashing out of the trees and sat at her feet, waiting for their next move. A car broke into Anna's reverie, however, its headlights dipping on the pavement as it came toward her, and she reluctantly relinquished the middle of the road to head to the shoulder, Wendy trotting beside her. Instead of driving past, however, the car slowed to a stop and waited, its engine idling. It was only then that Anna realized it was a cruiser. The window rolled down, and Steve looked out.

"Anna, is that you?" he asked. She stumbled to his car and paused beside it. She didn't want to talk to a single soul that night; not to Steve, nor to anyone else.

"What are you doing way out here? It's after ten. Something wrong?"

Anna shook her head. "No, everything's fine. I just needed a walk."

He shook his own head. "Sometimes I think you don't have the sense you were born with, girl. Get into the car. I'm driving you and Wendy home." Anna sighed and crossed to the passenger side while Steve put Wendy in the back. He shifted out of park and turned onto Wistler Road.

Steve didn't speak and, after a minute, Anna glanced at him. He kept his eyes on the road, waiting for her to talk or not talk, as she chose. Feeling compelled to say something, she said, "How's it all going to end?"

He looked at her. "What do you mean? The murder?"

"Which one?"

"There's only one murder – Henry's. There won't be any charges brought against Sherman for Cabrero's death, if that's what you're worried about, although there'll have to be an inquest. We'll keep looking for Greg Rae, too, but I have a feeling that he had a bolt hole all prepared just in case something like this happened."

Anna kept her thoughts to herself; actually, it had been Evelyn's death that had been troubling her. Not that Evelyn's death counted as a murder, and Sherman didn't need to be punished for it since he was doing such a good a job of punishing himself. Besides, she had promised not to share what he had told her with anyone else.

"What about Tiernay? How's she taking this?" Anna asked.

"She's pretty upset, that's for sure. She's coming to terms with her brother being a criminal, just like her mother was. It seems that forgery ran in the family. Both of them ended up deserting her, too. She hasn't had an easy life, you know. And on top of that, she's also discovering that she doesn't have any supernatural powers. She's just as weak and human as the rest of us. It's been quite a blow to her ego, actually."

"Sure," Anna said. She didn't really care.

Steve looked at her for a couple of seconds. "Tiernay could really use a friend."

Anna snorted, and Steve turned back to the road.

"Is she planning on staying in town?"

"She is, for now. She's got the business, and she'd like to give it a chance. I think she might make something of it, if people will forgive her for having a brother who was a counterfeiter. It's been pretty quiet at the store these past few days."

Anna nodded mechanically. She hadn't thought of that. Of course, the town was closing ranks against Tiernay, protecting one of their own against someone whose brother had left Anna to die in the cemetery.

Steve pulled the cruiser into her driveway and drove up to the garage. Letting the engine idle, he waited for her to say something.

Anna glanced at him. Steve had been a good friend, even risking his career by giving her confidential police information during her ex-husband's murder investigation. If he wanted her to be a friend to Tiernay, well, maybe it was payback time. Besides, Tiernay could have run away with Greg after they had left her in the cemetery, but she had stayed behind and called Steve for help. Maybe Tiernay had a good side underneath that lousy attitude of hers.

Out loud, Anna said, "My back's been bothering me lately. Does Tiernay give a good massage?"

"I'll say," Steve blurted. Anna turned to look at him, and they both burst out laughing until the tears ran down their faces.

"I sure can pick them, can't I?" Steve said, wiping his eyes and smiling at her.

Anna leaned over to ruffle his hair. "You sure can." She smiled at him fondly before reaching for the door handle and climbing out. Over her shoulder, she said, "You want to let Wendy out of the back seat?"

When Steve released her, the dog dashed to the house and sat down on the front mat, waiting for Anna. Anna motioned for Steve to roll down his window, and crouched beside the car as he stuck his head out.

"People here were good to me when I was new, even though I was so stupid I didn't realize my own husband was cheating on me. I'm sure May could use a massage. Stumping around town with that cast of hers has played hell on her alignment. And Mary and Frank are on their feet all day. So's Clive, for that matter. I wonder how long it's been since any woman laid hands on that man. Other than his mother, that is." She smiled and straightened, rubbing her lower back as it complained. Come to think of it, she really could use a massage.

"I'll spread the word, Steve." She tapped the side of the car. "Night."

"Night, Anna. And thanks."

She nodded and climbed the few steps to the porch. Taking a moment to scratch Wendy's shoulder, she inserted the key into the lock and opened the door. Steve tapped softly on his horn as he backed down the driveway. Waving without turning, Anna went inside and shut the door.

Epilogue

The sunlight was slanting across the cemetery lawn on the afternoon of Friday, November 2nd, the feast of All Souls' Day in the Catholic Church. Quite a few seniors had been by earlier to lay flowers on their loved ones' graves, but the burst of activity had died down, and the cemetery was deserted when the silence was broken by the roar of a lawn mower engine.

Sherman steered the mower carefully between the plots as May sat on the seat in front of him. She had propped her cast on the hood and cradled a bouquet of peach sweetheart roses in her arms. Sherman manoeuvered past the evergreens trees, around the bench, and parked beside Evie's grave. He switched off the engine, and they paused, drinking in the blessed silence.

May stirred first. "Take these, will you?" she asked, handing him the flowers. She swung her leg gingerly over the engine and wiggled off the seat with Sherman's free hand around her waist to steady her. Straightening, she balanced against the machine. Sherman climbed off the mower and removed his baseball cap, revealing a new haircut. The hair was combed straight back from his face, revealing his strong, broad forehead.

May looked around. "It's a pretty spot. I've never been here during the day before."

Sherman nodded. "Evie would have liked it. It's private, and there's some beautiful statuary in this part of the cemetery." He gazed at her tombstone. "I come every year with these flowers for her." His eyes shone with unshed tears.

"Evelyn knows, and she appreciates it," May said, resting her hand on his shoulder. His body felt tense to her touch.

"Do you think so?"

"Are you kidding? Look at the other graves around here," she said, waving her arm. "Potted plants and cut carnations. A couple of early Christmas wreaths. No one else has anything half as beautiful as her roses. She's lording it over Mrs. Weber over there, even if her husband's got the tractor dealership."

Sherman shook his head. "There was more to Evie than that. She couldn't help liking nice things. She had a pretty rough childhood."

May looked remorseful. "I know. I wish that I had gotten along with her, Sherman. We were two stiff-backed, proud women arguing about stuff that didn't matter. I didn't even know her, really."

Sherman squeezed her hand and released it, leaving her beside the mower. He walked to his wife's headstone and bent to lay the flowers on the banked earth in front of it. Pausing to whisper a prayer, he closed his eyes, and when he opened them again, they were dry. He brushed two fingers across his lips and rested them on her stone.

"I forgive you, Evie," he murmured.

Sighing, he made his way back to May, who smiled as he took her hand.

"Come on. Let's go lay the teriyaki jerky on Earl's grave," he said with an answering smile.

~ The End ~

Always a voracious reader, Cathy Spencer cut her teeth on Sir Arthur Conan Doyle, Agatha Christie, Jane Austen, and Charlotte Brontë. She is married to a singer/actor/university teacher. He didn't actually say "Marry me and see Canada" when he proposed, but that's practically what happened. They have lived on the west coast in Vancouver, on the east coast in St. John's, in Calgary, and are currently living in Ontario.

Town Haunts is the second in the Anna Nolan series, a cozy mystery with an amateur sleuth set in the Rocky Mountain Foothills of Alberta. The first novel, *Framed for Murder*, won the 2014 Bony Blithe Mystery Award; the third novel, *Tidings of Murder and Woe*, will be released in time for Christmas 2014. Cathy has also written a regency romance entitled *The Affairs of Harriet Walters, Spinster*, as well as two short story collections, *Tall Tales Twin-Pack, Mysteries* and *Tall Tales Twin-Pack, Science Fiction and Fantasy*. *The Dating Do-Over*, a contemporary romance about an elementary school teacher with abominable taste in men, will be released on September 18, 2014.

www.ingramcontent.com/pod-product-compliance
Lightning Source LLC
Chambersburg PA
CBHW070052260626
47160CB00004B/1191